Simon Burke

PENGUIN BOOKS

Only Human

Sylvain Neuvel has a PhD in Linguistics from the University of Chicago. He is an amateur robotics enthusiast and life-long fan of all things science fiction. *Sleeping Giants* is the first in the Themis Files series, followed by *Waking Gods* and *Only Human*.

D1325298

By Sylvain Neuvel

Sleeping Giants
Waking Gods
Only Human

Only Human

Book Three of the Themis Files

SYLVAIN NEUVEL

PENGUIN BOOKS

PENGUIN BOOKS

UK | USA | Canada | Ireland | Australia
India | New Zealand | South Africa

Penguin Books is part of the Penguin Random House group of companies
whose addresses can be found at global.penguinrandomhouse.com

First published in the United States by Del Rey 2018
Published in Great Britain by Michael Joseph 2018
Published in Penguin Books 2019
001

Set in 11/12.95 pt Garamond MT Std
Typeset by Jouve (UK), Milton Keynes
Printed and bound in Great Britain by Clays Ltd, Elcograf S.p.A.

A CIP catalogue record for this book is available from the British Library

ISBN: 978–1–405–93572–2

www.greenpenguin.co.uk

Penguin Random House is committed to a
sustainable future for our business, our readers
and our planet. This book is made from Forest
Stewardship Council® certified paper.

Eyaktept eket ontyask atakt oyansot ot.
Eyantsant eps.

Prologue

File No. 2101

Mission log – Capt. Bodie Hough and Lt Barbara Ball, US Marine Corps, Mecha Division

Location: Outside Dar es Salaam Hotel, Tobruk, Libya

—Central, this is Lapetus. Target in sight.

[*Copy that, Lapetus. Stand by.*]

Standing by . . . Right where we're supposed to be. Am I good or what?

—Oh, stop bragging, Bodie, you just punch in the numbers they give you. When you can make that giant robot moonwalk, then you can brag.

—Moonwalk? Like in slow motion?

—Seriously, Bodie? How old are you?

—That's Captain Hough to you, Lieutenant *Baaaalllll*. If I remember correctly, you tripped on a house the last time you had the legs. Fell face-first, broke Benson's wrists in the process. Am I right?

[*Lapetus, this is Central. If you could stop bickering for a minute, we have a job to do. Are you facing the hotel?*]

Affirmative. It's a nice hotel. Wouldn't mind spending some R&R in this place.

[*Do they have a clear view of the robot?*]

If you mean the people staring at us from the top floor, yeah, they see us all right. We're taller than everything else in this town. You can't miss us.

[*Roger that, Lapetus. We're talking to their chairman now. Stand by for orders.*]

Standing by. Why are we in Tobruk, by the way? I thought the government was in Tripoli.

—It is.

—Then what's here?

—Another government. Don't you do any research before a mission?

—But it's the same country.

—It happens from time to time. They had three governments for a while when I was a kid.

—Which one's the real one?

—Depends on who you ask. Pretty sure they all say they're the real one.

—That doesn't make any sense. Anyway, who cares, right? Twenty minutes from now, it'll be an American general running this place.

—You mean advising the democratically elected government of Libya.

—Yeah, that.

[*Lapetus, this is Central. The chairman isn't as receptive as we'd like him to be. Use your light beam and remove the north half of the building. Repeat, destroy the north half of the hotel.*]

Copy that, Central. We're –

—Captain, top floor, second window from the right.

—I see it. Central, it looks like there are people in that part of the building. Wanna give them a minute to evacuate? We can wipe out every car in the parking lot, that'll make 'em leave.

[*Lapetus, you have your orders.*]

—What do we do?

—What do you mean what do we do? You heard the man, Lieutenant. Start from the center of the building and swipe to your right. Aim low, maybe we can spare those houses behind.

—Yes, sir . . . In position.

—Activating beam. Say when.

—Uh . . . when. You can see the beam, right? You know when I'm done.

—Terminating beam. Wow, that thing's nasty. Doesn't even make a sound. Central, this is Lapetus. Target destroyed. Half of it anyway.

[*Copy that, Lapetus. We have it on satellite. Stand by.*]

Damn, I love this job!

—I can see that.

—What's that mean?

—It means what you think it means. You said you loved this job. I'm telling you that it shows. That's all. You have a problem with that?

— . . .

—Good! Moving on! We might be here awhile. What do you want to talk about? Books? . . . No? Movies? Have any hobbies I don't know about?

— . . .

—All right, I'll go first. I collect Cabbage Patch Kids.

—I don't know what –

—It's OK. I wasn't born then either. They were dolls, supposedly all different. You didn't buy them, you 'adopted' them. They came with a birth certificate, adoption papers, a little card to write down its first word, when it took its first step, its favorite food.

—They talked?

—No, Bodie. They didn't talk. They didn't eat either. It was just meant to look real, like you adopted a real baby that was born in a vegetable.

—How do you adopt a doll?

6

—You buy it, of course. They're in a store. You pay, but you call it an adoption fee. Anyway, they were a fad in the eighties. People went nuts. There were fights in stores, all sorts of crazy things. They were only that popular for a short while, but they were made by one company or another for about forty years. My mom had six of them. She gave them to me when I was a teenager, and now I collect them. The old ones are hard to find, usually cost a fortune.

—You collect dolls. That's not creepy at all.

—I sold one last year for five K.

—You sold a doll for five thousand dollars.

—Brutis Kendall, born in the Cabbage Patch on November 1. Near mint. With box. All the papers.

—That's nuts. I still think it's creepy, though. You shouldn't –

[*Lapetus, this is Central. The Chairman of the Council of Deputies of Libya has requested technical and advisory assistance from the United States. Job well done. Just sit tight. Navy is bringing in troops. ETA twenty minutes. Return to base when they arrive. Navigation will send your get-home numbers in a minute.*]

Roger that, Central. Over and out. One more for the good guys. Spreading freedom, one city at a time.

—I'm fairly certain they had freedom before.

—Well, now they have more.

PART ONE

When In Rome

File No. EE955

Personal File From Esat Ekt

Personal Journal Entry – Dr Rose Franklin

Be careful what you wish for.

About ten years ago – I was thirty-seven at the time – a giant robot from another planet visited Earth and decimated part of London. We succeeded in destroying it, but thirteen more appeared and dispersed a genetically engineered gaseous weapon in two dozen of our most populous cities. One hundred million people died in the process. Among them, this mysterious man whose name I never learned, who steered our every move ever since I was put in charge of studying that giant hand at the University of Chicago, and Kara Resnik, my best friend, who was also Vincent's wife, and Eva's biological mother.

With some help, I found a way to alter the metal these robots were made of at the molecular level and disabled one of them. That was enough to convince the aliens to leave.

I can't say that I knew that was going to happen, that millions would die because I had discovered Themis and brought attention to our planet, but I was afraid it would. I was afraid ever since I was brought back to life. I felt . . . out of place, and I wished that whoever built Themis would come back and take her away. I also said I hoped they would take me with them.

They did. After the alien robots left Earth, General Eugene Govender, head of the EDC, Vincent, Eva, and I went aboard Themis to celebrate our – I was going to say victory, but that's not what it was – survival. While we were there, the Council of Akitast – the group of aliens who decide how their world deals with others – had Themis brought back. She dematerialized on Earth and reappeared on Themis's home planet, with the four of us inside.

They call it Esat Ekt – Home of the Ekt, their people. In some small way, they're also our people. The Ekt first came to Earth some five thousand years ago – twenty-four of them or so. They were among us for a couple of millennia. They were ordered never to interfere, to stay out of history's way, but over time, some of them frayed and joined the natives. They had children – half-human, half-alien – who in turn had children – three-quarter human – and so on, until their descendants, indistinguishable from humans, had but a tiny bit of alien genetics left in them. Three thousand years later, there was nothing left to distinguish them from. All of us, every single person on Earth, were related, however remotely, with the handful of aliens who chose love over duty, back when the Titans walked the Earth.

We have been living here on Esat Ekt for nine years now, but we are still very much outsiders. Their entire society is built on the idea that different species shouldn't interact in ways that can affect them, that each should be left to evolve according to its own set of values. Centuries ago, their kind was nearly decimated by the inhabitants of a planet their emperor had displaced, exiled for personal or political reasons. After that, they replaced their monarchy with a very complex democracy, and took their noninterference policy to a whole new level. To the Ekt, 'polluting' an entire species with their genetics means robbing them of the future they should have. They view this as we would genocide. What happened on Earth was a tragedy for them as much as it was for us. They came to exterminate what they thought were a handful of Ekt descendants before they could contaminate all of us. When they realized they were too late, they had already killed millions. We are living reminders of what they consider a stain on their history, like the Holocaust Memorial, or a monument to the victims of slavery.

They will not be reminded anymore. One way or another, our time here ends tonight. We're going home.

File No. EE961

Personal File From Esat Ekt

Mission log – Vincent Couture and Rose Franklin

Location: Aboard Themis

[*Dad, don't do this!*]

—It's too late for that. Don't come any closer, Eva. I don't want to hurt him. Rose, can you hold her?

—Hold her? No, I don't think I can hold her. Come here, Eva. Let's not make this any harder than it already is. You don't want anyone to get shot by accident. We'll send him back, Eva. I promise. No one else has to get hurt.

[*What do you mean, no one else? What happened? What'd you do, Dad?*]

—Ekim, *eyyots ant ipyosk insot. Ekim! Eyekant!*

[*Ekim, don't do it. You know he's bluffing. He won't hurt you. Eyekant ops!*]

You're right, Eva. I don't wanna hurt him, so don't force me to.

{*It's OK, Eva*. Eyekant aktept eps.}

[*No! Don't do it for me! I'll stay! I'll stay here with you.*]

14

—You can't stay, Eva. Not anymore. You don't know what we . . . never mind. There's no time for this. Ekim, you're all strapped in? Here. Hold the gun, Rose. I need a minute to get into my harness, and we're gone.

—They're coming, Vincent, we need to go now.

—Dammit! I can't get my arms through.

—You can do it. Just relax.

—I'm not sure I can. I've never piloted the upper body. Last time I saw someone put this on, Eva was like ten, I . . .

—Can't you switch places with Ekim? He can guide you through the commands on the console.

—He said it's complicated. He had me at 'orbital defense system.' I don't think I – Got it! But I'll never be able to close the front. Let me put the helmet on, see if it works without the braces closed.

—Any minute now . . . We have to GO!

—Yes! She's powering up. Go! Go! Ekim, punch it in. *Eyyots!*

—How long until . . .

—Whoa.

—What? Vincent, where are we?

—I don't know. I think we're . . . It's nighttime. Trees all around us. Ekim, is this Earth? *Akt eyet Eteyat?*

{Ops eyoktiptet.}

—What did he say?

—Euh . . . It's an expression. Beats me. Something like that.

—Look at the stars.

—What?

—Look at the stars. Do you recognize anything?

—I don't see anything familiar . . . Yes! That's . . . *la grande ourse*. I don't know the constellation names. The big bear?

—The Great Bear. Ursa Major.

—Yeah, that. We're here, Rose. This is Earth.

—Wow. I can't believe we made it. Eva, say something.

[*Dad, what did you do?*]

—Not now, Eva.

[*Tell me what you did!*]

I said not now. It won't be long before someone notices us. Let's lay Themis down so we can get out.

[*Just tell me?*]

Eva, what do you think they'll do to Ekim if they find him here? He needs to get back. Ekim, *eyost yeskust ak eyyots esat.*

{Eyekant ets ops. Ethemis eyet onsoks.}

—What did he say? Empty Themis?

—He said Themis is empty. Drained. She used up all her energy to get here. There's enough left to power the helmets but I can't move the arms anymore.

—How long do we have to wait, Vincent?

16

[*Dad, I'll kill you if anything happens to him.*]

—Easy, Eva. When you and I drained her in New York, it took only a few minutes before she was able to move again. Looks like we're in the middle of nowhere. With any luck, no one's spotted us and we can get out before the sun comes up. Heck, it might take days before we're found. Just like last time.

[*Last time we almost died.*]

Then *not* like last time. Look, there's nothing I can do. If I knew how to speed this up, believe me I would.

—Go talk to Ekim, Eva. You have some time. You should talk to him. You might not see him again after he's gone.

[*I hate you, Dad. I really hate you.*]

—I know.

—She'll get over it, Vincent. Just give her time.

—I don't know, Rose. What we did, it's . . . Anyway, she's home, that's all that matters. Now we just need to get Ekim home safe.

—He could stay here.

—No, he couldn't. They'd put him in a cage, stick needles in him all day. A hundred million of us died the last time his people were on Earth. It's been a while, but I don't think folks here would've forgotten.

—What will happen to him when he gets back home?

—Well, he'll tell them we kidnapped him – we did. Hopefully, they'll end it at that.

—Do you think they'll believe him?

—I don't know, Rose. What would you have me do? Write him a note?

—He looks scared.

—He's a kid! He's millions of miles away from home, and he may have just committed treason. I'd be scared too.

—You put a gun to his head.

—Like I said, I'd be scared too.

—We just traveled millions of miles ourselves, you know.

—Weird, isn't it? We've waited all this time, then, boom. We're here.

—Our . . . friend once told me it took ten days to get from there to here. It just feels instantaneous. I'm not sure how they'd know.

—Know what, Rose?

—How long it takes to get from there to here.

—They'd probably check the date?

—How? We can get the date here, but what we'd need to know is the date over there, now. How do you get that? You go back, divide by two?

—I have no idea. I . . .

—You did what you had to do, Vincent.

—Did I? Did I *have* to do this?

—Don't go there, Vincent. Don't.

—What's worse is I don't feel nearly as bad as I think I should. Shit.

—What?

—Can't be. Not that soon.

—What's happening?

—Lights. There are a bunch of vehicles coming our way. Trucks, maybe. Ekim, *eket eyyots apt aks.*

[*Who's coming, Dad?*]

I don't know, but they seem to be in a hurry to get here.

[Yokits! *Now what? We can't do anything!*]

Well, if it's just trucks, neither can they. We're fifteen floors high.

[*They can bring a crane.*]

It takes days to put together a crane this high. A crane isn't what I'm worried about.

[*What then?*]

They might just be locals in some pickup trucks. If they are, we're still good. We can just transport Themis when she's charged and disembark somewhere else.

[*And if they're not?*]

Well, if they're military, they won't just bring trucks. They'll come with . . .

[*With what?*]

That.

[*What?! We can't see, remember?*]

A helicopter.

—Is it military?

—It's big, Rose. It's not a TV helicopter. Nothing you fly tourists in either.

—What's it doing?

—It's coming . . . Hovering above us now . . . Side door is opening. Shit. Shit. Shit.

—They're coming in?

—Two guys on ropes.

—Vincent, who are they?

—I don't know, but they have guns. One's at the hatch.

—They might be happy to see us.

—They might be ecstatic. Eva, you should stand in front of Ekim, just in case they're not. Whoever this is, he's in the shaft between the hatches.

—The inner hatch is opening.

<*Derzhite ruki na vidu*>

Vincent, what did he say?

—I have no idea, but I'm pretty sure he said it in Russian.

File No. 2106

Interview between Major Katherine Lebedev, Russian Main Intelligence Agency (GRU), and Dr Rose Franklin, PhD

Location: GRU building, Saint Petersburg, Russia

—Good morning, Dr Franklin. I trust you had a good night's sleep. I'm sure you did. We have really good drugs . . . Don't tell anyone, but I take some from time to time when I need the rest. I never thought I'd get to do this, but on behalf of the Russian Federation, and the entire planet, I suppose, welcome back! And welcome to Russia!

—We're in Russia?

—Yeah! You are! Sit down, Dr Franklin. You're making me nervous.

—I'm sorry. I *am* a bit nervous. I don't know what I'm doing here.

—Oh, you have every right to be nervous, Dr Franklin. I said you were making *me* nervous. I'm supposed to look superconfident. That's hard to do if I'm fidgeting in my seat. But this is so exciting! Please sit!

—I don't suppose you'll tell me who you are, or where I am.

—Who I am? Doesn't it say on . . . Where is it? There's a little plaque with my name on it . . . Oh, here it is. I'm Katherine Lebedev.

—You don't sound Russian.

—I hope not. I spent most of my life in New Hampshire. I went to Brown. Law school.

—You were a spy.

—I wa . . . No! I was a kid. I was born there. I played with dolls. My *parents* were spies. I didn't find out about any of it until it was time to leave. I moved back here eleven years ago, and here we are! I was saying something. Oh yes. I'm Katherine Lebedev. I'm a major in the GRU.

— . . .

—You don't know what that is, do you? The Main Intelligence Agency of the General Staff of the Armed Forces of the Russian Federation. Mouthful, I know.

—It sounds like the KGB.

—The KGB – it's called the SVR nowadays, by the way – is for kids. Don't tell them I said that. We're ten times bigger than the SVR. OK, maybe not ten times, but we're it. This is where the fun is. We have six times the numbers of agents, spy satellites, James Bond stuff. What else did you wanna know? Oh yes, you're in – we're in Saint Petersburg. Government office. Big grey building.

—Are you the head of this . . . GRU?

—Me? I wish. No, I'm a lowly major. I run a small – tiny, really – division focused on alien tech. We don't have any, so, like I said, it's small. Which is why you'll understand how happy I was, how happy we all were, when you landed in Estonia. Only a few hours away, really. What are the odds?

—Estonia? You said we were in Russia?

—*Right!* You don't know! I'm sorry. Where are my manners? You have a lot of catching up to do. What do you wanna know? Ask away.

—How long were we gone?

—Nine years, three months, six days – ninety-seven days – nine years and ninety-seven days. I'm sorry, I don't know the scientific way . . .

—Nine years? We thought it was less than that.

—Oh! Our scientists talked about that. Something about time dilation when traveling at near-light speed. I don't understand any of it, but they said you might come back a thousand years old. No, that can't be. A thousand years would have passed *here.* Can you tell I'm not a scientist? So how long did you think you were gone for? A few seconds?

—Eight years, seven months, maybe eight.

—Oh . . . Wait? You don't know exactly?

—We . . . Do you know where we were?

—I'm waiting for you to tell me, but everyone assumed you went to the planet where those robots are from.

—Right. It's called . . .

—What? It's called what? Oh, you don't know if you should tell me . . . It's really up to you. No, it's not *really* up to you, but you know what I mean. It's not like we'll torture you on your first day. I'm kidding! GRU humor . . . I know. How about this? Do you think telling me the name of the place will *for ever upset the balance of power*? Besides, you worked for the United Nations when you left. We're in there. It's your world!

—What?

—It's your world. The motto of the United Nations.

—I didn't know it had a motto.

—Awful, isn't it? So, what do you say? *Please!* I'm dying here.

—It's called Esat Ekt. It means Home of the Ekt. That's what they call themselves. We couldn't keep Earth time, but they . . . They use a unit of time that's somewhere around a minute, so . . .

—You didn't have a watch? Or a phone?

—We did before the batteries ran out. So like I said, we counted our heartbeats during that unit of time – Vincent and I know our normal heart rate – and we did the math.

Obviously, we were a bit off. It's possible the air was different. More oxygen, maybe.

—Oh, like when you're on a mountain.

—Well, that would be the opposite. But yes, that's the idea.

—Sorry. Law school, remember? Oh, before I forget. When you left, General Govender was with you. Now he's not, unless he somehow got transformed into an alien teenager. What happened to him?

—He died.

—I'm sorry . . . How? Did they kill him?

—He died of natural causes.

—So sad . . . SO, the people on that planet are called the Ekt. That's what he is, your friend that came with you? He's an . . . Ekt?

—I thought you wanted to answer my questions.

—I did it again, didn't I? I'm *so* sorry. I get too excited. I am! I am *so* thrilled! But I do that. I steal the conversation, and I don't even notice it until I've offended someone. Please forgive me? I swear – No, I won't, because then I'll do it again five minutes from now, and I'll feel even worse. Stop talking, Katherine. PLEASE! Dr Franklin. What do you wanna know?

—I'm sorry, Ms Lebedev, I –

—Did you just call me Ms Lebedev? It's the office, it does that. I don't even know what it's called. Victorian gothic? Ms Lebedev is my mom. I'm Katherine. Call me Katherine.

—OK. Katherine. I don't know if it's the traveling or if the drugs you gave me are still working, but I'm exhausted. Would it be possible to continue this conversation tomorrow?

—Of course! You traveled, I don't know, millions of miles, and here I am asking you all these questions. You get some rest. We'll talk when you feel you're ready.

—Thank you.

—Don't even mention it. I want you to know that we're doing everything we can to help your friend, even if you're being less than forthcoming with us, being exhausted and all.

—My friend?

—Yes, your friend. The young Ekt – I love saying that – who came with you. He's a bit sick, I'm afraid. Don't worry, though, you need to rest. I'm sure he'll be fine. He's got the best doctors with him.

—What did you do to him?

—What did I – ? What makes you think I would hurt him?

—There was a scientist working for you before we left, she . . .

—You mean Dr Papantoniou. What about her?

—She had no problem submitting people to very invasive procedures to get what she wanted.

—That was before my time. I did hear some pretty nasty things about her, though, but she works for the Americans, now.

—Alyssa does? What does she do?

—Oh, we can talk about that tomorrow. You need rest, remember?

—Please.

—She finds pilots for them. Some kind of blood test.

—Pilots for what?

—For their robot. Giant one, like Themis. I told you you had a lot of catching up to do.

—What robot? Where did they find it?

—Well, you gave it to them.

—Me?

—Yeah, you. Nine years ago, you disabled one of them in New York. It fell to the ground in pieces, remember? How long do you think it took for the US military to grab it?

—But it didn't work.

—Well, it does now!

—How do they even pilot it? Do they have someone with legs like Vincent?

—I have no idea. But that geneticist finds pilots for them. I hope you don't think I'm anything like her! I seriously hope you don't, because . . . *woooo* . . . crazy. I mean, sure! I like to get what I want – I usually do get it – but I don't want anything bad to happen to your friend. I really don't.

—What *do* you want?

—From him? I want him to get better. I *really* want him to pilot that big robot for us, but he can't do that if he's sick, now, can he? So I want him to get better. He seems nice. A nice Ekt.

— . . .

—That's a lot to take in all at once, I know. Go get some rest. We'll talk later.

—Am I a prisoner?

—What? Of course not! You're free to leave whenever you want, go wherever you want.

—I could leave this building and no one would stop me?

—Your escort will take you anywhere you want to go. Take in the city! It's beautiful. It's a lot better than Moscow, if you wanna know what I think. See the cathedrals. Walk along Nevsky Prospect. If you want to visit the Hermitage, I'd love to go with you. I haven't been in years.

—Can I see my friends?

—That's a great idea! Why don't we all have dinner together? After you get some rest, of course.

File No. 2108

Interview between Major Katherine Lebedev, Russian Main Intelligence Agency (GRU), and Vincent Couture

Location: GRU building, Saint Petersburg, Russia

—How are you feeling, Vincent? I can call you Vincent, right? You had a *lot* of wine last night. Wish I could have. Appearances. You know how it is.

—I'm fine. Thank you.

—You barely touched your plate, though. Rose and Eva didn't eat either. Should I tell them to fire the chef?

—It's not him. On . . . Where we were, the people have more sensitive taste buds than we do. The flavors there are a lot more subtle.

—Bland.

—Yeah, that's how it feels at first. I guess we've gotten used to it. I'm sure the food was great. Thank you for dinner.

—You're welcome! I knew you and I would get along! So glad, especially after meeting your daughter. She's *soooo* confrontational! Wow! I don't think she and I'll be BFFs.

—You never met her mom.

—I wish I had. I know I'm a few years late, but I'm terribly sorry for your loss. I meant that in a good way, about your daughter, you know. She has character. I like that. How old is she now? Nineteen?

—Yes she is. How's our friend?

—You mean Ekim? Eva told me. Oh, don't make that face. What difference does it make if I know his name? He's not well.

—Do you know what's wrong with him?

—A lot of things. He's got the flu, for starters. His immune system is completely out of whack, and he's infected with toxoplasmosis.

—What?

—I know. The Marine – yes, they're called marines here too – who got you out of the robot has cats. They tell me about half the world's population is infected with toxoplasmosis – did you know? – almost everyone in some places. Most people don't show any symptoms, apparently, but your friend does, a lot of them. And he's not responding to antibiotics, antimalarials, nothing. To be honest, we're afraid the meds will kill him if the disease doesn't.

—Please save him. I'm begging you, find a way to save him.

—You really care about him.

—He's my friend.

—Are you sure that's all he is? I thought maybe . . .

—Yes . . .

—Nah. You'll think it's silly. Ah, what the hell! I like to listen to people, in restaurants, everywhere. My parents were spies, you know, or maybe you don't know. Well, now you do. Anyway, maybe eavesdropping is a genetic thing. It's like a game. I try to guess things about people. Sometimes I even think I'm good at it. So yesterday at dinner, I couldn't help noticing a bit of tension between you and your daughter. I didn't make anything of it at first, but come dessert I'm thinking Eva's mad at Daddy for something. What if she's mad because Ekim got sick? What if Ekim's the boyfriend? Maybe she blames Dad for what's happening. Now Dad, he loves his daughter, he really doesn't want anything to happen to the boyfriend because he feels responsible and he's afraid his daughter won't forgive him . . . That's it. That's all I got. Am I close?

—I'm afraid not.

—I told you you'd think it was silly. Are you sure you don't want some Advil? You look a little pale.

—Coffee would be good.

—What was I thinking? I've been up for hours, I forgot it's still early. Coming right up. Black, right?

—Does it work?

—Does what work?

—That bubbly, friendly routine?

—Oh, that was rude, Vincent. I *know*. Big bad Russia, right? We're the bad guys. You might want to rethink that.

You won't believe it now, but you and I really want the same thing.

—How could you possibly know what I want?

—Well, right now I know you really want to get out of here, but that will pass when you learn a bit more about what the world is like now. Where would you go, if you could? Back to the US? Home to Montreal?

—Sounds about right.

—Which one? Don't answer that. It doesn't matter. They're pretty much the same now.

— . . .

—OH. COME. ON! You're not even gonna ask? I get why none of you'll say anything, but I don't understand why you won't ask questions. You've been gone nine years. Nine years! Aren't you the least bit curious about what you've missed? Seriously, even if I only gave you half the truth, that'd be a lot more info than the diddly-squat you have right now!

—You're saying the US has invaded Canada.

—No, they didn't need to. But there are forty thousand American troops there now. There's a Marine base in Montreal.

—So we're allies.

—You're a little more than that. Your parliament hasn't met in over two years, and your prime minister is assigned to residence. General Scott is running your country.

Yours isn't the only one. Venezuela. Half the Middle East. North Africa too. They just took Libya. The Mexican president was a lot more defiant than your prime minister – good for him – but it didn't do much good. The United States now extends all the way to Panama.

—How?

—The robot, of course. Iapetus. There's a big crater in the middle of Mexico City to remind everyone that it was in their best interest to 'join' the United States.

—What about you?

—Me?

—Russia. I may not ask a lot of questions, but I was listening last night when you told us we landed in Estonia.

—And?

—And, we're here. I take it Estonia isn't as sovereign as it used to be.

—Oh, that. Yes, Estonia is now a proud member of the Russian Federation. So is Georgia, and pretty much all the -stans. To be fair, about half of them asked for it.

— And the other half?

—Do you drink soda?

—What?

—Pop! Soda!

—I –

33

—Imagine Coke is taking over everything, buying every brand they can get their hands on, and Pepsi is the only thing they can't afford. Now, maybe you like Dr Pepper and you wanna keep drinking it, but you can't. There is no Dr Pepper anymore. There's Coke and Pepsi. Some people accept that, but for some it takes a little longer to sink in. Georgia, for example, they couldn't let go of their Fanta.

—So you send in tanks, a hundred thousand men and have them take the Pepsi challenge with an AK-47 to their head. I don't see how that makes you any different than the other guy.

—We're protecting our borders. They're taking over the world.

—What about the EDC?

—You're funny. That lasted for about a week after Themis disappeared.

—There's no United Nations anymore?

—No, there's a UN. On paper at least. But that robot is All-American. Red, white, and blue through and through. And it's not defending widows and orphans.

—And you want to do the same thing with Themis.

—I would like to even things out a bit, yes! I don't see anything wrong with that. The only thing stopping them from beaming into the square across the street is the threat of a nuclear strike. Mutual assured destruction. Dun dun dun . . . The MAD doctrine is the only play we have left without that robot. You understand how that's a bad thing, right? They know we don't really want to push that button – because of that mutual part where everyone ends up extra crispy – so they keep backing us into a corner until we have nowhere to go, then boom. No Coke *or* Pepsi, just muddy radioactive water.

—You do realize there's no way I'm ever gonna pilot Themis for you, right?

—Oh, Vincent, Vincent . . . Why do you do this to yourself? . . . I know you've seen the way the guards look at your daughter. Do you know how long she can hold her breath? Repeat after me. Exacto knife.

—Fuck you.

—Well, you kind of asked for it a little bit, don't you think?

—I'll –

—I know, I know. You'll kill me if I hurt her. I don't doubt for a minute that you mean it. Don't worry. I was just messing with you. I would never hurt your daughter.

—How do I know you mean that?

—Because you know I don't need to. I could give her a haircut, and you'd be in that robot asking for orders before I get to her bangs. Let's talk about something else, OK? This is just depressing. Let's do something constructive, like maybe saving your friend. To be honest, I'd much rather have *him* pilot Themis for us.

—What do you want me to do?

—That's the right attitude! Thank you for asking. You see, our doctors, they won't say it because they're afraid of what'll happen to them, but they have *no idea* how to save your friend right now – like *none* – and I'm thinking: Maybe *he* knows. Maybe he could save himself. Only he won't talk to us. Either he can't understand or he doesn't want to, but I'm sure he'd like to talk to a friend.

—What makes you think I can talk to him?

—Really? Let me see. Hmmm, he was *with* you, inside Themis. It would make for a boring ride if he couldn't talk to anyone . . . Oh, yes, you also spent NINE YEARS on his planet. Oh, and you're a linguist. Like, that's the *one thing* you actually trained for. What else? Hmmm. No. That's it. That's all I have.

—I meant what makes you think it's even possible? They could communicate with something other than sound. They could use chemical reactions, pheromones, touch, telepathy, sign language. Even if they did use sounds, in order to communicate, you'd have to be able to make the sounds, and recognize them. They could have a very different articulatory system. They could have no larynx, two of them, something entirely different. Even with the same physiology, they could produce sounds we can't replicate, or can't hear. Some of their sounds could be ultrasounds to us. Some could be indistinguishable from one another. They could have a thousand different sounds where we only hear one. They could produce a dozen at the same time. There are so many ways this could not work. I can't hear tone the right way in Mandarin, let alone reproduce it. I hear it backwards, up is down, down is up. That's with humans. Imagine the odds on another planet with folks who walk like ostriches. Even with the sounds out of the way, what they express could be impossible for us to grasp. They might not use a logic similar to ours, they might not conceptualize things as we do.

—Wait, wait . . . How stupid of me! Duh! I completely forgot I asked Eva if she'd like to talk to him just before you came in. She's with him right now. I'm *such a scatterbrain*. Seems I *don't* need you to talk to him after all. But thank you *so much* for that little lesson just then. That was superinteresting. No, don't make that face again! It really was! They seem close, Eva and Ekim. How long have they known each other? The whole nine years? Less than that?

—What difference does it make?

—Exactly! What's the point in not telling me? I can just ask her, you know. I'd rather you tell me because the security protocols are a lot tighter with her, and I hate the paperwork. But it's OK, you don't *have* to. Do you know how many forms I have to fill out just to talk to her through a glass wall?

—I don't understand. Why would things be any different with her? We all spent the same amount of time over there.

—I know! Right? I asked the same question when they put her inside that sealed room. Well, for starters, she has more alien DNA than just about anyone we've come across.

—That's still just a tiny fraction of her genetics.

—Well, tiny fractions matter now. She's an A5.

—What's that mean?

—It means she'd have a real hard time getting a job. I'm an A1 and I can only make colonel. Most countries keep their A3s in camps. Anyway, that's strike one. Your daughter, being more alien than most, also spent almost half her life on another planet. She was a baby for a few of the years she spent here, so, really, most of her life is over *there*. I'm gonna make a fool of myself again, but I'd be willing to bet that . . . she didn't wanna leave! Yes? No? Anyway, strike two. Then, of course, there's the whole dating an alien thing. You know, the same kind that killed one hundred million people here on Earth, the kind that destroyed Moscow.

—I thought you bombed Moscow yourself.

—Potato, po-*tah*-to. The point is she doesn't inspire a lot of trust right now. I *was* glad when I found out she's held on to some Earth customs – she gave me the finger the first time I saw her – but still, she speaks friggin' alien.

—She's as human as you are. We lived by ourselves. *I* raised her. Rose did. She was with us.

—See! That's the spirit. Now I have something more positive than the finger thing to share with my boss. What else can you tell me? Come on! Anything! OK, tell me what happened when you landed on Esat Ekt – yeah, Rose told me. It's a good name. What'd you do? Was anyone there to greet you? Did you just walk around aimlessly until you ran into people? Please?

—We didn't do anything . . . We were waiting to die.

File No. ~~1641~~ EE001

Party Log – Eva Reyes

*Location: Inside Themis, EDC Headquarters,
New York, New York*

—This is Eva Reyes. We're on board Themis, celebrating. I'm with my dad, Dr Franklin, and General Govender. I . . . I don't know what I'm supposed to say! Hey, Vincent?

[*Yes, Eva?*]

Why do I have to wear the headset?

[*Because we're recording this. Rose likes to record everything.*]

I know that, but why me? Why can't any of you wear it?

[*Let's see. I have a broken shoulder and a bent-up leg. Rose has a broken tibia.*]

It's a headset. It goes on your head.

[*You can move around more than we can. Stop complaining, will you?*]

The general could wear it.

[*The general is slightly inebriated.*]

{*I heard that, Couture!*}

[*Sorry, sir. I meant to say you're drunk as a skunk.*]

{*It's that damn champagne. Why can't I get a real drink? And why is it so dark in here? I can barely see my glass!*}

That's the other thing I wanted to ask about. Why am I the only one drinking juice?

[*So you can do the recording. Oh, that and you're ten.*]

Come on, Vincent! I just kicked some giant robot's ass. I just want one glass of champagne.

[*Technically, Rose kicked his ass —*]

<*Come here, Eva. I'll give you a glass. A small one!*>

Thank you, Dr Franklin.

<*I told you to call me Rose.*>

I'm not sure I —

<*Vincent does it. If you don't, I'll start calling you Ms Reyes.*>

OK, then, Rose. How does it feel?

<*Champagne? It's — *>

No, I meant you were right. Your plan worked.

<*I guess it did. Why are you making that face, General?*>

{*Show the aliens that humans could be just as tough without them messing with our DNA, by shooting some green goo full of bacteria out of a keg —*}

What are you saying, General?

{*I'm saying . . . What was I saying?*}

<The general was saying he didn't think my plan had any chance of success.>

Is that right, General?

{Not a chance in hell.}

Haha! What about you, Vincent? Did you think it would work?

[Me? I –]

<You thought it was stupid. Come on, Vincent! You can say it!>

[No, Rose! I understood the logic behind it. I just wasn't sure that, even if the bacteria worked, the aliens were gonna get the right message.]

<We don't know that they did.>

How can you say that, Dr Franklin? They left, didn't they!

<It's Rose, remember? We don't know why they left. We don't know if that's what they really wanted us to do. This is just what Mr Burns told me. He knows more about them than we do, but he hasn't talked to them. He was probably guessing as much as we were.>

Why else would they have left?

{Because Dr Franklin sprayed them with some goddamn goo!}

[General, maybe you should try some of Eva's juice.]

It's apple juice.

{Shut up, Couture! That's an order!}

Seriously, Rose. Why else would they leave?

<*Your father can guess. Ask him!*>

Vincent?

[*I don't know! I think, maybe, they could have been scared by the bacteria. What if all their robots, their ships, maybe their homes, are made using the same technology. Imagine for a second what would happen if some of that bacteria made it to their world.*]

. . .

What was that?

[*I can't remember what I was saying. Did the light just get brighter?*]

Maybe.

[*I think Themis just powered up.*]

<*Without any of the helmets on?*>

Can she do that?

{*I don't know! I've never been in this damn robot of yours.*}

Vincent?

[*The console is lit up. Eva, get up there and put your helmet on.*]

Sure. But we're in a garage! What do you expect me to see?

[*I don't know, Eva. It's just a hunch.*]

I'm putting it on. I . . . I don't think –

[*What is it, Eva?*]

<*Eva?*>

{*Goddammit, kid! What do you see?*}

Guys? I don't think we're on Earth anymore . . .

[*What?*]

<*What do you mean not on Earth? Vincent, put your helmet on.*>

Giant robots. They're all around us.

{*The ones that attacked us?*}

I don't know, General. There are . . .

{*Goddamn it, kid! It's a simple question. Are these the same ones that attacked us?*}

I don't know! I don't know if they're here.

{*Couture, what the hell is she talking about?*}

[*Shit! She means she can't tell. There are hundreds of them.*]

Thousands. They're all lined up in perfectly straight rows. Behind us too.

[*She's right. It looks like the Terracotta Army. And we're smack dab in the middle of it.*]

I'm scared, Dad.

[*Yeah. Me too.*]

File No. EE002

Personal File From Esat Ekt

Personal Journal Entry – Eva Reyes

Location: Inside Themis, on unknown planet

My name is Eva Reyes. I'm ten years old. My dad wants me to keep a journal in case we don't make it back to Earth. I . . . We've been inside Themis for three days. At least that's what his phone said before the battery ran out. I'm not sure that's true. The sun hasn't gone down once. We don't have any food or water. All we had was a quart of apple juice. That also ran out. I . . . I don't know what else to say. Dr Franklin? What should I say?

[*Talk about yourself. Where you're from. How you got here. And call me Rose.*]

Ehhh . . . I was born in Puerto Rico. My parents, the people who raised me, they worked for the government. We lived in a nice house in San Juan. I went to English school at Saint John's. I had good grades, but no one liked me there. The teachers thought I was trouble. I would have been expelled if my dad wasn't on the board. I didn't have a lot of friends. People thought I was crazy because I saw things, things that would happen sometimes. They made fun of me, called me names. My friends, the ones that didn't call me names, they never said anything, but they worried about me. My parents too. They worried all the time.

[*I'm sure your parents loved you very much.*]

I know they did. But they thought I was sick. They believed me in the end, but they died because of me.

[*Eva!*]

They did!

[*It wasn't your fault!*]

I didn't do anything, but they still died! If I hadn't been there, those mercenaries never would have come. I wasn't even their daughter, really. I was made in a lab. My mom carried me in her belly, but I was made in a test tube. My biological parents turned out to be Kara Resnik and Vincent Couture, the EDC pilots who control Themis. That's why I was made, so I could pilot Themis someday. What else? I was kidnapped. Kara rescued me, but then she also died. Earth was attacked by giant robots from another planet, and she died trying to save me.

[*Eva, I . . .*]

What?

[*I don't know. I just . . . There have been good things too, right? Can you talk about the good things?*]

I . . . Yeah. I met my dad, Vincent. He's cool.

{*Did you hear that, General? I'm cool!*}

He taught me how to pilot Themis. We went to Egypt. I saw the pyramids. Then we fought one of the alien robots. I thought we were gonna die, but you –

[*Pretend I'm not here.*]

. . . but Dr Franklin – she's really smart – destroyed the robot, and they all left.

[*Thank you, Eva. That's very kind.*]

It's true. Then . . . Then we had a party, but Themis powered up in the middle of it. Somehow, we ended up here, wherever this is. Themis is standing in the middle of a whole army of robots, just like her. We can't see anything else, and we can't get out.

OK, now what?

[*That was . . . a little short. I'm sure you have a lot more to say.*]

I feel sick. I'm hungry.

[*We all are, Eva. Think about something else. What did you do in San Juan? What was your life like?*]

I don't know. I didn't go out much. I played video games.

[*You never went out?*]

I played with Essie before she moved away. We used to look for rocks together. She had this huge collection. I was better at spotting the good ones than she was. She really liked rocks. Her parents took us to the Rio Camay Caves one summer. I didn't think my parents would let me go, but they did. It was amazing. Essie was so excited.

I've never seen anyone so happy. We stopped at the Arecibo Observatory on the way back. Her dad said that they
used it to talk to aliens. We knew he was messing with us,
but I thought about it for months after that. I imagined a
girl like me on another world. Both of us staring through
giant telescopes, talking to each other with big cardboard
signs.

[*That would have been a really slow conversation. Arecibo is a radio
telescope, and radio waves would take a long time to get there. Your
friend's dad might have been joking, but they did send a message into
space from there once.*]

Did anyone answer?

[*No. I don't think they were looking for an answer. I think they
were just showing off their new toy. I don't know much about it. It
was a long time ago. Before I was born.*]

Did you ever dream of going to another planet when you
were my age?

[*I thought I was from another planet when I was your age. Ironic, I
know. I . . . Have you ever felt like your parents weren't really . . .
Never mind. I felt misunderstood. I guess every kid feels that way at
one point or another. I had this idea that I was from another planet
and that, someday — some night, actually, somehow that had to happen
at night — my 'people' were going to come back for me, on a spaceship.
Only there were also bad guys — probably from another planet, I don't
remember — who were hell-bent on preventing that. Of course, the bad
guys were hiding under my bed, because . . . Well, because that's where
bad guys hide. I had to make sure that my entire body was on the bed
all the time. If a single toe was sticking out, they were going to get me.*]

47

Why wouldn't the bad guys just get out from under the bed and grab you?

[*Because my bed had special powers. A force field, maybe?*]

Like the robot we fought on Earth?

[*Exactly like that. Maybe my bed was made here.*]

I wish I . . .

[*Eva, are you OK?*]

I'm dizzy. I'm hungry. I don't wanna do this anymore.

[*I know. I know. But try to keep your mind occupied.*]

You said that everyone on Earth has blood that comes from aliens.

[*It's not blood, it's DNA. It . . . It's a code.*]

A secret code?

[*You could say that. But your cells know how to read it. It's like a recipe that tells your body what it should grow into, how it should function.*]

And everyone has some that comes from this planet?

[*Well, we don't know where we are. But if this is the planet where they built Themis, like we think it is, then yes.*]

Do I have some too?

[*You do. Your mom and dad have more than most people, and you might have more than either of them.*]

48

Maybe the aliens wanted to bring me back here, like the ones you imagined when you were my age.

[*Eva. The part of your DNA that isn't from Earth is a tiny, tiny part of your genetic code. Imagine that you are that code, your whole body, then the alien part of it would be . . . smaller than the nail on your little finger. It's not impossible that they brought us here because they wanted to meet you, but I seriously doubt it. If they wanted to meet any of us, they would have come when we arrived.*]

Dr Fran . . . Rose?

[*Yes, Eva.*]

How long can we survive without food?

. . .

Rose?

[*Vincent, I think you should be the one to answer that one.*]

{*It's OK, Rose. You can tell her.*}

[*I'd rather you did.*]

Tell me what, Dad?

{*We can go for a couple more weeks without food, but we won't last long without water. You can probably go for another three, four days. The rest of us had all been drinking alcohol, so . . .* }

So what?

{*So less than that. Do you want to try Themis again?*}

We tried an hour ago. She won't move.

{*Do you have anything better to do?*}

I don't understand. These . . . whoever brought us to this place, they're just gonna let us die up here? Why won't they come?

. . .

Rose?

[*I don't think they know we're here. I think they brought back Themis, and we just happened to be inside.*]

Dad, what do you think?

{*I think . . . I think we should try to move Themis again. I know it won't work, but they might pick up that there's someone inside.*}

What if they don't?

{*I don't know what else to tell you, Eva. We can't jump. We ran out of stuff to throw outside.*}

We have to do something. I think the general is getting sick.

{*She's right, you don't look so good, General.*}

<*You worry about yourself, Couture. I'll be fine. It's that damn champagne.*>

{*You —* }

<*You what? I need water? Tell me something I don't know. Make yourself useful. Go and empty the ice bucket. It stinks in here.*>

Don't look at me. I'm not touching that thing again. Ever.

File No. EE003

Dear Kara,

I wonder what you'd hate more, that I'm writing to my dead wife, or that I'm opening with Dear Kara? This isn't the first time I picked up a pen and paper to write to you. Rose said I should, a couple days after you died. She said it would help me to deal with the loss. I told her I didn't do stupid. Truth is, I tried that very night. I just stared at that piece of paper for an hour, then I gave up. Second time's the charm, apparently. Everyone's asleep. I didn't want to wake them up using the recorder, so this seemed like a good idea. You should see Eva. She looks so peaceful.

I miss you so much, Kara. And I want to believe in God right now. I've never wanted anything so badly. I'll be dead soon, and I want to believe you'll be there waiting on the other side with something snarky to say. My whole life, I thought that just being a part of the universe was grand enough. I thought it was much better than my little self sticking around for eternity. I suppose I still do. I don't care what happens to my 'soul.' I don't care if there's still a me, but I really want for there to be a you. The world makes more sense if there's a you.

I know what you'd say if you were around. Stop whining, Vincent, and find a way out of this mess. I'm trying. Believe me, I'm trying, but I'm running out of options. We're stuck in a ball of metal fifteen floors high with no food or water. The controls have somehow been turned off, and Themis won't move. We can't call for help, we can't get out. Kobayashi Maru. I'm all for not giving up, but I can't just will *us out of here. It seems so anticlimactic. Fight an alien invasion, get whisked away to another planet, then slowly die of thirst in a room that smells like piss. What was the point of getting this far? I could have just stayed with you.*

I'm not complaining. I guess I am. But one hundred million people died last week. What's four more if this is the end of it, right? I've lived plenty. I know Eugene has seen his fair share. Rose . . . Well, Rose lived twice and saved a planet. That's hard to top. I mean, really, what do you do after that? Stare through a microscope all day? Open a restaurant? When we realized no one was coming to get us, I could tell the three of us were ready for what comes next. But Eva isn't. She's scared shitless. She wants to live. We all do, but she wants it in a pure, animal way. She's a lioness. She's like you. There's such strength in her. It's beautiful to watch, and it's heartbreaking.

She's just a kid. She's been through more grief in her short life than most war heroes, but she's still a kid. There's no 'good death' for a ten-year-old, but she sure deserves better than this. This is a shit way to go. I feel like I'm failing her, again. That's what hurts the most. I want her to live, of course, but I wish I could have given her a normal ten-year-old day, one week, something of a regular life, if only for a short while. These aren't normal times, I get that, but I wish we could play pretend.

It was probably never in the cards for her to be a regular kid. Imagine those robots never came. Maybe we broke Themis? I don't

52

know, but let's say you and I were together, raising Eva. Can you picture us with a regular job, coming home after work for a family meal? Neither of us can cook. Poor kid would be raised on pizza. This is going to sound insane, but I think the end of the world is the only thing that remotely qualified us as parents. We could have done well, though, you and I, under extreme circumstances. I don't know how we'd fare at a PTA meeting, but we sure could rock World War III together, 'together' being the operative word. Without you, I'm not sure I can do anything.

Don't tell me I'm being too hard on myself. Believe me, my standards as a single parent are about as low as they can be. She didn't come with a manual, but if there is one, I'm pretty sure there's a bit in it about not stranding your child on another planet, dying in front of her, letting her deal with your body. I know. Keep her alive. But part of me sometimes wishes she would go first. We haven't had the how-to-survive-a-plane-crash-in-the-Andes talk yet. I'm not even sure what I'm going to tell her. I don't think there's enough water in human flesh to keep her going. Is there? I wish we had Internet. How do you even start that conversation? 'I'm not hungry, but you should eat Eugene, honey.' I don't know if I'd do it. Would you? Yeah, you would.

It's hard to test your principles against hypotheticals. We'll know soon enough, I suppose. Eugene won't last the day. He just moans, rambles for a few seconds, then he's unconscious again. I wish there was something we could do for him. I wish Eva didn't have to watch.

It's frustrating. I don't mean the we're-dying part – obviously, that is – but I feel like I'm missing something, like someone's explaining things to me and I'm too stupid to understand. What was that thing Wittgenstein said? Something about a man imprisoned in an unlocked room because it doesn't occur to him to pull instead of pushing on the door. Blame the scientist in me, but I want things to make sense. This doesn't. Themis has been gone for thousands of years. You'd think they'd be curious enough to inspect her, hose her down, something. They have to know she's back. They're the ones that brought her back, they must be. We didn't do anything in the sphere.

They can't wait indefinitely. If I can just keep Eva alive a bit longer, someone will come. I don't know if that's even a good thing. Whoever comes, you can bet it won't be a friend. These are the people that attacked us. They killed millions. Rose thinks that might not have been their intent, but regardless of why they came, we also killed a few of them. And by we, I mean me, and Eva, and Rose. The only three humans to have hurt any of them are inside this sphere right now, slowly dying of dehydration. That might not be a coincidence.

How do they treat their prisoners of war? That's probably how they'd see us. Do they even take prisoners? I'll do everything I can to save Eva, but I'd rather she died here, peacefully, than be tortured for months on end, then die. I don't even know if I'm making the right choice looking for a way out, but I am. It's a puzzle. One piece at a time. For now, I just have to keep her alive for another day. If I'm still around tomorrow, I'll try to do the same. And the next day, and the next. You don't have to worry about me trying, Kara. I am. I'll do anything to keep her alive. I'll set myself on fire if I have to.

Come to think of it, that might not be such a bad idea. This is a fairly small confined space, kind of like a submarine. What's the one thing you don't want on a submarine? Actually, I have no idea if that's true, but it's true in movies anyway. Themis doesn't have a radio or A/C, but there might be a fire alarm. Rose, the other Rose, used to carry a lighter around in her purse. I hope that *was an old habit. Gotta go, love. If this works, I promise to write every month. Yes, every month. I'm not writing to my dead wife every day. Our daughter already has visions. I'd like to keep the crazy to a minimum in our family, if I can.*

This is a shitty thing to say right now, but I wish you were here with us.

Stay out of trouble.

Love,
Vincent

File No. 2109

Covert Russian recording –
Dr Rose Franklin and Vincent
Couture

Location: Private quarters, GRU building,
Saint Petersburg, Russia

—She's telling the truth, Vincent.

—Who is? About what?

—That Russian major, Katherine. And about everything as far as I can tell.

—How could you possibly know that?

—She said – Katherine said I needed some new clothes.

—Oh, did she? Rose! Is she your friend now? Are you doing each other's hair?

—You're missing the point. I went shopping. I went out.

—Where?

—A place called TsUM. It's a . . . big department store. Fancy, like Saks.

—You went shopping. With what money?

—Hers. Theirs. I don't know. Will you let me finish? I didn't go there for clothes though I'm happy I'm not wearing those sweats anymore. There's an Apple store inside there, one that doesn't have anything from Apple anymore, just some Russian rip-offs. My escort was looking at fake iPhones, so I used one of the laptops and went online. I'm telling you, what Katherine said is true. Canada, Mexico, the whole thing.

—It doesn't make sense. Why would the US invade its allies?

—I don't think there's such a thing anymore. My guess? Corn, tomatoes, whatever else they grow in Mexico. Factories, perhaps. I'm not entirely sure, but from what I gathered, there seems to be very little foreign trade going on anymore. Borders are closed. Everyone has to be somewhat self-sufficient to survive.

—And the robot?

—Also true. It's everywhere online. They call it Lapetus.

—Is it the one you knocked out?

—Seems to be. It's missing part of the leg I sprayed bacteria on. They've attached a huge metal structure in its place. It's ugly, scary as hell.

—How? Themis wouldn't work at all without all the pieces. And who pilots it? I thought we were —

—I don't know, Vincent. I think Alyssa has something to do with that.

—Alyssa?

—That's what she said.

—Who?

—Katherine.

—Rose! You do realize she probably planned all this, your going to the store where there happens to be a bunch of computers. She's manipulating you, me, all of us!

—Are you saying she's created a whole new Internet for my benefit? I went on local newspaper sites, small ones. I can see the government making a fake CNN, but not all of this.

—Don't tell her anything, Rose. Don't tell her what we did.

—I won't tell her, Vincent. And I know she has an agenda. I have absolutely no doubt she'd lie to us every step of the way if she thought for a second that it served her interests. I think for now she's using the truth because most of it seems to be on her side. I'm not saying I trust her. But there *is* a giant robot running around scaring foreign governments into submission. There are internment camps at home, Vincent. Here too.

—For whom? People with too much Ekt blood?

—Yes. Foreigners too, I think. Something about Muslims. I don't know what happened while we were away, Vincent, but it hasn't gone well.

—If you're telling me I should pilot Themis for them, you've completely lost your mind.

—Of course not. But I wouldn't send her back to the US either. Remember how scared we were at the beginning about what they'd end up using Themis for? We were right to be scared. This is it. Our friend knew. That's why he wouldn't let just one nation control Themis.

—People died, Rose. Lots of people. Things would be bad without that robot, I'm sure.

—You don't feel the least bit responsible?

—My God, Rose! When does it stop? No! I don't feel like I owe anyone anything. Neither should you. They did this to themselves. You weren't even here! You saved this planet, Rose. The whole planet. You did that. Just you. Whatever debt you feel you had for falling into that hole, I'd say it's been paid, with interest. How about we just find a way out of here? Get as far away from this place as we can. They've been playing nice with us, but how long do you think it will take before we're strapped to a chair and pumped full of sodium thipental . . . thiopental?

—I don't know, Vincent. I don't think they can.

—What's there to stop them?

—Well, you, for starters. They might want to know more about what happened on Esat Ekt, but they want you to pilot Themis more than anything else. They could coerce you, but that wouldn't be my first choice if I were about to hand over control of the most powerful weapon in the world to someone.

—What about you? What do they need you for?

—I'm not sure they really need me for anything. I think the only reason I'm not strapped to that chair right now is you. If they think there's a chance they'll convince you to help, they're not gonna jeopardize that by roughing me up. Besides, the US *has* to know Themis is here. I'm an

American citizen. Sooner or later, they know they might have to turn us over. That's easier to do if we're still in one piece. My point is we can't just leave. That's not good enough.

—You just said they need me for Themis to work. Isn't it better if I'm gone?

—The Americans have a working robot and pilots. They obviously don't need you. If the US can put back together a robot that was disabled, how long do you think it'll take the Russians to get their way with one that's perfectly functional? It's only a matter of time before they start pounding at each other.

—Good for them. If what you're saying is true, then the world's gone mad while we were away. I don't think there's anything either of us can do about it.

—Why did we come back, Vincent?

—What kind of question is that?

—I'm serious. Why did we go through all this just to leave Esat Ekt?

—You know why we did it. We did it for Eva.

—So she could have a normal life, here. How's that working so far?

—Dammit, Rose! What do you want from me? I'm tired. I'm so fucking tired.

—I know. But we're not done, Vincent. That deal we made? We're not done yet. You can see that, can't you?

File No. 2113

Interview between Major
Katherine Lebedev, Russian Main
Intelligence Agency (GRU), and
Eva Reyes

Location: GRU building, Saint Petersburg, Russia

—I want to see Ekim.

—Not now, Eva, you can't.

—I WANNA SEE HIM!

—Calm down. *Jeez!* I just wanna talk. Chit-chat! I brought beer! Do you drink beer? I bet you don't – me, I like wine – but this is all I could find in the office fridge. I thought we could have a drink, get to know each other a little. You're allowed, right? Of course you are. You're nineteen.

—Fuck you!

—Really? Is that about the beer? Because I can get vodka . . . No? I know you don't like me, Eva, but I'm trying to help you here.

—If you really want to help, start by getting me out of this aquarium. Oh, wait, you're the one who got me locked in here in the first place. Like I said, fuck you!

—All right . . . No beer. I'll be straight with you, Eva. You can choose to believe me or not – that's entirely up to you – but this wasn't my idea. I'd like nothing more than to let you out, but I'm not the boss here. I *want* to help you, but you have to give me something. Maybe you don't realize it, but you, your dad, and Dr Franklin leaving, going to the place those robots came from, that's –

—You *astast yokits* . . .

—I don't know what that means.

—It means there were four of us over there. I know you don't give a shit about General Govender, but I do. He was my friend.

—Yes! Him too! All of you going to that planet, that's a *big deal*! People wanna know, Eva. Everyone does! And if I can tell my boss that you're cooperating –

—Cooperating with what? What is it exactly that you want me to do?

—I told you the same thing I told your father. In time, I'd like you to pilot Themis for us. But first, I want to know more about the planet you were on.

—Bullshit. This whole pilot thing is utter and complete bullshit. You'd let me and my dad inside a giant robot that can lay waste to your entire army and disappear in an instant. Yeah, sure. Where do I sign up?

—So what do you think is going on here, Eva?

—I think I'm just leverage, so you can get my *dad* to work for you. He's probably worth the risk, with the leg thing and all, and you're betting he won't do anything stupid as long as you keep a gun to my head. That means you'll need another pilot for the upper body. You've been running every kind of test there is on me since I got here, so I'd say you're trying to replicate that genetic test the Americans are using to find one. What I don't get is why you keep wasting your time talking to me. You don't need my help to keep me hostage, and you *have* to know I'm not gonna tell you shit.

—Well, you must be right. I just come here, every day, because I enjoy your company so much. You know, maybe I got this whole thing wrong. Maybe I should get *you* to pilot Themis for us and use your dad as leverage.

—Try me.

—Maybe not, then. But you see where that leaves us, right? I mean you. You see where that leaves you. I . . . Well, I'm not the one who spends my days inside a pickle jar . . . That was fun! As always. You let me know if you change your mind. Toodeloo!

—Why can't you just let me leave? I won't do anything.

—Oh, come on, Eva! You're better than that. You know why! I can't let you go back to the US, not with the way things are.

—Wait, you think that's where I wanna go? To the old US of A? Do I look like a patriot to you? From what you tell me, the place has gone to hell like the rest of this world. I don't care what you tell yourself to justify all the crazy shit you're doing. I don't care if you do it for the motherland, or because you think you're the only one with freedom. I don't give a shit about any of that. I don't give a shit about you *or* them. You say I don't like you. You're right. I don't. I think you're a conniving psycho bitch. Maybe I'm wrong. That's true, I mean that. I don't *know* you. But I don't *wanna* know you. I just wanna take Ekim and get the *yokits* out of here.

—And go where!

—Home! I just wanna go home!

File No. 2116

Interview between Major Katherine Lebedev, Russian Main Intelligence Agency (GRU), and Vincent Couture

Location: GRU building, Saint Petersburg, Russia

—I've been nice to you, Vincent, haven't I?

—What's that supposed to mean?

—It means it's time for you to be nice to *me*. I'm trying really hard to keep things civil here, but there's a lot happening. Like, a *lot*.

—Like what?

—Oh, I don't wanna bore you with my day. It's just your usual brink-of-war political nonsense. I'll tell you this, though. I'm a major. Information goes through a lot of hands before it gets to me, and at every step, people lose a bit of their manners. Ambassadors meet, they have some food, a bit of wine, maybe some caviar if they really wanna threaten each other. Generals meet over coffee and croissants. Colonels will skip the croissants. By the time information gets to *me*, it doesn't come with anything to eat *or* drink. They also lose all the remotely positive things

along the way. I just get a manila folder filled with negativity. Well, today, that folder is the size of a phone book.
Remember the Twinkie in *Ghostbusters*? Well, like that, but
in a manila folder, so now would be a really good time to
start talking.

—What will you do to me if I don't?

—I'm not gonna do anything to you, Vincent. It makes
me queasy when I break a nail. I'm afraid of spiders . . . I
am! I hate those little legs. The worst are the ones with
long, long legs and nothing but a little beige ball in the
middle. Ahhh! Anyway, can you picture me with pliers
and a blowtorch? I hope you can't. But I don't run this
place, Vincent. Soon enough, if I don't give my boss
what he wants, it'll be someone else asking you questions.
Trust me, you don't want to talk to that someone else. I
don't want you to either because that'll mean I failed, and
that doesn't go well in this place. Nooooo. Not well at all.
So what do you say? Do you wanna help me? I have
cookies!

—What do you want to know?

—Everything! Jesus, Vincent! I wanna know everything!
I wanna know how to beat the Americans. I wanna know
how Themis can disable their robot. I wanna know if the
aliens are coming back! I wanna know if we should be
preparing for a war and against whom. People are afraid,
Vincent. You show up out of nowhere after nine years,
they don't know what it means. *I* don't know.

—The Ekt are not coming back.

—How can you be sure?

—I suppose I can't. I'm telling you that they don't mean us any harm, and that based on what I know, they're not coming back to Earth. But you're right, I can't be sure. They could change their mind. If they did – and I know this is not what you wanna hear – there is absolutely nothing you could do about it. Nothing.

—We've been making more bacteria, the kind Dr Franklin used against Lapetus.

—Good for you. Here's a thought. Why not use *that* against the Americans? What do you need *me* for?

—That bacteria is useless against it now. The *one thing* the EDC managed to do before they were shut down is to develop a chemical shield they could put on Themis so she'd be protected if the aliens ever came back. It kills those bacteria on contact. They have it. We have it. We sprayed Themis the minute you got here. You see! I *do* need you! With Themis, with the other robot, we –

—You don't get it, do you. They didn't send a dozen robots here because that's all they had. They thought it was enough to wipe out a few people scattered across the globe. They have thousands of these robots, Katherine. *Thousands!* More than that. They could carpet this place so that every single person on Earth would be able to see at least one of them. They wouldn't need to, though. They have ships, and weapons . . . If you wanna do something useful, find a way to stop all this nonsense with the US, and the camps. Just . . . make the world like it was, before all that.

—I'm not sure anyone can do that, Vincent.

—Why not? You broke it. You fix it.

—Did I? Break it? You dug up pieces of a giant robot all over the world, then the aliens came, and they killed . . . They killed a lot of people . . . I'm sorry, I just . . . No crying, Katherine! My point is if anyone 'broke it,' Vincent, it's *you*. You, and your wife, and Dr Franklin.

— . . . Whom did you lose?

—Whom did I lose? Does it matter? A lot of people lost a lot of people. I'm not . . . *special*.

—Who?

—My husband. My . . . daughter. She was eight months old.

—I'm sorry.

—No, Vincent. *I'm* sorry. You, and the Americans, you started all this. You don't get to be sorry. You get to live with it, that's all.

— . . .

—And the camps? You're surprised about that? You're the ones who told us we're all kind of related to them, some of us more than others. You told us they only came for a few of their kind. You're still saying it. Dr Franklin said it on television the same day you disappeared. I know you think it's supposed to make everyone feel better, knowing that these Ekt, or whatever, didn't *really* want to kill all of us. But it doesn't Vincent. It just doesn't. My

68

baby's dead. She's not coming back. And they're still here. The people they came for, some of them are still here. Millions of us died, and they're still here, walking the streets, like nothing happened.

—I'm sure they feel responsible.

—Yeah, I'm sure they do. But they shouldn't. They shouldn't be feeling anything at all. They should be dead. We'll never be safe until they're all dead.

—Are you saying they're killing people in these camps?

—Only the A5s, for now.

—Eva . . .

—Well, I told you –

—You told me she'd have a hard time getting a job. You –

—We keep her in a glass jar, Vincent. What would you have us do? The aliens came for those people. As long as they're here, there's no reason the Ekt shouldn't come again. You just told me we can't stop them.

—Eva's not one of them. She . . . She's my daughter. I'm human. I'm like you.

—No, Vincent, you're not like me. Don't look at me that way. It's not my opinion, it's a measurable fact. You're an A4. You're less human than I am. *I'm* less human than Dr Franklin.

—But those people you're talking about, the ones they came for, they're . . . different. They're . . .

—What are they, Vincent? . . . See. You didn't get it before, but you're getting it now, aren't you? They came for a handful of their kind, but they realized their blood had mixed with ours along the way. So who would they come back for? The ones that have *more* alien DNA? How much more?

—I don't –

—I know you don't. No one knows. No one knows where they'd stop. No one knows what would make them say: 'OK. We'll leave now. We'll stop killing everyone.' So we're guessing. Start from the top. Work your way down. Right now, we're rounding up A3s and up, but we're stopping the purge at A5. Not everyone is, by the way. I wouldn't go to France if I were you.

—That's insane. This has to stop.

—Then help me stop it. Tell me what happened.

—I don't know what you wanna hear.

—Start from the beginning. You end up on another planet. You're stuck inside Themis for days. You can't get out. You think you're all gonna die. Then what? Obviously you *didn't* die in there.

—I made a fire. That set off an alarm. People came.

—What people?

—People! I don't know who they were. We didn't understand what they were saying. We were weak, scared, confused.

—And?

—I don't know! I woke up inside a small room with no windows. I was there for days, a couple weeks maybe.

—Alone?

—Yes.

—They put each of you in a different room.

—No, Eva, Rose, and Eugene were together.

—Why just you?

—I . . .

—I what?

—I punched one of them, sorta. He . . . He grabbed Eva, and I tried to punch him. Then they put me in a different room.

—That's funny . . . OK. Maybe it wasn't funny back then, but it's funny *now*. No? What then? Did they hurt you?

—No. They're not like that.

—Not like what? You punch someone in the face, they don't need to be anything to wanna punch you back. It's just –

—Human nature?

—I see what you did there. OK, so they're *supernice*. And you spent a week or two in a dark room, alone.

—Yes. Well, someone came. He . . .

—He what? Brought you flowers? Some tea?

—He taught me how to speak.

File No. EE006

Personal File From Esat Ekt

Interview between Opt Enatast and
Vincent Couture

Location unknown

—*Ast eyet Enatast.*

—My friends and I have been separated. I want to see them.

—*Ast eyet Enatast.*

—Where are you keeping my friends? My friends? I just want to know if they're safe. You have absolutely no idea what I'm saying, do you?

—*Ast . . . eyet . . . Enatast.*

—Good for you. I don't understand. But you already knew that.

—*Ast . . . ey . . . et . . . En . . . at . . . ast.*

—So you keep saying. I guess that means there's no tiny robot coming to inject me with translator microbes. That was a joke. I take it you didn't watch *Farscape*. DRDs, little yellow things. Never mind . . . How about this? Shaka, when the walls fell.

—*Ast . . . ey . . . et . . . En . . . at . . . ast.*

—Dear God. Do you know why they have everyone speak English on television? It's because learning a language takes fucking for ever! Sorry. Bad word. Don't learn that one. That's why I did linguistic theory, so I wouldn't have to do *this, ever.* Fieldwork sucks. Again, bad word.

—*Ast* –

—I know. I know. Now you're touching your forehead. Is that a greeting? Let me try. *Ass Enatat . . .*

— . . .

—Blank stare. I guess not. Is that your name? My name is Vincent. Vincent . . . Vincent. This is my head.

—*Eps eyet Yincent!*

—You're smiling. *Eps eyet Vincent!*

—*Ast.*

—What? Ah wait. I just said you're Vincent, didn't I? *Ast eyet Vincent. Eps eyet Ena . . .*

—*Enatast!*

—Yes! I can say my name! I'm a genius. I'm gonna need something to write this down. Your turn. You are Enatast. I am Vincent.

Oh, don't look at me that way. I have a feeling I'm not the smart one in this room. An hour from now, you'll feel like you're trying to teach a cat to do tricks. I learn yours, you learn mine. That's the deal. You . . . are . . . Enatast . . .

73

—Yout . . . ay . . . Yincent.

—Close enough! Now where are my friends? Friends. Here. Let me mime them for you. Eva, tiny human. Eugene. Big Man. Rose. I can't mime Rose. My friends!

—*Optept akt.*

—Yes, *optept akt*! Where are my friends?

—*Eyet onyosk.*

—Don't *eyet onyosk* me. You know what I'm saying. *Optept akt!* I have no idea what it means, but I mimed my friends and you said *Optept akt. Ast* . . . see, with my eyes, *optept akt*!

File No. EE011

Personal File From Esat Ekt

Interview between Brigadier General Eugene
Govender and Dr Rose Franklin

Location unknown

—Wake up and smell the coffee, Rose! We're goddamn prisoners!

—They're just being cautious, General.

—Cautious! Is that what you call it? The doors lock from the outside. There are armed . . . teenagers outside the door. This is a jail.

—What did you expect? They don't know us. They don't know what our intentions are.

—Of course they know what they are. Our *intention* is to get out of this shithole and go back home, which is precisely what they seem to be hell-bent on preventing.

—I don't think they mean us any harm.

—You don't think . . . Goddammit! They killed a hundred million of us! That's pretty unambiguous if you ask me.

—I'm certain that's not what they came to do. And you know I meant the four of us. They could have killed us on the spot when they found us inside Themis.

—Is that good? Who's to say they don't want to torture us, dissect us, make us watch while they cut us into little pieces? Maybe that's what they're doing to Couture while you and I are talking.

—Shhhh!

—The kid's sleeping, Rose. She can't hear us.

—And what if she's not? She's ten! She's scared enough as it is. Don't put ideas in her head. Vincent's coming back. He could be in the next room. You saw what he did to that guard when he grabbed Eva.

—Goddamn idiot. I thought he was gonna get us all killed.

—That's my point. They *didn't* kill us. In fact, since we arrived, the only violence came from us, not them.

—If I didn't know you better, Rose Franklin, I'd say you're taking their side.

—There are no sides. There are no good guys and bad guys here. Everyone is just trying to do the right thing. I'm trying to understand where they're coming from.

—The right thing? Have you lost your goddamn mind? They're killers, Rose. They kill people, by the million.

—So do we.

—And if we were holding four of them prisoner on Earth, they'd have every reason to be scared shitless. We *would* probably dissect them. I'm not saying we're better than they are. I'm saying these aren't the righteous evolved beings you make them out to be. They're the dominant species on their world. They're predators.

—You're afraid of them because they are . . . well, alien. Europeans had these maps of North Africa at the times of the Crusades. They marked the regions where giants lived, where two-headed people could be found. People fear what they don't know.

—Yeah, they do. People slaughter what they don't know, they keep it in chains, they enslave it. I understand what you're saying, believe me, Rose. I understand better than you do. This is what I'm afraid of. These people out there, they're not alien. This is their home. We're the aliens, Rose. We're the two-headed monsters.

—I understand that the events of the last few days might indicate otherwise –

—Can you hear yourself? You're talking like him, now.

—Just trying to be clear. But I truly believe that their intention, when they came to Earth, was not to slaughter millions of us. What do the military call it? A surgical strike. I think that's what it was supposed to be. In a way, I think they came to Earth to help us.

—I don't buy that for a goddamn second, but say you're right. Does it change anything? No, it doesn't. Not a god-damn thing. It's *not* the intention that counts when it comes to genocide. They didn't give us an ugly sweater for Christmas. They violently killed millions of us. You're curious. I get that. But don't lose sight of the facts. We know they're killers because they killed millions. I don't really give a damn if or why they wanted to do it. You want to study them, fine! Let's bring one back with us. We'll lock it in a cage and you can have a tea party with it every night if you want to. First order of business, though, is to get the hell out of here, get our butts back to Earth.

—How? Seriously, how do you propose to do that, General? Yes, I'm curious. Maybe my curiosity is skewing my judgment a bit. I'm willing to admit that. I *want* to know more about them. Now you might think that's a bad idea, but I don't see us having any other choice. We don't know how we got here. We don't know if Themis has the capacity to get back to Earth on her own, and even if she did, we wouldn't know how. Besides, she's disabled right now, and we don't know how to fix that. It seems to me, and correct me if I'm wrong, that if we want to get our butts back to Earth, as you say, these people are gonna have to do it for us. I think the odds of that ever happening increase exponentially if we don't treat them as enemies. We need to get on their good side. Whether you're sincere about it doesn't necessarily matter, but I'm sure it wouldn't hurt.

—And how do we go about that?

—You can start by not calling them 'it.'

—You think they're listening to us? Even if they did, this ain't *Star Trek*. They can't understand anything we're saying.

—Do you want to ask them, just to be sure?

—I think I liked you more when you were on the verge of depression.

File No. EE013

Personal File From Esat Ekt

Interview between Opt Enatast and Vincent Couture

Location unknown

—Yincent! Yout yeyn enoy.

— . . .

—Yout.

—You. I got that one.

—Yeyn.

—Yeyn? I have no idea wh— Learn! You learn more! No! I don't learn more! And *you* have to learn some consonants, my friend. This is nuts. We're not doing this anymore, not until I see my friends. I've been here for . . . You've had me cooped up in this stupid room with no windows for days now. I'm starving. I hate that white stuff you keep bringing me. Is it tapioca? I stink. I think I've been peeing in the sink. I wanna see my friends!

—*Yok yosk.*

—What?

—*Yok yosk.*

—Now? *Yok* is now, I think. I can see them now?

—*Yosk.* Enow . . . epyus one.

—Now plus one what? One hour? One day? Do you mean tomorrow?

—How etut yout esay eton . . . oyow?

—What? How . . . you say? How do you say tomorrow! No. 'How do you say' is with *your* words. 'What does X mean' is with *my* words.

—What etos X enean etonoyow?

—You don't say X, you put the word where X is. What does tomorrow mean? And that's . . . That's a very good question. The sun was up the whole time we were inside Themis. You probably don't care about the planet's rotation . . . Sleep. How do you say sleep? Like this. Not sure the hands under my cheek are helping. Eyes closed. Over there. In the bed. I sleep in the bed.

—*Iksyokt.*

—*Iksyokt*? This . . . eyes closed, is *iskyokt*?

—*At.*

—I can see my friends now, plus *oneiskyokt*?

—*At.*

—Yes? Yes I can see them?

—*At.*

—Yessssss. Thank you!

—*Iskyokt* is eyes.

—What? No. These are my eyes. This, with my eyes closed, is sleep. *Iskyokt* means sleep. Now, plus one sleep is tomorrow.

—*Yok yosk* is etonoyow.

—Yes, sir! Let me write this down. *Yosk.* Could mean something like *after*, maybe *next*. At this rate, you and I will be able to talk to toddlers everywhere in no time.

—*Eyyots esat yok yosk.*

—What did you just say? You sounded real serious all of a sudden. What's happening tomorrow?

—*Yout ekot etut Eteyat etonoyow.*

—I . . . to Terra tomorrow. I go to Terra tomorrow?

—*At.*

—We're going home?

—*At At.*

—YES! Thank you! Do you guys do hugs?

File No. 2116 (continued)

Interview between Major Katherine Lebedev,
Russian Main Intelligence Agency (GRU), and
Vincent Couture

Location: GRU building, Saint Petersburg, Russia

—Who was this Opt guy? A language teacher or something?

—Enatast. He . . . He's some sort of scholar. He can't pronounce an l to save his life, but he's good with the law. He
was sent there by the Council, the government.

—To teach you how to speak.

—No. Well, yes. I think he was helping them figure out
what to do with us. They had no idea.

—Like whether they should kill you or not?

—No! They didn't know what to make of us. They figured out we're related to them when they came here, but
we're still . . . We're very different. They have laws that tell
them how to deal with full-blown aliens, and laws that tell
them how to deal with people that are part Ekt, but those
were intended for people that were born there. They
weren't prepared for a whole planet full of hairy people
with a tiny bit of Ekt in them.

—Hairy people?

—Yeah – well, you saw Ekim – they don't have body hair.

—We don't have a lot . . .

—We have enough, apparently. People stopped us on the street to look at our arms. Kids wanted to touch our eyebrows. We were like Wookiees to them.

—You're making this up.

—I swear. It was like Chewbacca landed in New York.

—I don't get it.

—What? Chewbacca?

—These people, these *Ekt*, they come here and they kill *millions* of us. Then they take you there and they just . . . what? Get you to learn their language. Feed you, clothe you, I suppose. For years. That doesn't make sense to me. Were you prisoners the whole time?

—No! It's complicated. They don't . . . We were some sort of legal, more like a philosophical, hot potato to them. They debated, a lot. The way their government works, it's . . . slow.

—So you didn't spend nine years in a room with that Opt guy.

—No, but I did talk to him a lot. He's a good person and for a long time, he was the only one I could really talk to on their planet.

—I thought you learned their language.

—It takes a while before you can carry a real conversation with people. Enatast could meet me halfway. With everyone else, I felt like a tourist in Cuba. *Donde esta la playa?*

—Did they have beaches?

—They have oceans, but we've never seen one. They had plenty of sand . . .

—What does it look like, their planet?

—Well, it's a planet, so it really depends on where you go. They have oceans, two continents. Each is divided into . . . regions . . . Osk, where we first stayed, was really . . . clean. Have you ever been to Singapore?

—No, why?

—Never mind. It was just really well kept. Beautiful, lots of old buildings. It's where their . . . planetary government – I guess you can call it that – meets. The imperial palace is there. It's gorgeous.

—Skyscrapers?

—No, everything was low. Nothing above two or three floors. We were in a government compound, though, so we didn't see everything there was to see in Osk. They moved us to Etyakt next. Another region. It's a weird mix of old and new. Lots of people from different places –

—You mean planets?

—Well, yeah. Planets, other regions. They were all born on Esat Ekt as far as I know, but some had ancestors that were from other worlds. Lots of different customs, all sorts of weird food. It wasn't as pretty as Osk, but more . . . lively.

—Why did you have to move?

—Like I said, we were in some government building. Eva, Rose, and Eugene – I mean General Govender – were bunking together. There was a lot more room in Etyakt. We each had a house. Well, not Eva.

—They gave it to you? Like, a real house?

—I don't think it was *really* ours. I never asked. It's not like we were going to sell it.

—Go on.

—That's it. We moved to a new place.

—And you watched TV for nine years. The end.

—There's . . . no TV. There's information you can watch, but they don't act. No . . . fiction, just info.

—Why not?

—I don't know. They just don't. They write books, novels, but nothing visual. To have someone pretend to be someone else is just . . . not something they do. Anyway, we didn't need TV. We had a whole world to discover. It took us weeks to figure out the house. How to use the kitchen, how to –

—Uh-huh.

—What? Too mundane for you?

—I don't know, I think alien world, I don't think Martha Stewart.

—What did you expect? Space combat? We ate and we slept and we washed dishes. I know it sounds boring, but . . . how do I explain this? Imagine yourself in a place that kinda looks like here, but every little thing is just different enough to make you feel like an idiot. It's familiar, but you don't know how to use the door handles, the toilet. You don't know if the thing you're holding in your hand is a fork or some kind of screwdriver. Is that box food, something like salt, what you clean the toilet with? We were . . . lost.

File No. EE026

Personal File From Esat Ekt

Interview between Rose Franklin and Vincent Couture

Location: Assigned residence, Etyakt region

—Can we do this quick, Rose? Eva wants to take a walk, and I don't want her to go outside alone.

—It won't take long. I just want to keep some record of our time here if we're leaving soon. Do you mind?

—No, it's fine. Go! Go! Let's talk.

—So . . . What can you tell us about where we are?

—Enatast told me this is a residential neighborhood somewhere in the Etyakt region. I'm not sure what these houses are for, but he said we can stay here until we leave. It's pretty. There are trees everywhere. Weird, alien trees.

—They're not that weird. I'm actually surprised at how *not weird* everything is. I mean, sure, it's all different, but it's also . . .

—Not different?

—There are houses, for one thing, streets, neighborhoods. They have government. Some of it makes sense.

They've spent a couple thousand years on Earth near what was the epicenter of civilization. It's possible they've influenced us a lot more than we thought – don't tell them I said that. But there are things I really didn't expect. Look at how close their vegetation is to ours.

—Rose, I've looked. Have you ever seen a tree with multicolor bark?

—I have. Rainbow eucalyptus. I think that's what it's called. Has bark just like that. The street is a lot weirder if you ask me. That black sand, it looks volcanic. I wonder if all the streets are like that.

—You're free to walk around, you know. You wanted to see more of the place. Here's your chance.

—Do we know if it's safe?

—I don't think they would have us stay in the middle of a war zone, Rose. There aren't any guards at the door.

—I saw one walk by earlier. Her uniform looked different, but she was armed.

—Different government. I know they call them regions – well, I call them regions, they call them *etyeks*. It means a part of something, but from what I gather it's really more like a country. Different rules, different . . . everything. We were in the Osk region before, this is just south of that. And by south, I mean lower on the map that Enatast showed me. I don't know if there's really a south.

—Vincent, did Ena . . .

—His name is Enatast.

—Did Enatast tell you why we're here?

—He said we'd be more comfortable.

—Did he say when we're leaving?

—He says he doesn't know.

—Do you believe him? We were supposed to leave right away, and it's been days.

—Do I believe that he doesn't know when? Yes. I'm sure he knows what the holdup is about but that he won't say.

—I have a feeling we'll be here a while.

—Why do you say that?

—They've given us a place to live, Vincent. It seems like a lot of trouble to go through for a few extra nights. We could have stayed where they were holding us before.

—I don't know. He says we're leaving soon. There's obviously a lot he's not telling me, in part because I can't understand half of what he says, but I don't think he has any reason to lie to us. He's getting good, though. He can pronounce d's now, sorta, and r's. He *growls* them. He still adds vowels before everything, but you can barely hear it anymore

—He's right about one thing. This place is way more comfortable.

—You like it here, don't you?

—I just said it's a lot more comfortable.

—I didn't mean the house. You like being here, on this planet.

—It's a bit eerie, but yes, I do. It's a new world, aren't you the least bit excited?

—Looks a lot like Havana, without any windows.

—I've never been to Cuba.

—Sorry, I forgot you weren't allowed back then. I went on vacation a few times. You could get an all-inclusive for five hundred bucks, booze included. Anyway, that's what it looks like. Spanish architecture, intricate details, bright colors. Only Havana's falling apart. It looks great from the street, but go on a rooftop, and it looks like Beirut. Gaping holes everywhere. This place is in great shape.

—And empty.

—We can't complain about the neighbors.

—It's not just our block, Vincent. Eugene and I went outside. We didn't see anyone, anywhere.

—There's a market about a twenty-minute walk that way, supposedly. Enatast said there are people living on the other side of that.

—OK, but you don't think it's weird that there are empty houses for miles on end? Also, there are no . . . cars, no vehicles.

—There weren't any where they kept us before either. I noticed that when we left. Maybe they . . . beam themselves anywhere they can't walk. And yeah, of course it's weird, Rose. Everything is. Have you tried the bathroom?

—I have.

—Do your legs touch the ground?

—No, they just hang. But I understand the concept. Their legs have to bend underneath, and they have these extra joints so they can keep their feet on the floor.

—Does your . . .

—Vincent, we don't need to talk about the toilet . . .

—Yeah, but my . . .

—I know. I know. Can you ask him about all the empty houses next time you see him?

—Sure. But seriously, Rose, what do you care if we're going home?

—I'm curious.

—And? Come on, I know when you have something on your mind.

—I . . .

—What? You can say it.

—I don't think we're going home.

—Oh, we're going, Rose. I don't care if you want to stay. We're going home.

—I didn't say I don't want to go home. I just don't think they're sending us back.

—But if they are, you'd like to stay awhile before we go, is that it?

—Is that so bad? We're on another planet, Vincent. Another planet!

—Well, I'm sorry, but I really hope you don't get your wish.

—I understand. But imagine for a minute that we're staying here, for a while. Don't you wanna make the best of it?

—Rose, I don't want you to take this the wrong way, but I want to be absolutely clear. I don't care what happens to me, to Eugene . . . to you. I don't care if we live or die. I'm sorry for the way that sounds . . . I'm getting my daughter home.

—I know you want to keep her safe.

—I'm not just keeping her safe, I'm getting her back to Earth.

—She could be happy here, you know.

—You mean you.

—I'm surprised, Vincent. I thought the scientist in you would be more excited. We're the first humans to set foot on another world. This is a . . . Once in a lifetime doesn't even *begin* to describe this. This is a truly unique opportunity. We can learn so much from these people, use the time we have to understand how their society works.

—What's the point if we can't tell anyone?

—Do you really mean that, Vincent? That doesn't sound like you at all.

—Maybe I'm getting old.

—Vincent, we're the same age.

—We are, aren't we? I keep thinking you're older than me because . . . well, because you were older than me before. You're right, though. I should be all over this. But I'm not.

—You should try to –

—I've never bought her clothes.

—What?

—Eva. I've never bought her clothes. I've never bought her a toy, a stick of gum. I never took her out for pancakes on Sunday, haven't helped her with homework.

—Those are all things *you* haven't done. Are you sure this is about her?

—Maybe you're right. Maybe I'm being selfish. I want her to have . . . I want to give her some semblance of normalcy. I want that to be my gift to her. I think she deserves it. Besides, you're talking about staying here as if it were just another option, like moving to France or something. It's not. She won't be going to the prom with a bunch of her alien girlfriends. It's not safe here, Rose. It's not safe for us, and it's not safe for her. You're like a volcanologist staring down the crater of an active volcano. It's cool and all, but I'm not raising my daughter on the edge of it just to satisfy your scientific curiosity.

File No. EE027

Personal File From Esat Ekt

Personal Journal Entry – Dr Rose Franklin

Location: Assigned residence, Etyakt region

I think I just tried to pet a rat. I was playing with the sand on the pathway outside the house I'm staying in. I thought it was ground volcanic rock – I guess it could be – but there's a lot of metal in it. It's insanely heavy, it won't move at all when I blow on it. This . . . thing, about the size of my hand came out of nowhere. A red fuzzy fur ball. Something like a large hamster, but red. And I mean red. When I was a kid, my favorite crayon was called Torch Red. That red. The little thing didn't have a tail, you could barely see its eyes. Just a red ball zipping across the path. It stopped dead in its tracks when it saw me. I tried calling it, slowly moved my hand towards it. That's when a . . . security person showed up. She screamed, at me or the animal, I'll never know. She said something else while she whooshed away my little friend. The whooshing part I understood. Red ball certainly got the message. I don't think I was in any danger, but the guard looked at me like my mother did if I ate an earthworm on a dare, or chewed on a piece of gum I'd found on the car's floor. I take it red ball isn't the most beloved animal on this world.

In many ways, this place is a lot like Earth. Gravity is roughly the same. There's just no way to measure that with what we have. Atmosphere is obviously similar to ours, but the air feels a bit thicker. Atmospheric pressure might be a bit higher. That, or the air is just drier. It also smells different. The air is . . . sweet. Sugary.

Vincent said Enatast told him we didn't need to worry about diseases. I wonder why. I don't want their entire species gone because of something like a cold sore. I guess the people doing the space travel probably know more about the dangers of space travel than I do. We didn't understand a lot of what was going on when we first arrived, but I assume some of what they did was meant to prevent the cold-sore apocalypse. Hopefully, we won't die of alien gum disease either.

I know there are more important things to worry about, like dying, but I can't stop thinking about that little red ball. I wonder if it's considered a pest for practical reasons — maybe it eats crops, or carries diseases — or if it's just cultural. Maybe red ball is mean as hell and would have ripped my finger off, but it seemed kind of friendly. It's completely stupid and crazy — and I won't do it, I swear I won't do it — but part of me really wants to try and tame one, bring it inside the house. I have a feeling this is the kind of thing four-year-olds get scolded for around here.

We might as well be four years old. We're children here. Ignorant and naïve beyond belief. We're in awe at the simplest and most insignificant things, playfully swimming in the unknown, gobbling information faster than we can process it. I am, anyway. Everything is science. Everything is discovery. Needless to say, I'm happy.

I wish Vincent and Eugene were that happy. All they can talk about is going home. I understand. Or I *want* to understand. Eugene is suspicious of everything and everyone. He doesn't trust a word out of Enatast's mouth. I don't think he ever will. Vincent just wants to keep his daughter safe. That part I really get. I just wish . . . I wish they'd make the best of whatever time we have here. We all see the same things, but I wish they could see them as I do. I feel like I'm enjoying a movie no one else in the room is paying attention to. It's a selfish feeling. I really just want someone to share the wonder with.

I don't know how long we have, but I don't want this to end. I'm so curious about everything, I can't sit still. I'm not the only one who's curious. We all stick out like sore thumbs here. Vincent and I, especially. We're both freakishly pink. We're also the only ones I've seen with long hair. Either theirs doesn't grow long or they keep it short on purpose. I see more people walking in our neighborhood every day, no doubt hoping they'll 'accidentally' bump into us. I help with that as much as I can. I love the look on people's faces.

I should get ready. We're going to the market today.

File No. 2116 (continued)

Interview between Major Katherine Lebedev,
Russian Main Intelligence Agency (GRU),
and Vincent Couture

Location: GRU building, Saint Petersburg, Russia

—Look, Katherine. I can talk to you about what the weather was like, what we ate for breakfast, but I don't think you're that curious about it. What do you *really* wanna know?

—The same thing *everyone* wants to know, Vincent. I want to know if they're coming back!

—They're not! I told you already. How many times do you want me to say it? The Ekt aren't coming back here. I really, honestly – cross my heart and hope to die – don't think they are. The whole Earth debacle is a *huge* deal for them. They'll talk about it for ever, but there's no way they'll ever agree on anything. It's all about interference. Everything is. Coming here to remove the alien descendants is definitely interfering, but they agreed to it thinking it would only affect a few people, and it was better than having our entire species 'infected' with their genetics. Realizing that's exactly what had happened was really bad. Killing millions of us while figuring this out is also bad, not so much because people died but because that's even more interference. It's like trying to wipe an oil stain off your shirt, only to realize your hands are dirty and you're smearing more shit all over. They can't fix this. They won't do anything.

—I wish I could believe that.

—Well, that's your choice, now, isn't it? But stop asking the question if you don't care about the answer.

—It's just hard to believe, Vincent. You said they came here to find a few people. They left when we all started dying, but they still haven't found those people. They're still here. Won't they want to come back and finish the job?

—I'm telling you, they don't want a war with us. They told us in so many words. They were Ekt words, so there might have been fewer.

—They did?

—Tell us? Yes! General Govender was there. He made peace with their government.

—Officially?

—What does that even mean? Yes. Officially. He met with them, in an official manner. It was all ... very official.

File No. EE028

Personal File From Esat Ekt

Interview between Eugene Govender and Opt Enatast

Location: Assigned residence, Etyakt region

Translated by Vincent Couture

—Sit down, Couture. You're making me nervous. What does he want with me?

[*He said: 'Take me to your leader.' I'm only half kidding, that's sort of what he said. He wants to talk to the boss. I explained to him what a general was, and he said he wanted to meet you.*]

What's his name again?

[*Opt Enatast.*]

Do I call him Opt? Mister Opt?

[*No. Either the whole thing or just Enatast. Or you don't call him anything.*]

I have to call him something.

[*How often do you use someone's name when you talk to them? But whatever, call him Enatast. That's what I do. I don't think it's rude, but even if it were, he had to teach me how to use the toilet, I'm sure he'll cut us some slack on etiquette.*]

And you'll translate everything back and forth.

[*He might understand you if you keep it simple. If not, I'll do my best, but you still need to keep it simple.*]

Goddammit!

[*Here he is.* Eyyetist, *Enatast.* Eyet *General Eugene Govender.*]

—*Eyyetist*, Vincent. *Eyipot otot eps*, Yeneyay.

—What'd he say?

[*I don't know. Something polite.*]

Did he call me Yeneyay?

[*Yes. He called you General. Just shake his hand, will you? I showed him how that works.*]

It's an honor to meet you, Opt Enatast.

—*Eyitokt aktept otok apats Akitast* —

[*Whoa. Stop! Slowly.* Ansyets. Ansyets.]

Eyitokt . . . aktept . . . otok apats Akitast.

[*Speak like Great Council of Akitast. I speak for the Council, on behalf of, something like that.*]

Ast eyapetent ekukt eteyans.

[*I apologize, or I'm sorry for the death of the Terrans, humans.*]

. . .

[*You have to say something now, General.*]

—Ask him why they attacked us.

[*How about you apologize for their four pilots first?*]

A hundred million to four. We're not exactly even. Ask him.

[Ekt eyepsats iset akt.]

—*Eyekant ops. Aks eyepsats apepoks Ekt. Ast eyapetent.*

[*We didn't. We attacked Ekt criminals. I'm sorry.*]

—That's it? A hundred million dead, and he's sorry?

[*Look, General, he's not the one who sent those robots. I'm sure he'd have a lot more to say if his interpreter didn't have the vocabulary of a three-year-old. Just take the man at his word, will you?*]

Ask him if he knows how many of us they killed.

[*No, I won't. Even if I could, I'm not asking him that.*]

Fine. Tell him . . . Tell him we don't want a war.

[Aks eyapat ops . . .]

Vincent?

[*EEEEEEEEEEEEEEEEEEE. BOOM! TATA-TATATA! AAARGH!*]

What the hell are you doing?

[*I'm miming a war. I told you to keep it simple.*]

—*Oyokyets!*

[*Maybe?*]

Aks anyoks eyapat ops oyokyets.

[*We don't want a war either. There!*]

—Tell him I don't speak for our entire planet. Tell him no one does. Tell him it won't be easy to convince the people on Earth that they don't mean us any harm, not after what they've done. It might take a few generations before we're able to start a relationship with a clean slate. Tell him I'll do my best to explain to our leaders that this was . . . Goddammit, how do you tell someone one hundred million dead was an accident? It wouldn't hurt if they took some responsibility. This five-year-old thing: It was an accident. I don't think it's gonna sit too well with anyone who's had their biggest city turned into a mass grave. Are you sure he can't understand me? YOU! I'M TALKING TO YOU! Did you hear what I just said?

[Aks eyyots Eteyat anesk akt.]

What did you tell him?

—*Eyakosk. Eyapetent* Yincent.

[Eyesunt.]

—Why is he leaving? Dammit, Couture! What did you tell him?

[*It's OK, sir.*]

Whatever you said, it was suspiciously shorter than what I told you to tell him.

[*There was no point, sir. Like you said, you can't speak for everyone on Earth. He knows that. He can't speak for his people either. This was just for show.*]

Why?

[*If I had to guess, I'd say he wanted to make us feel better about staying here.*]

What the hell are you talking about?

[*You wanna know what I told him? I asked when we were leaving.*]

That's it?

[*Well, yeah. What else matters at this point?*]

And?

[*He said it's complicated.*]

What the hell does that mean?

[*I think it means we're gonna be here a while.*]

Are you OK with that?

[*Like I told Rose, I don't really care what happens to me, but I don't want my daughter to grow up here. We need to get her home.*]

Then I suggest you start making friends.

[*Was any part of 'We need to get her home' unclear? I don't want to make friends. I don't want to be here long enough to make friends. What we need is a plan.*]

No. What we need now are friends. I wanted a plan, but Rose shut me down faster than a rocketful of monkeys.

[*Don't pay attention to her. She likes it here. She's —*]

She's right! Trying to come up with a plan is just stupid. We don't know anything. We don't know how we got here. We don't know how to get back. What are we gonna plan for? What we need is someone who knows how to get us off this goddamn rock, so I suggest you get out there and start making friends. Lots of them. We need friends in the government, friends that hate the government. We need friends, Couture.

File No. EE031

Personal File From Esat Ekt

Interview between Vincent Couture and Esok

Location: Aptakt Market, Etyakt region

Translated by Vincent Couture

—What is your name?

—You forgot already? You asked a minute ago (at a time four moments in the past).

—I know I did. It's for a . . . I don't know how to say 'recording.'

—I'm Esok.

—Just Esok?

—Do you see anyone else?

—No. Thank you, Esok. Can you tell me what this place is?

—Here? This is the Aptakt Market. It's the largest one in the Etyakt region. People come here to buy food and things.

—We get our food on that street in another market.

—Yes. Yes. Etyakt dispensary. Government.

—The food over there is a lot better. There's more too.

—Much better.

—OK, so what's the difference?

—There the food is free. Here you have to pay.

—Then why do people come here?

—Here is where the market is.

—I . . . I don't understand.

—Yes. Yes.

—No, I meant –

—What is your world like?

—My world? It's . . . Parts of it are like here. We have trees, like here. Other parts are much colder . . . We have – I don't know how to say ocean – lots of water, large things of water.

—Yes. Yes. Here too. Is everyone like you?

—Like me? What does that mean?

—You have hair on your face, and on your arms.

—A little bit of hair on our arms, yes.

—Lots of hair. Does everyone have arms?

—Yes, we have arms . . . and legs.

—No one lives in water?

—Yes. Animals do.

—What is an-im-al?

—Hmmm . . . A living thing? Something that eats, and sees, and moves.

—Like you.

—Yes, but different . . . less intelligent.

—Some people are less intelligent.

—How do you say self-aware? (I said me conscious of me. Blank stare . . .) Humans – I'm a human – are conscious of their own feelings, of what they think, what they do.

—You believe that thinking about you makes you better?

—No, I . . . Actually, yes. Humans think that.

—Interesting.

—Your . . . pad. It's doing something.

—Oh. Just a vote. I can do it later.

—A vote on what?

—Let me see . . . It concerns you.

—Me?

—Yes. Yes. Someone suggested we plant more trees on your side of the market, now that someone lives there.

—And you get to vote on that?

—Why wouldn't I? You don't need any special skills to decide on a tree! Besides, I vote on all things that concern trees and plants. You don't think I should?

—I . . . I didn't mean . . . I'm sure you're really good at . . . How do you know I live on the other side of the market?

—Everyone knows.

—Why does no one else live there?

—There aren't enough people to fill those houses.

—That's what I mean. Why are there houses if there are not enough people?

—You don't know?

—I don't know anything!

—This planet, it used to be a *yatsak* nest. You could barely walk these streets. There were people from many worlds, buying things, selling things. Then, thousands of months ago, there was a war. The emperor had done something very wrong, and the people that were hurt attacked this planet. Many died. Many, many. After the war, they decided that Esat Ekt would never interfere with other worlds again, in any way. Everyone not of this planet was sent away.

—How many?

—*Yokokt*.

—I don't understand.

—Show me your hands . . . Both hands. This is how many people lived here before. Now put one hand down. This is how many people lived here after.

—Half? Where did they go?

—Anywhere but here. Most were born on Esat Ekt, but they were not Ekt. Many went to the planet of their ancestors, but many were not welcome there either. Many refused to go. Many many died.

—But you're here. All these people are here.

—How do you know I'm not Ekt?

—You're blue.

—Not blue enough. I couldn't go to my ancestor's planet, even if I wanted to. There they'd call me grey. My fifth father was really blue. My fifth mother was Ekt. Those with Ekt blood did not leave.

—They were allowed to stay.

—That depends on your point of view. My fifth mother would say they weren't allowed to leave. My fifth father was not Ekt. He had to go. But my fifth mother could not go with him. My fourth mother, their daughter, was half-Ekt, so she could not leave either.

—Why?

—She could have babies on another world, babies with Ekt blood. The Ekt can't have that.

—Interference.

—Yes, yes. It's a very important word on this planet.

—I'll try to remember that.

—I've seen you with a young girl. Is she your daughter?

—You have? Her name's Eva.

—Good. She will like it here. There are other kids her age.

—There aren't elsewhere?

—Not where the Ekt live. Most of their children go to school in the city, or they work.

—They work?

—Someone has to work. The only Ekt children left here are the little red ones.

—Red ones?

—Imperial cadets. They wear red. They train to be soldiers in the Imperial Guard. There's one over there.

—You don't seem to like them.

—Yes, yes. They're still nice at that age. It's what they'll grow up to be I don't like . . .

—Your pad. Another vote?

—Not for me. The Etyakt Council voted. You've been made citizens.

—Us? Why?

—You can't be on this planet if you're not.

—So it's a good thing?

—It depends on whether or not you planned on ever going home.

—You mean we can't leave?

—Yes, yes.

—What?

—I said yes. You can't leave Esat Ekt.

—For how long?

—For ever.

File No. 2116 (continued)

Interview between Major Katherine Lebedev, Russian Main Intelligence Agency (GRU), and Vincent Couture

Location: GRU building, Saint Petersburg, Russia

—So you chose to stay there, for nine years . . .

—They offered to let us stay.

—And you said?

—We said yes. It was a unique opportunity.

—You stayed voluntarily.

—That's what I just said.

—Willingly?

—Wholeheartedly. We're gonna run out of synonyms soon.

— . . .

—What? Is that so difficult to understand? We had the chance to spend some time on a new planet with another species. We jumped on it. Rose and I are scientists, remember? It was a unique –

—A unique opportunity. You said that already. Then one day you decided you wanted to come home and they just . . . sent you back, is that it? You didn't have to do anything. You just asked: 'Can we go home now?' and they said: 'Sure! Hop on!' Nothing happened in between, nothing worth mentioning. At all. For nine years.

—I don't know what to tell you. Everything was interesting. Everything was new.

—What did you do?

—What do you mean?

—I mean what did you do all day, for a decade? Did you have jobs?

—Eva did for a while. She worked in a soup kitchen.

—An alien soup kitchen?

—Well, it wasn't alien *there*. But they did serve people from other worlds.

—That's so nice. Eva feeding people without money. You must have been so proud.

—Was that sarcasm? I can't tell. And yes, they were poor, but they did have money. In fact, they were the only ones who did. There's no currency, officially, in any of the regions. Everything essential is more or less free, and you can trade for most other things. You only need money to buy things outside the system.

—Communism!

—Not quite. People own things. Some people own much more than others. If they produce something the government doesn't regulate. Art, for example. Sculptors, dancers, writers, they all lived better than most if they were any good.

—Sculptors? What about doctors?

—Well, most people work because they want to. No one there would get up every morning to do something they don't like just so they can get more food or clothing than everyone else.

—How cute. And boring. There must be some crappy work no one wants to do.

—Sure. Farming, mostly. Kids do that, for a few years before they go to . . . I guess you could call it university.

—Child labor. Lovely.

—They're more like teenagers. They just look very young.

—What about you and Dr Franklin? What did you do all day?

—We didn't have jobs if that's what you're asking.

—Why not?

—We were totally unqualified for . . . everything.

—Poor things. Did people make fun of you?

—They stared, mostly. They did call us hairy. Point is it probably never occurred to them to offer us work. I spent a few hours a day teaching English to Enatast while he taught me Ekt. I'm not sure how much he really wanted to learn. After a while, he might have come just so I'd have something to do. But he kept coming, so I didn't ask. Rose . . . Rose spent some time with scientists of theirs, but she really didn't have any skills they could use. I 'hung out' with them for a while, especially at the beginning, so I could translate for Rose, but I stopped when I got good enough at spotting condescension. Except for the knee thing, Rose was much more interesting to them.

—Why is that?

—She knocked one of their robots out, all on her own. They were impressed.

—They weren't angry?

—No. Not where we lived, anyway. We're not enemies to them. We're more like . . . They think they made us . . . sick, in some way, by messing with our gene pool. We're also much less evolved technologically, scientifically, and we're physically weaker, shorter. There's nothing remotely menacing about us. I don't know how to explain it . . . Have you ever seen a baby squirrel?

—I don't think I have, but what's that got –

—Kara found one on the sidewalk once. It was right after they founded the EDC. We'd just moved to New York. We didn't know anyone. Anyway, she saw this baby squirrel. We both didn't want anything to do with it. We didn't want it to die, but we also didn't want to take care of a squirrel because . . . because it's a squirrel, and we'd be stuck with it if its mother didn't take it back. It was about nightfall, so we knew the cats were probably gonna get it, but we were ready to let nature take its course. Only the little bugger crawled on to my foot and curled up into a ball, then it fell asleep.

—Ohhhh . . .

—Yeah. That. We took it home for the night and dumped it in the same tree the next day.

—What happened to it?

—I have no idea. It probably died. That's not the point. The point is it was a pest, a glorified rat with a fuzzy tail, but it was cute, and helpless, and we felt responsible. Fortunately for us, the Ekt are more patient than Kara and I were, so they took care of us for more than a day while their government decided what to do next.

—And what did they decide?

—Nothing.

—Vincent. I get that you don't trust me, but if you're gonna come up with lies, they should at least be reasonably believable. And this is coming from someone who'll believe just about anything. No, really! I'm supergullible. I buy all these stupid things on television, then I'm too ashamed to return them.

—I told you before. The way they work, it's slow.

—Nine years slow?

—Yeah! They have a very strict democracy. Some things are hard to decide for them.

—I thought they had an emperor.

—They do, it's an empress now. But she doesn't do anything. It's a lot like the queen. The people make most of the decisions directly. Everything that involves another species, another planet, the decision belongs to the Great Council of Akitast.

—OK, so they vote on things. We do that. I don't see what's so hard about it that it would take a decade.

—It's not like us. What we do, it's baby vote. These people are major-league voters.

—What does that mean?

—Well, here, we vote on a few things, like government. Some places require an absolute majority, 50 percent of the vote plus one. Some places don't care, they just pick whoever got the most votes. But we choose from a list; there are a limited number of options. Imagine that instead of a list of candidates, we let everyone write in the name of whoever they'd like, and to be elected to something, you'd need more than half the vote, from everyone. That's how they decide things. Getting the votes isn't a problem. These people vote on everything, all day every day. Getting things done depends on the question. If they can formulate it as a yes/no question, then it's all good. If it's multiple choice, it gets complicated. The Council had no clue what to do with us. That's an endless number of possibilities, and they couldn't agree on any of them. When we left, they were still debating whether they should allow us to stay.

—How stupid do you think I am, Vincent?

—What do you want me to say?

—Hmmm, I don't know. The truth, maybe?

—That *is* the truth. What part of it is bothering you? That they're not a threat?

—Tell me about their army.

—Really? There isn't much more to say other than what I've already told you. We didn't exactly go on a tour of their military. They have a shit ton of robots. We've seen some transport ships, but they said they had . . . Are you listening to anything I'm saying?

—I'm sorry. We're gonna have to do this another time.

—What is it?

—It's . . . not good. We have a bit of a problem.

—What kind of problem?

—Your daughter.

—Has she done anything?

—Well, she's gone. I suppose that's something.

—What do you mean, gone? Where?

—Hmmm. That was gonna be *my* question. Where is she?

—How the hell should I know? You have me locked in a room all day. I'm not even allowed to see her.

—That's a bit of an overstatement, Vincent. That room isn't locked, it's well guarded. There's a difference. But you do have a point. Let's say I believe you. Dr Franklin was also in her room. Besides, I really don't think she's the prison-break type. Are you sure it's not you?

—What? No. Yes, I'm sure.

—Fine. It wasn't you. It would just be so much better if it were you.

—Why's that?

—Because if it's not your people who broke her out, then it has to be one of my people. You can see how that's a problem, can't you? Yesterday, I had three people who could pilot Themis. Three pilots. Now one of them is dead and one's –

—Ekim's dead?

—Oops! I forgot to tell you, didn't I? He is *very* dead. He died two days ago. From cat poo, no less.

—You should have let him go. I told you to let him go home!

—You were serious about that? Well, had I known . . . We'd have let the alien kid go, *with* Themis, because why not? That certainly would have solved my pilot problem. Because now . . . Now Eva's gone missing. I'm not super-good at math, but I know that robot needs two pilots and three minus two is less than that. As if that weren't enough, it would appear I have a traitor working for me . . . CHYORTVOZ'MI! I'm sorry. I'm a little ticked off at the moment. Do you know how much trouble I'm gonna be in for this? I had to fill out three forms just to talk to her. Imagine the paperwork for losing her altogether. We're, like, not supposed to lose people. That's a big no-no. It's kind of our thing, really.

—Am I supposed to feel sorry for you?

—You could! That would be nice. I could use a hug. You could also help me find her before this gets any worse.

—Why would I do anything to help you?

—Good question. There doesn't seem to be any, does there? I mean, right now you're just happy she found a way out of here. Right? About five seconds from now, you'll realize she now has the entire Russian Army and secret service after her. You'll think: Hmmm, my daughter isn't the most restrained person in the world. I hope she doesn't do anything stupid when they catch up to her. And they will, they're very good at finding people. Soon – OH! I think it's happening! Now you have this mental image of her getting shot eight hundred times and –

—You so much as touch her, and I'll –

—Oh, for God's sake, Vincent! Run that through in your head one more time! Are you sure that's the right play? The words you're looking for are: 'Please, Katherine! Pretty please! Isn't there anything you can do?'

—Is there?

—NO! Not unless I find her first! Are you sure you don't know where she is? Where would she go to? Where would she hide?

—In Russia? She's never . . . We've never been here. She doesn't know anything. She'd have no idea where to go.

—She left you a note.

—What did it say?

—It said: 'Dad, how the hell could Katherine possibly know what I wrote? She just found out about the note.'

— . . .

—Don't worry, you can have it, after everyone else takes a look at it.

File No. EE066

Personal File From Esat Ekt

Personal log – Eva Reyes and Vincent Couture

Location: Aptakt Market, Etyakt region

—Yours sees the world in only two dimensions. These ones are born and ready for adoption.

—Eva?

—What?

—Why are you telling me? I wrote the clue. I already know what it is.

—I'm just thinking out loud, Dad. I don't get it. It's hard.

—It's a treasure hunt. It's supposed to be hard. Otherwise, it's a treasure stroll or something.

—You still haven't told me what's in that jar.

—I'll tell you when you figure out this clue.

—What's in the jar?

—Really, Eva?

—I wanna know!

—A couple strands of hair.

—Yours?

—Yeah, mine. Do you think I go around cutting other people's hair for no reason?

—I don't know! . . . Do I really need to ask?

—Ask what?

—Dad! Why do you have your hair in a jar?

—Oh. That. You'll see.

—That's not funny, Dad. Tell me!

—You'll know when you figure out the clue. It's the last one.

—I don't know what it means! Mine sees the world in two dimensions. My what?

—Why do you see things in 3D?

—I . . . because my eyes are facing forward?

—How many eyes?

—Two eyes.

—So . . .

—What do I have that doesn't have two eyes? . . . I don't have anything!

—Not here. Back home.

— . . . Kara's plush gopher!

—Yes!

—All right. These ones are born and ready for — The little furry animals next to the fruit stand?

—Yes! They're called yotyot, by the way.

—Do you mean . . . ?

—I do mean. We're getting a yotyot! You said you liked them, and it's the closest thing to a cat I could find.

—Thank you! Thank you! Thank you!

—Hey. It's your birthday. At least I think it's your birthday. The guy said they'll eat anything, and they won't grow any bigger. They only pee in water, apparently.

—Can we get it now?

—In a minute. There's some sort of scuffle going on o— Shit! EVA! WATCH OUT!

—AAGH!

—Eva, are you OK?

—Yeah, I — He bumped into me pretty hard.

—HEY! ASSHOLE! YEAH RUN AWAY, YOU CHI—

—DAD! I'm fine.

—Are you sure? There's a guard trainee coming this way. I can get the asshole arrested if —

—I said I'm fine.

[Eps eyiskeks akt?]

Ops. Eyesunt.

[Ast eyet Ekim.]

Eyet Eva.

[Eps eyesat Eteyat akt? Eps ast eyyetsek onyosk ant ot.]

At, at. Aks eyek ant asteks onsoks.

[Ast eyyekt. Ast eyapat yetsek eps epokt, Evat.]

Anyoks! Aks eyyekt eket ops. Bye!

—What did he want?

—Dad! He just wanted to know if I was hurt.

—Why did he ask for your name? By the way, how did you get so good at their language?

—He didn't ask. He told me his name was Ekim. I gave him mine. I didn't know it was a secret. And you taught me, Dad.

—I didn't teach you all that! What does *onsoks* mean, anyway? Empty?

—Yes. I don't know, Dad. I just . . .

—Don't apologize for learning quicker than me. Just be careful with strangers, OK? And stop telling people we don't know anyone, will you?

—He was just being nice, Dad.

—He's a trainee in the Imperial Guard.

—And?

—And nothing. You're right. We don't know him. That's all.

— . . .

—You think he's cute, don't you?

—Dad!

—What?

—Can we go get my yotyot now?

—Yes. Let's. It's right over th— Eva, don't run!

. . .

I said don—

—Can I take this one?

—Let me catch my breath for a second.

—Can I take him?

—Eva, you can take whichever one you like. They all look the same.

—This one looks sad.

—You can pick any one of them, and you want the miserable one?

—Maybe he'll be happier living with us.

—That is . . . very nice of you, Eva. Happy twelfth birthday! Can you carry him? I don't have anything to put him in.

—Sure. Come here little fellow!

—*Eyesunt.*

—What did you just do?

—I thanked the man. I paid him, and I thanked him.

—You gave him the jar!

—Yes. I did.

—With your hair in it!

—I did. That's what he wanted.

—That's . . . You don't feel bad?

—Why would I feel bad?

—You paid him with hair, Dad!

—Well, the hair is just something I threw in at the end. I already gave him my belt yesterday, but that wasn't enough. Oh, and my New York MetroCard. Basically, I traded a thirty-dollar belt for some game. If anyone's getting rip—

—It's not a game! It's a pet!

—Not that kind of game. Meat! You know people eat these things, right?

—What? Nooo!

—The . . . I don't know what they call themselves. The . . . tall, lanky bald fellows.

—They're all sorta bald, Dad

—The naked ones.

—Oh. Them.

—Yeah. They eat those. That's why they sell them.

—That's horrible! They're so cute!

—Like a bunny rabbit?

—Yes!

—Well . . .

—Don't listen to him. No one's gonna eat you, Mr Yotyot.

—That's his name?

—What's wrong with Mr Yotyot?

—Nothing. It's just like calling your cat Mr Cat.

—I like Mr Cat!

—Mr Yotyot it is, then. Welcome to the family. How do you know it's a he?

— . . .

—Oh. I see. Eva, before we take him home . . . You know we might go back soon, right? To Earth? I don't know how long we'll stay. I sure didn't think we'd be here for eighteen months. And I don't think we should – I don't think we can take Mr Yotyot back with us when we leave.

—I like it here, Dad.

—That's good. I just don't want you to get too attached if we're going soon. I don't even know how long these things live. Mr Yotyot might be like a hundred years old already. Oh, before I forget. Rose is having all of us over for dinner tonight.

—You said we'd spend the day together.

—We are. We'll be together, with Rose and Eugene.

—But it's my birthday!

—I know! That's the point! Rose even found something that resembles a cake!

—I thought we could just . . . hang out, just the two of us.

—How about this? We'll have dinner with Rose and Eugene, then we'll go home and . . . hang out all you want . . . I think I might be too old to use that phrase.

File No. 2117

Letter from Eva Reyes to Vincent Couture

Vincent,

*If you're reading this, it means that guy came through on his
promise, and I'm gone. I guess it also means that everyone in the
GRU has combed through it looking for clues, some sort of secret
code. How's this? The pigeon is well done. The blind man can't see
a thing. Fuck you all.*

*This is it. I don't think I'll ever see you again. The truth is, I
hope I never do. I wish I could tell you all this in person, or at
least in private, but this will be easier on both of us. Katherine
already knows I didn't want to leave Esat Ekt, and I don't give
a shit what else she knows about me.*

*You took everything from me, Vincent. Everyone I knew.
Everything I cared about. It was my home! My* esat*! You may not
have liked it, but that was my home. I liked it there. I belonged.
I had a life,* my *life, and you took it away. You chose to.*

*Even Ekim. You know he didn't deserve this. He was
innocent. All he cared about was helping people, and me. It
probably doesn't mean much to you, but it meant the world to me,
having someone look at me that way, like I could do nothing
wrong. It didn't matter how much I tried to push him away, how
mean I was to him, he kept looking at me that way, always. He
also kept telling everyone I was his* eputet*. That made me mad to
no end. He knew, that's probably why he kept doing it. Every*

now and then, I'd let him get away with it. No shoving him against the wall, no mean joke. You should have seen his face. I don't know if I was in love with him, but I loved how he made me feel. I liked me *when he was around, and that hasn't happened a lot. Now he's gone. You took that away too.*

There's nothing for me here but bad memories. My parents, Kara. Everyone I ever cared about here is dead, dead because of me. People here made fun of me because I was different, they mocked me for who I was. Now I'm even more of a freak. They put me in a glass room, stick needles in me all day. What made you think I could possibly want that? Everything I had, Vincent, you tore it from my hands. You took the good away and sent me back to where it hurts. I hate you for it.

Was it worth it? Was it worth killing Ekim? I hate you if you say yes. I hate you if you say no. I hate you, Dad. I bet you tell yourself you did all this for me. Well, I didn't yokits *want it. That should have meant something.*

I don't know what I'll do or where I'll go from here, and I wouldn't tell you if I did, but wherever I end up, it will be my choice. I choose *this. Me. I want you to remember that. You'll probably never admit it, but you're better off without me, and I really don't think I can be worse off. I know you tried your best. I know it wasn't easy, and I'll always love you for it. But I hate you all the same.*

E.
P.S. Hey Katherine! Toodeloo!

PART TWO
Hell Out Of Dodge

File No. EE098

Personal File From Esat Ekt

Personal Journal Entry – Dr Rose Franklin

Location: Assigned residence, Etyakt region

We've been on Esat Ekt for almost four years, yet some-how, we're still strangers. There's a distance between us and them, an invisible wall we can't traverse. I want to break that wall, but I don't know how. They smile at us, give us the occasional elbow grab, a sign of affection, but there is no warmth, no real connection. It feels like wear-ing gloves all the time.

We don't know what we are. No one knows. On the one hand, our species has some of their genetics. By law – their law – that should make us Ekt. That's why we were made citizens. If that's true, we can't leave this planet, ever. On the other hand, only a very small portion of our genetic makeup is affected by theirs. I for one show no signs of genetic interference. None. By that reasoning, we have no business on this planet at all. They don't allow aliens. The Etyakt region can't give us citizenship. If we're aliens, we go home. So, either we can't leave or we can't stay. The Great Council of Akitast stepped in to settle the matter, three years ago. While they debate, we remain in limbo. We've also become the topic of a lot of debate. Our region, Etyakt, is very diverse. More than half the population is from other worlds, at least in part. They identify with us. They see what happened on Earth, the Ekt killing millions of us, and they fear they could be next. There are a lot of protests. Those in Osk – the population there is much more homogeneous – blame us for what is happening. They want us gone as fast as possible. I think that's why the Council can't come to a decision. Let us stay – force us to stay if you ask Vincent – and you anger people in Osk. Send us away and you risk making the part-alien population even angrier.

I can tell that people here are extremely curious, about us, but also by nature. We are living treasures to them, a gold mine of information about a world they know almost nothing about. I'm certain that everyone here wants the Council to call us Ekt. Because if we're not Ekt enough, if we're aliens, then we shouldn't even be here, and every second they spend talking to us risks affecting us in the worst possible way. So they wave at us on the street, chitchat – it would be rude to exclude us, and the Ekt are anything but rude – but they will find an excuse to disappear if the conversation elevates itself above small talk. They are astonishingly good at it, experts at walking this very fine line. They do it without unease or awkwardness, something we could never do if our roles were reversed.

There are exceptions, of course. Most of them involving Eva. She's . . . raw. Vincent and I are constrained by what we think is expected of us. She's not. She can be rude, always say what's on her mind. People in Etyakt love her for it. Of the three of us, she's the only one who's managed to develop genuine relationships with people. Vincent and I have . . . acquaintances.

There's a rift forming between the four of us as well. Eugene only talks about leaving. Vincent doesn't want to be here either. People here are hesitant to get close to us, but Vincent won't let anyone in at all. Except for Enatast, and Esok, of course. She really likes him, and I think it runs both ways. If it weren't for Eva, I think there might be more there. But he won't allow himself. He won't betray Kara's memory – that's how he'd see it – not with Eva reminding him of her with every breath she takes. She's so much like her mother. Eva and I don't see eye to eye on a great many things. She and her father are also growing apart.

Despite all this, I feel right at home here. I hope we don't go back to Earth anytime soon. I love this place. I love these people. There is so much knowledge here. I remember going downtown when I lived in Chicago. The life, the energy. I could just sit alone on a bench somewhere and feel those eight million lives around me. The same is true here, but what I feel is wisdom, and I find myself bettered for just bathing in it. I'm a child on this planet. The most complex science, the most abstract concepts I can grasp are so mundane on this world, it is almost impossible for the Ekt not to teach me new things. They try their very best, but some things are so obvious to them, they'll slip into conversations about the weather.

I was foolish enough to think I could be useful when we first arrived. I spent some time with their scientists – they seemed very eager to meet me – but when I explained what I was working on, I could tell by their faces I could just as well have told them I was trying to boil water. They were curious about me, but nothing I could ever do would qualify as scientifically relevant here. I got them to let me use one of their school labs. That only took two years and twelve votes. They are . . . let's just say *reluctant* to do anything that could affect human knowledge in the tiniest way, but I eventually convinced enough committee members that it couldn't happen in a school lab. It's the one good thing about never having long conversations with anyone, they never fully grasped the extent of my ignorance. Holy cow! The things their teenagers – they're not even that old – play with! They won't let me read a book, but they'll explain how the equipment works if I ask for something specific enough. It makes sense. If I can devise the experiment myself, it's probably something I could have done without their help. I wish.

I started with very simple things, things I already knew. That way I'd know if the results made any sense or if I did something wrong. Then I upped the ante, little by little. They always asked for more explanation, to make sure I wasn't fishing for knowledge. Over time, I found ways to trick them into letting me use more sophisticated equipment. I had noticed what I thought was a hunk of germanium among the samples in the lab. These guys have really good rocks. It turned out to be germanium-76. I told them germanium was rare on Earth, which is true, and that I'd never seen that particular isotope, which isn't. I told them I'd like to see if it was capable of double-beta decay – two protons turning into neutrons at once, instead of just one. That took surprisingly long to explain – I suspect they don't intuitively see matter as being made of discrete things – but I did it well enough that they assumed I had seen that happen with my own eyes, and they didn't object when I asked if I could test their isotope. They gave me a box. Not a nuclear reactor and an underground detector, not a particle accelerator the size of a small city, they walked in with something the size of a shoe box under one arm. I watched them tinker with it for a minute, probably to make it display things in a dumb enough way for me to understand. They explained how the controls worked in baby terms, and they left me alone with it. It took me a good week to figure it out, but today I observed neutrinoless double-beta decay. I didn't detect it in some convoluted way, I saw it happen right in front of me. I was so giddy, I told everyone I ran into on the way home. They all looked at me funny, as if I were some deranged person screaming: 'The Earth is round! The Earth is round!'

It took me a few hours to realize I couldn't talk about it to anyone. The Ekt would think I was an idiot, and they would throw a fit if they knew I had learned something of value because of them. Vincent knows a bit about physics, but not enough to understand this. Eva and Eugene couldn't care less. It was the strangest feeling. What I'd seen was *really* important. I had proven that neutrinos are Majorana, meaning they're their own antiparticles. I had proven neutrinos had mass. I even helped constrain the mass scale by measuring the decay rate. That was a *huge* step in physics. It might give us a way to explain why the universe is full of things instead of nothing. It could help explain how primordial stars formed, what dark matter is made of. It was an incredibly far-reaching discovery. On

Earth, I'd be a shoo-in for the Nobel prize. Here, it might get me a B– on a high-school exam. It should have been a world-changing moment, but I was in the wrong place at the wrong time. I felt like I had just invented the wheel, only to realize I was standing in the middle of Broadway during rush hour.

I can live with that. I can see myself doing great science all day even if it's primitive by everyone else's standard. In many ways, it's the best kind of science. It's stimulating yet free of consequence. Nothing I do in that lab will get anyone killed. No one will use what I do to hurt people. I hope we get to stay. I hope Vincent and Eugene change their mind about this world. Fortunately for me, our fate is in the hands of the Council, not mine, and I see nothing wrong with enjoying what this planet has to offer while we wait.

File No. EE108

—Can we eat the cake, Dad?

—I was waiting for Eugene.

[*He's not coming. He wasn't feeling well.*]

Again? Well, more cake for us then! Sorry I couldn't find any candles. Fourteen years old! I just want to say how grateful I am that I got to spend these last four years with you, though I wish we could have spent them on Earth. Watching you grow into a rebellious teen has been . . . pure torture. I *am* grateful there aren't any black clothes anywhere on this planet so you couldn't go full goth on me. Oh, and one big thank-you to Itit at the market, who finally managed to recharge the batteries for our recorders.

—I'm not rebellious.

—Well, you leave the house on your own, and you talk to people. That's rebellious enough. Esok said you spend a lot of time with one of the guard trainees. What's his name?

—Ekim. And we're just friends!

—Yeah, well, I hope so. He's like twenty years old.

—They age superslow! He's younger than me!

—Then he's too young for you. Wait . . . That's not what I meant.

—What *did* you mean?

—I mean . . . I mean you should stay here. Never leave the house, or do . . . anything. And whatever happens, never, ever, show up here with a boyfriend.

[*I wanna meet him! Bring him over some time!*]

Thank you, Rose . . . That was sarcasm, by the way. It's bad enough you talked me into letting her take a job, we're not doing the boyfriend thing just yet. MR YOTYOT! OFF THE TABLE!

[*She's helping others, Vincent, feeding people. You should be proud of her.*]

—Can you stop talking about me like I'm not here?

—Hey, have you seen Eva? You know, the awkward one?

—Very funny, Dad. And you're one to talk. I see the way you look at Esok.

—I use my eyes. That's how I look at Esok. If I didn't, then I couldn't see her.

—It's OK, Dad! She likes you. She and I are friends. It's perfect.

—Why don't we talk about something else? Turn on the wall, please. We can't see a thing in here.

[*Did you just say: 'Turn on the wall'?*]

—He did. He's been saying it for four years. You never noticed? Dim the wall. Turn off the wall.

—See what I'm up against, Rose. We're the only people on this entire planet who speak English, and I still don't sound cool enough for my kid. What do you call the wall thing, Rose?

[*Let more light in?*]

Oh, you're so clever. Let's eat that cake!

[*Eva, tell me about the soup kitchen. What do they have you do over there?*]

—There's not much to tell. It's a soup kitchen. I stir the pots. I hand out bowls of soup.

—How many people do you feed in a day?

—I don't know. Hundreds. A thousand. A lot.

[*How can that be? They're allowed the same amount of food as everyone else. You've seen what they give us. We could eat twice as much and still have leftovers.*]

Where have you been for four years, Rose? Half of these people don't exist. They don't get *anything*. Their children don't get anything. Their grandchildren won't get anything. It's only gonna get worse unless they get rid of that stupid Council.

143

—Eva. Someone could hear you.

—They're evil, Dad! Everyone here hates them.

—I'm serious, Eva.

—They're nothing but a bunch of racist assholes.

—They're the only ones who can help us.

—You said they haven't ruled yet. They couldn't come to a decision in four years! They'll never do anything.

—They will. They'll send us home. They're the only ones who can. You wanna go home, don't you?

— . . .

—Eva?

—Yeah, I do. But the way they treat everyone, everyone who's not 100 percent Ekt, it's wrong. Someone has to stop them.

—I know you don't like them, Eva. I'm just asking you to watch what you say in public. The last thing we want is to rock the boat any more than we have to. They're already blaming us for all those protests.

—Did you know that Esok's people are dying?

—I didn't know she had any family left.

—She doesn't. On the planet where she's from. They're dying. All of them.

—She was born here.

—Don't be an ass, Dad. They could cure them, you know? They could. It's like supereasy, apparently, but the Council won't do a thing. They'll let a whole planet die.

[*They have a law that prevents them from interfering, Eva.*]

—Rose, I don't think you wanna go there. Eva has . . . strong feelings about those great Ekt principles. I don't want us to fight on her birthday. Besides, all of this is more or less your fault.

[*My fault?*]

Where do you think she gets all these ideas? Certainly not from me.

[*You think I . . .*]

No, I don't. You love the Council. You're –

[*I don't –*]

I'm not done yet. You're the one who convinced me to let her work at that soup kitchen. That place is filled with nothing but starving aliens, most of them with a bunch of illegal kids to feed. Not exactly the most Council-friendly place around.

[*I didn't realize. I'm sorry.*]

Hey. You're not the one telling them how many children they can have.

[*The Ekt don't have a lot of children. They're trying to keep a balance between –*]

—They're trying to weed them out!

[*That's not . . .*]

Oh, come on, Rose!

—I'm afraid Eva's got you on this one, Rose. That's not a political opinion, it's just math. One child per person. That's half as many children every generation if they reproduce the way we do. These people wouldn't be here at all if they followed the rules.

—Why do you keep defending them, Rose?

[*I'm not defen . . . maybe I am. I just think it's not as simple as it seems. They didn't pick those principles out of a hat, there's history behind them, there's a reason. I agree that there might be some consequences to —*]

Might be?

[*There* are *some unfortunate consequences, but there's a lot more to the Ekt than their noninterference policy. They have as close to a pure democracy as I've ever seen. They vote on everything, from the color of lampposts to medical-research priorities. These people have more control over their own lives than we've ever had.*]

—OK, Rose, that's enough.

[*I was just . . .*]

I know. I know. Let's just change the subject.

—I can't listen to this. I'll see you guys later.

[*What? Why?*]

—Eva, come on! It's your birthday!

—Save me some cake, will you?

—Eva! Come back inside!

[*Vincent, I'm so sorry. I don't know what to say.*]

It's OK, Rose, she's . . . She's . . .

[*She's what?*]

She's a teenager without a mother. She's trying to make sense of the world around her, only it's not her world. It's . . . She's also right, you know?

[*About what?*]

You do sound a little brainwashed. A 'pure democracy'?

[*I said close to.*]

OK, so you know about physics. If we lived here, officially, you'd get to vote on anything that has to do with physics. If you knew about bugs, you'd get to vote on bug stuff. You'd also get to vote on mundane things you don't need any special knowledge for, but for the important things, you'd need to know what you're talking about.

[*I don't see how that's a bad thing.*]

But who decides if you know what you're talking about?

[*There are committees that assign credentials.*]

And who decides who sits on those committees?

[*The committees choose their own members. They . . .*]

Now you're getting it. If you live in Osk and your skin isn't the right shade of olive, you don't get to vote on anything but where to plant trees. The people here, they get to be on committees and stuff, but the policies that affect them most, anything having to do with people of alien descent, that's not done locally. Do you think there's anyone that looks like Esok on the Great Council of Akitast? Do you think there'll ever be?

[*You're saying the system is rigged against them.*]

They're saying the system is rigged against them. I'm saying they're not even a part of it, not in a meaningful sense anyway. They've been sold the illusion of democracy. And they bought it! They really bought it. They don't want to get rid of the system. They're asking for more representation *in* it. They don't even realize that the whole thing is purposely built to keep them out. The Ekt basically renounced a whole empire, power over thousands of planets, just to get rid of all the aliens here. Half-aliens were just never part of the plan. They're a compromise. They're like bicycles in a city without bike paths. It wasn't designed with them in mind.

[*I don't think their decision to take power away from the emperor had anything to do with race.*]

You don't think so? I heard the story. The emperor did something stupid, they got their ass kicked, and they wanted to make sure it wouldn't happen again. But there's a big difference between not meddling with other worlds, and kicking out everyone who doesn't look exactly like you. This is entirely about race. These people got scared, 9/11-style, only much worse, and they started to fear anything and anyone that wasn't Ekt. This is populism on steroids. These people went all in. They got rid of the scary people, the political elite. Hell, they got rid of central government altogether.

File No. EE109

Personal File From Esat Ekt

Personal Journal Entry – Eva Reyes

Location: Assigned residence, Etyakt region

I thought I was done. They told me it was over, then it happened again. They said my visions would go away, that I'd stop getting them as I got older. I did. Then this happened. I was at the Aptakt market with Esok. We weren't looking for anything in particular, just nosing around. Whoever found the weirdest object would win. We play that game often, but I suck at it. It's not that I can't find things, but even after four years – almost five, wow – I still don't know about the everyday stuff. Imagine someone screaming: 'Hey! Look at how crazy this is!' while holding a toothbrush. That's usually me. That time, I knew exactly what I had found. My socks. I couldn't figure out how my old socks – I was wearing them when we got here – ended up at the market. There were holes in both of them, and I threw them away, I don't know, two, three years ago. Esok said there, the four of us were kind of . . . famous and that there was a market for just about anything having to do with us, but socks? Anyway, no way I could lose with that. The funniest thing, I thought, is that they weren't here before. I come here pretty much every day, and I would have noticed my green socks. Someone had rummaged through our garbage, found my stinky socks. Maybe they changed hands a few times, but now, whoever owned them was either desperate enough for food to sell their prized possession or realized after a few years that socks weren't everything they were cracked up to be. I was explaining what a sock is, to Esok – I thought that was funny as hell, she didn't. That's when I saw it.

Hundreds of giant robots, maybe more, walking together towards a city . . . It was confusing. I think it was here, in Osk. I saw the imperial palace . . . Hundreds more, a lot more, thousands of robots were waiting for them in line. They started fighting. More than I could count all firing at each other. It was hectic. So fast. Robots disappearing into thin air, reappearing behind the enemy. So many flashes of light, too bright to look at. It went on for a while, then it stopped.

It was quiet. The air was fresh, like morning. I was standing where the fight took place. Half the city was destroyed. Vaporized. Giant robots standing over the ruins. They were everywhere. I could see them in all directions, all the way to the horizon. I saw people running. I – They weren't . . . They were Ekt, then human. Morphing superfast from one into the other. Flickering. The palace was still there. But for a moment I thought I saw a silhouette, a skyline. Tall buildings, not like here. Maybe New York or Chicago. There was a woman, she was clearly from Earth, so scared. Terrified. I was too. She was holding a baby in one arm, running, running as fast as she could away from the robot. She was coming towards me. She kept getting closer, and closer, until she ran *inside* me. I looked at my hands, my legs, and I was Ekt. Then it stopped.

Esok was in front of me, holding my shoulders. I could see her lips move, but there wasn't any sound. It took a second or two for me to realize I was screaming at the top of my lungs. I heard my name, and I stopped screaming. There were . . . lots of people around us, everyone from the market, I guess. Esok told them I was experiencing the *askat yetost* – that's what they call it, the visions. I was still scared of what I'd seen, mortified for making what must have been quite a scene in front of all these people. When they heard those two words, *askat yetost*, their faces changed. Suddenly, they were all smiles. All of them. Some just left, smiling. Others put their hands on me. You're fine, girl. Don't worry about it. That's what it felt like. You're one of us. A minute later, everyone was carrying on with their day. Business as usual.

Esok said no one knows when my visions will stop. They've never seen a human, let alone one that sees things like their kids do. But she says it has something to do with becoming a woman. If she means what I think she means – I don't know anything about her . . . body, or anyone else's here – the visions should have stopped two years ago. I don't know. I'm hoping this is the last time I see things. It reminds me of school. Everyone staring at me. *La Evita loca*.

No soup kitchen for me today. I asked Esok to tell Ityets. I'm sure he'll manage without me. I need to lie down for a while.

File No. 2120

News Article – Liz McCormack,
Reporter, *The Arizona Republic*

Arena Gunmen were A2s

The coroner released his report today on the two armed
men who opened fire inside the Tempe Arena, killing
nine and injuring thirty-one before being gunned down
by police. Both men scored A2 on the Bashir xenogenetic
scale.

Gene Lundman and his son Patrick were both active
members of the Council of Concerned Citizens. In the
video they posted online minutes before the attack, they
describe their imminent actions as retribution for the
government's failure to protect God's children and their
refusal to expand the encampment to all nonwhites in the
United States.

Other advocacy groups have seized on the report to
demand that A2s be required to at least register with state
and local authorities so that they can be more closely
monitored. The coroner's report comes out just as a new
government-sponsored study establishes a correlation
between criminal behavior and higher scores on the
Bashir scale.

The ACLU was quick to call the study a self-fulfilling
prophecy, pointing out that the data used by the

researchers came from camps where law enforcement is almost nonexistent, and simple things like attempting to communicate with the outside are considered criminal. They also argued that any measures aimed at restricting the rights of A2s are not only immoral but also impractical since A2s represent nearly 40 percent of the population.

White House Press Secretary Abendroth said the government is taking note of the coroner's findings but warned against drawing broad conclusions based on an isolated incident. Asked if the administration was ruling out expanding security measures to the A2 population, he said: 'Nothing is off the table at this point.'

File No. 2121

Personal log – Eva Reyes
(with unknown Russian)

Location: Safe House in Saint Petersburg, Russia

—*My nie mozhem segodnya puteshestvovat'. Oni nas budut iskat' vezdye. My mozhem zdes' nochevat'. Eto dom druga. Zavtra my uyezzhayem pro pervom rassvete.*

—You know I don't speak Russian, right?

—Yes. *Tebye nado shas' spat'. Naydu nam mashinu na zavtra.*

—You know, but you just don't care.

—Yes.

—What's your name?

—Bob.

—Really?

—No. You should sleep.

—Why are you helping me?

—A friend of a friend.

—That makes absolutely no sense.

—My friend, he is friend with your friend. Sleep, Eva.

—Wait. Who's my friend?

—Dr Franklin.

—Oh! OK, and who's *your* friend?

—I not know his name.

—Good friend . . .

—He tells good stories.

—OK . . . Well, whoever you are, thank you for getting me out of there. Wait, is that a map? Show me. Where are we going? Saint Petersburg is . . . here. All we have to do is get here, to Finland, right? That's what? A couple hours by car?

—Yes. But we go *through* Finland. Finland is Russian-occupied territory. I use GRU papers to get to Helsinki. Tell them I take you to genetic-research center there. From Helsinki is . . . complicated.

—What does that mean?

—We need to get to Turku, here. Take ferry to Marie-hamn in Åland. There we take other boat to Sweden.

—Why go all the way there? Why not get a boat in Hel-sinki to   anywhere.

—Too many Russian Army in Helsinki. Port is very protected. Gulf of Finland very protected. Åland is much safer.

—The map says it's still Finland? Won't there be just as many Russians there?

—No. Åland is *avtonomnaya territoriya*, independent place. No military. Russia not send army to avoid war with Sweden, Europe. Still, much travel between Turku. Easy for us to go. You go where you want after that.

—You're not coming with me?

—No. I come back for your father.

—Don't. They'll know you're the one who let me go. You won't be safe here anymore.

—You do not want your father free?

—I don't want you to risk your life a second time for him, no. I don't think he's in any danger. Just let him be. He can take care of himself.

—Family is all you have.

—Believe me, I know. That's part of the problem. All I have now is his blood, and people are chasing me for it. Besides, I think the world is much safer with the two of us not being in the same place.

—*Sem`ya eto te kto paderzhat tebya v trudnoiy situatsyiy.*

—What the hell does that mean?

—Hmmm . . . When trouble come, it is family that support you. What happen with your father?

—Look, *Bob*, I'm grateful for what you did. I am. But can we skip the family counseling?

— . . .

—No? Oh, what the hell. You probably don't understand half of what I'm saying anyway. I don't know what happened, *Bob*. He . . . I was gonna say he changed, but I'm not sure that's true. Things changed. He was everything to me after the aliens came. He was my whole family, my *one* friend. Oh, don't give me that pitying look, or I'll knock your *yokits* teeth out. We had this . . . bubble. This tiny bubble with just the two of us, and I felt safe inside it. Maybe that's just not the way it's supposed to be. Then we get whisked away to another world, and things change. I . . . No one knew me there. My visions, they . . . their whole species has them. Do you get what I'm saying? I wasn't a freak anymore. No one looked at me the way you just did. I wasn't . . . *normal*, but no one was. Shit, I hung out with a blue girl and some dude who was nearly two hundred years old. I found this band of misfits in the slums of an alien planet and I fit right in somehow. For the first time in my life, I belonged. My dad, he just didn't understand. Maybe he did. Who the hell knows? Was that personal enough for you? How about we talk about something else?

—No.

—Well I don't know what else to tell you, Bob. We grew apart. That's it.

— . . .

—My whole life, before we left, I felt . . . defective. Broken. With my dad, I felt lucky. I felt really *yokits* lucky that *anyone* would love someone like me, that much. And I *was*. I was lucky. I don't know, I guess, over time, he started reminding me of that. Of how I saw myself before. How shitty, and ugly, and undeserving I felt, and I just . . . I didn't wanna feel that way anymore.

We disagreed on things . . . more and more. What's that face? You think I went out of my way to argue with him? Sometimes. Yeah, I'm not stupid, I know. Sometimes I'd hold my ground for no good reason, just to piss him off. It was like a victory, somehow. A small one. I was . . . *smaller* when I was around him, so I stopped being around him. Then, things got really messed up, and before I could do anything to fix it, he dragged me back here against my will, and I'm a freak again. They put me in a glass jar, for *yokits* sake, like a . . . deformed baby in a sideshow. A pickled punk.

—Bad person.

—Who? Katherine? Yeah, well, she's a lawyer.

—Katherine is not lawyer. She is nuclear physicist.

—What? Why am I surprised? I can see her blowing up shit. Betcha she stuck firecrackers inside frogs when she was a kid.

—Katherine did bad things to you. Your father –

—Weren't you listening? He took away my home!

—*Sem'ya aznachayet, chto nikto ne astanetsya pazadi ili budet zabyt.*

—That's another Russian saying thing, isn't it?

—Family means no one gets left behind or forgotten.

—I *wanted* to be left behind. That's all I wanted. Was that too much to ask? I was happy. Why couldn't he just let me be happy? He didn't *have* to do this. He sure as hell didn't *have* to drag my friend into this. He *kidnapped* him, put a gun to his head. Do you have a proverb for that? He didn't ground me on prom night. He killed my best friend. There's no apology for that. There's no . . . do-over. You can't take that back.

File No. 2122

Letter from Daniel Moensch,
US ambassador to Russia, to the
Russian Minister of Foreign Affairs

The Government of the United States, prompted by a genuine desire to come to an amicable understanding with the Russian Federation, has continued negotiations with the utmost sincerity since September 10, date on which the device known as Themis appeared in Estonia for the advancement of Russian-American relations. We have done so with the utmost sincerity in order that our two countries, by their joint efforts, may contribute toward the realization of world peace.

In that spirit, it is my honor and duty to reiterate the following points:

1. It is the immutable policy of the United States Government to promote world peace and, in accordance with that policy, it has consistently exerted its best efforts to prevent the extension of warlike disturbances.

2. Subsequent to the dissolution of the United Nations Earth Defense Corps, we have made claims regarding ownership of the device known as Themis based on established principles of

international law. To this date, the Government of the Russian Federation has not challenged these claims in any recognized court of law or through the proper administrative procedures at the United Nations. The Government of the United States considers these nine years of inaction to be a tacit agreement on the part of the Government of the Russian Federation.

3. The detention of foreign nationals without proper notice of the names of the detainees and the motives of their detention is a violation of Article 36 of the Vienna Convention on Consular Relations, to which both our governments are parties.

4. The Government of the United States demands the immediate return of its property and of any and all American citizens present inside that property at the time of its reappearance.

In view of the aforementioned facts, and of the continued refusal by your government to respond to our reasonable and legitimate request, I have been instructed to inform the Government of the Russian Federation in the name of the government of the United States that a failure to comply with this request by midnight on the evening of September 22 will be considered an act of aggression and that a state of war will therefore exist between our two countries. I have the honor to be, with high consideration,

Sir,
Your obedient servant,
Daniel Moensch

File No. 2124

Interview between Major
Katherine Lebedev, Russian Main
Intelligence Agency (GRU), and
Dr Rose Franklin, PhD

Location: GRU building, Saint Petersburg, Russia

—So, Dr Franklin, Vincent tells me he does not think the . . . Ekt will come back.

—I think he's right. I don't think they'll want to interfere any more than they already have. Their last visit sent their world into turmoil. You can trust that they won't make the same mistake again anytime soon.

—Turmoil? No one's mentioned turmoil before. What are you not telling me?

—Maybe turmoil isn't the right word. Unrest. No, that's –

—Unrest isn't much better than turmoil.

—I'll let you choose a better word. They . . . A lot of people disagreed with their decision to come here. It goes against their principles. After it went . . . bad –

—Bad? Millions of people died, and you call that bad. I can't begin to imagine what turmoil looks like.

—The Ekt are a peaceful race. Almost to a fault. They don't deal well with violence. There were protests –

—What kinds of protests?

—It's not what you think. There were vigils, letters. A lot of letters. Here, people protest about anything and everything, so this would be par for the course, but that sort of thing doesn't happen over there. It was a big deal. They won't make the same mistake twice, believe me.

—So I'm supposed to feel safe – everyone on Earth is supposed to feel safe – because they have principles.

—They take them very seriously. You should try it some time.

—Noninterference. What does that even mean? We interfere all the time. I'm interfering with your day right now.

—You could say it means let nature take its course . . . It's not as crazy as it sounds. Look at what happened when *we* tried to play God with nature.

—What happened? I feel like I should know these things.

—Some good things, actually, but once in a while some pretty bad things too.

—Like what?

—Oh, I don't know. Man-made plants invading the ocean floor. Killer bees.

—We made the killer bees?

—We did. They were supposed to make more honey.

—That's crazy. I hate bees. Still, you can understand why I don't find that particularly reassuring.

—I suppose if I were in your shoes, if I hadn't seen what I've seen, I'd be skeptical too.

—I knew you'd understand. I feel like we have a connection, you and I. Don't you? We're roughly the same age. We could be like sisters. Oh, wouldn't that be fun?

— . . .

—OK, maybe not *sisters*, but you know, friends! We could talk, we could help each other. I sound superneedy now, don't I? But that's what friends do, right? They help each other? I'm sure you could use a friend.

—I have a friend. You have him locked in the room next door.

—Speaking of, I'm sure you know Vincent's been . . . *reluctant* to help us with Themis.

—He'll never go around the world scaring people for you if that's what you have in mind.

—Scaring people? Why do you always assume the worst? Oh, and while we're at it. Why does everyone keep saying I have you locked in? The doors aren't locked. They're not! You make me sound like Cruella De Vil. I'm not chasing puppies to make fur coats. I just . . . I just want everyone to get along. Where was I? Oh yeah, Vincent. It's like you said, he doesn't want to help.

—I don't want to help you either.

—Well . . . We can work on your motivation later. I'd really like you to help me find another pilot. Make me a test or something, like that crazy doctor did for the Americans. 'Cause, you know, I had a bunch of pilots, and now I don't. But we'll get to that later. My point is I kind of need his help *now, today.*

—Why now?

—I'm glad you asked. The thing is, your government – the United States government – they're not happy that you're here. They probably think you're prisoners, but that's not the point. They're mostly unhappy that Themis is here. *Really* unhappy, like superpissed. They asked us to give her up. You too. They asked nicely at first, but now . . . Not so much.

—Why not just turn us over to them?

—You're funny. I like you. That's just . . . not gonna happen. They'll, my bosses, they'll retire you before they turn you over.

—You mean they'll kill us.

—Retire sounds so much better. But yes, you're not alive anymore afterwards. I'm not sure what we'll do about Themis, though. We can't shoot her. We're not giving her away either. You see where this is going, don't you? Every submarine we have is already approaching the US coast. The Chinese sent out their whole fleet yesterday. They might bump into American subs on the way there because the US also deployed everything they have six hours ago. Funny how everything happens underwater now.

—Why is that?

—We can't send troops anywhere; Lapetus would get rid of them in seconds. The only things we have that it can't touch are subs. The problem is subs are only good for one thing. They're not superintimidating because no one can see them, so for them to be a good deterrent, the other side kinda has to believe you're willing to push that launch button.

—Are you?

—Oh yes. We're all in, as they say! Do they? Say that? I don't play cards . . . See, if you're not willing to launch those missiles but the other side thinks you are, you're fine. The worst? The worst is if you *are* willing to strike but the other side thinks you're not. Guess what situation we're in now? This isn't gonna end well. You think: Yay! The US is here to save me! Then you get shot in the head. Then . . . then it's raining nuclear warheads. Poof! Just like that. Bad day all over.

—I don't know what I'm supposed to say. I don't know how to stop this.

—I do! I think I do. No, I really do. But I'll need your help to convince Vincent . . .

File No. 2127

Mission log – Capt. Bodie Hough and Lt Barbara Ball, US Marine Corps, Mecha Division

Location: Aboard Lapetus, Muskö Naval Base.
Near Stockholm, Sweden

—Two robots, Barbara. We're gonna have two robots. You know what that means, right?

—I'm not so sure they're just gonna hand over Themis, Captain.

—They better if they don't want to get blown to . . . whatever it is we do to things. You didn't answer my question.

—What was the question again?

—Do you know what that means? Two robots. It means twice the missions. No taking turns. No more sitting in our room while Benson and Smith get to have all the fun.

—All the fun?

—They're the only ones who got shot at. Our guys always surrender. What's taking so long?

—They're changing some bolts on our leg. There's time.

—Two minutes. Which one would you like?

—Which what?

—If we get assigned to a robot all the time, which one would you like?

—I like Themis.

—That's because you're a girl. I like this guy. He's bigger.

—He's wearing a prosthesis. Did you just call me a girl?

—He's like a pirate! I want this one, and I want the arms.

—You don't like driving?

—I'd rather shoot at things.

—You're the one pushing the button. I just raise my arm. Anyway, that's fine with me. I'd take the legs.

—There. It's settled. I think it makes sense. I'm the captain. I'm higher than you are in the chain of command, I should be higher than you are inside this thing.

—Really? That's your problem? You can't deal with me standing three feet above you? If you were up here, I'd be in front of you. You're OK with me being in front of you.

—Yeah. I'd be higher.

—You're the captain.

[*Lapetus, Navigation here. Are we ready to move?*]

—Affirmative. Just get the grease monkeys off our foot, and we're good to go.

168

[*They're leaving now. Get ready for a two-jump trip. Swing around to seventy-nine degrees, one minute.*]

Roger that. Wiggle, wiggle.

—You good?

—Yeah, I just . . .

[*Lapetus, what's taking so long? We're on a schedule.*]

Gimme a sec. I just can't get the minutes right. I keep jumping from zero to four.

—You're turning with your feet.

—Want me to use my butt? I've done this before, Lieutenant.

—That's not what I meant. It's hard to be that precise moving your feet. Once you get the degrees right, keep your feet straight and turn your head a little towards where you wanna go. Then just shift your weight from leg to leg. The big man'll turn without you knowing it.

—Hot damn! You're right! Seventy-nine degrees, one minute, two seconds.

[*Calculating. Lapetus. Punch in. Unit size: ninety-eight. That's one, four, two in base-8.*]

Roger that. One. Four. Two.

[*Distance: three hundred and sixty-six. Base-8: five, five, six.*]

Five. Five. Six. Engaging. Aaaand, we're underwater.

[*You're good, Lapetus. That is the Gulf of Finland. We have you less than ninety miles from Saint Petersburg. Second heading: eighty-nine degrees, seven minutes.*]

On it ... All set. Eighty-nine degrees, seven minutes, twelve seconds.

[*Roger that. Set unit size to thirty-two. That is four, zero. Repeat. Four. Zero. Distance: two-eighty-six. Base-8 is four, three, six.*]

Confirm. Four. Zero. Distance: Four. Three. Six.

[*Confirmed. That should put you right in the middle of Palace Square.*]

Ready, Lieutenant?

—No, but that's as good as I'll get.

—Off we go . . . What the? Central, this is Lapetus. Seems you were a little off on those coordinates. We can see the square, we're right in front of it, but we crushed part of a castle or something.

[*Sorry about that, Lapetus. We have you on satellite. You're on . . . You're standing on the Hermitage.*]

—Jesus Christ!

—Calm down, Lieutenant. These things happen.

—No, Bodie. Leveling the Hermitage doesn't just happen.

—Central. We're onsite. We're staring at a big yellow building.

[*Roger, Lapetus. The General Staff and Ministries Building. That's your target. Sit tight. We're talking to the ambassador now.*]

—Look at this place!

—Yeah, it's cool. Too bad it'll be a hole in a few minutes.

—They might find a diplomatic way out of this, you know.

—Yeah, sure. I don't see Themis anywhere.

—They think she's underground somewhere.

— . . .

—It was in the briefing notes?

—Lieutenant?

—What?

—Shut the hell up.

—Do you have *any* idea what's going on, Bodie? Do you get how bad this is?

—No one can touch us.

—Yes, Bodie. We're in here. The rest of the world isn't. They're fucked if this goes wrong.

—Well, they asked for it. We gave them an ultimatum.

—I don't mean here, you dumb-ass. I mean everywhere. Home, Bodie! Home! Your mom, your friends.

—Do you always talk this much?

—What? You don't wanna think about bad shit, so you pretend it doesn't exist? Reality doesn't give a crap whether you pay attention to it or not. It's still there.

—What do you want me to do, Lieutenant? Just tell me. What do you want me to do?

—Someone has to stop this insanity, Bodie. Someone has to.

—Well, it won't be me. And it sure as hell won't be you. So what's the point in talking about it?

[*Lapetus, this is Central. It's 23:58. Stand by to commence firing in two minutes.*]

—Are you sure about this, Central? Maybe we should give them more time.

[*Negative, Lapetus. Stand by for strike order.*]

—All right, Central. Standing by.

—Don't do it, Bodie.

—What are you saying, Lieutenant? Are you suggesting I disobey a direct order?

—I'm not –

—'Cause that's what it sounded like.

—I'm saying you don't have to do anything you don't want to do, Bodie.

—Are we gonna have a problem here?

—There's no problem, Bodie. It's just that forty-five seconds from now, you'll be asked to start World War III. We will. Not the whole army. Not fifty thousand men. Just you and me. Now I'm thinking maybe that's not something you want on your conscience. Remember how

172

many people died when this big guy showed up? We're about to do it again. You and me. You and me, Bodie. Whoa, don't you *ever* point a gun at me. Did you hear what I said? Holster that weapon, Captain.

—Central, we have a bit of a – HOLY FUCKING SHIT!

[*Lapetus, this is Central. What did you say?*]

It's Themis! She just appeared right in front of us.

File No. 2128
Broadcast statement from
Vincent Couture

Location: Inside Themis, Saint Petersburg

Hello, everyone. My name is Vincent Couture. I prepared a short statement. If you don't mind, I'm just gonna read from it. Here it goes.

To the United States government, and to the women or men piloting the alien device in front of me. I am inside Themis. I have recently returned from the alien world where this robot and the one I am staring at were built. I was brought there by the inhabitants of that planet along with General Eugene Govender, Dr Rose Franklin, and Eva Reyes, my biological daughter.

I have been told that you are requesting our immediate release and are threatening to destroy the government building behind me along with everyone inside if that demand is not met immediately. Before you do anything you can't take back, let's all be clear on what that would mean. You would declare war on the Russian Federation. They would retaliate with . . . everything they have. Now, I know you might be thinking: Russia won't start a nuclear war over this. They'd be hit just as hard, if not worse. Common sense will prevail. You'd be *wrong*. Don't believe me? Imagine a battalion of Russian tanks turning the White House into a pile of rubble. Can you think of a scenario in which you say: Yeah, we'll let this one slide? They *will* retaliate. So the real question is how many people are you willing to kill over this? Because it's not hundreds, or thousands, or tens of thousands, or hundreds of thousands.

Now let's talk about those demands.

First, you should know that General Govender did not return with us. He died on the alien planet five years ago, so you're not getting *him* back. As for my daughter, Eva Reyes, she is no longer here. Neither I, nor the Russian authorities, are aware of her location, but she is most likely on her way to the United States right now.

Second, Dr Rose Franklin and I were never prisoners. We do not need to be *rescued* though we appreciate the thought. We are guests of the Russian Federation and have been treated as such since our arrival. However, given the tense nature of this situation, Dr Franklin has agreed to return to the United States and should already be in US custody.

That leaves me. Let me remind you that I am not an American, so your request for my release is touching but baseless. I have no doubt that you can get the Canadian government to issue a formal request, but let me save you the trouble. I choose to stay. Let me restate that to avoid any misunderstanding. I am here of my own volition, and I choose to remain here. Your help is not required. Any attempt to remove me by force would amount to kidnapping.

Now for the main course, you're not getting Themis either. I have agreed to pilot her and defend the Russian Federation against foreign aggressors until I feel it is no longer necessary. I have entered this agreement of my own free will. I have been assigned a Russian copilot, and Themis is now fully operational. We are ready to engage your robot and will do so in sixty seconds if it is still here. I can't tell you how that fight will end, but I'm sure you know that I have disabled one of these robots in the past. In fact, I'm the only living person to have ever fought one of these robots and won. With that in mind, I implore you not to test my resolve.

Now that we've covered your demands, let's talk about mine. Yeah, I have some too. I demand that the United States remove any troops from Canada. I . . . I demand that the sovereignty of my country be restored fully, and immediately. I want my parliament to be allowed to meet. I'm not gonna let you bully everyone with that robot of yours anymore. That's not what these things are made for. They're supposed to be instruments of peace. I want the EDC restored. I want things back the way they were. Did I just ask for world peace? I think I just did. So until you can deliver that, don't mess with me.

Oh yeah, I have also been asked to inform you that, as a precaution, Russian and Chinese submarines, each carrying a full complement of nuclear warheads, are currently under way to North America. But you knew that already.

So . . . Your call. I'll even let you throw the first punch. Just make sure we don't get up again.

That's all I have to say. This is Vincent Couture. Over and out.

. . .

. . .

. . .

Oh, thank God! There. I've done it. They're gone now. You can put the gun down.

Katherine, tell your man to put the gun down. Please.

[*Oh, sorry. I'm just . . . WOW! Thank you, Vincent. Well done! I knew you could do it. What was that 'I demand' bit at the end? I thought we'd agreed on your speech.*]

I improvised a bit. I thought it would sound more convincing if I put something more personal in there. I mean, no offense, but what reason do I have to 'help defend the Russian Federation'?

[*Hey, I'm not complaining. You were great. Were you scared? I was. I almost wet myself, and I wasn't even there. Woo! I need a drink!*]

What would you have done if they'd attacked? We'd have had no choice but to surrender.

[*You could have fought back! You could have gotten away, made Themis disappear or something. Couldn't you? I hope so because that soldier had orders to shoot you if you lost.*]

Shoot me how? He's just standing there. One punch from that robot and he would have bounced around here like a rubber ball.

[*I'm sure he's glad to hear that now.*]

There's no fighting back, Katherine. We can't even move our arms without another pilot! No escaping either, not if it's anything like the one Kara and I fought. Themis won't beam while it's holding us. Something about the energy field.

[*Oh, don't be so negative, Vincent! You won!*]

We bluffed, and they fell for it, but that's as far as it goes. I can't pilot Themis by myself.

[*Then we better find you a copilot.*]

How are you gonna do that?

[*I have an idea! Another one, I know! It's crazy. I never think of anything, then boom! Two in a row.*]

File No. EE149

Personal File From Esat Ekt

Interview between Vincent Couture and General Eugene Govender

Location: Assigned residence, Etyakt region

—Goddammit, Couture! I'm not dead yet.

—I don't know what to say. Did they tell you what it was?

—Well, your Opt friend told me, but I don't understand anything he says. Something about my cells being out of control.

—Cancer?

—That's what it sounded like to me.

—I'll ask him.

—Why? I'm still dying. What difference does it make if I know what's killing me?

—Maybe they can cure it.

—Do you think they'll be able to cure it more if *I* know what it is? Besides, he's already told me they can cure it. They just won't.

—What?

—You heard me. He said they don't want to in—

—Interfere.

—Exactly. I swear I'll die if I hear that goddamn word one more time.

—That's not funny, sir. I'll talk to him. Maybe I can –

—What? Change his mind? I don't think he makes those kinds of decisions. I *know* the people who do don't give a damn about what you have to say. And it *was* funny! Maybe not fall-off-your-chair funny, but enough for a polite laugh.

—I'm serious, General. There has to be a way to convince them. There has to be. Rose knows some of their scientists, she –

—She can't do anything. You know that. When they say they don't want to interfere, they really mean that horseshit.

—But the Council. If they rule that we're part Ekt. They'd have to take care of you then.

—That argument is what got us stuck on this rock in the first place. I don't wanna be cured if it means spending the rest of my even longer life here. You'd be stuck too.

—We'll cross that bridge –

—Screw that bridge, Couture. We're not crossing it, ever.

—We can try!

—Goddammit! Listen to what I'm saying! I don't wanna be saved! I don't want you to do anything because I don't want their stupid cure.

—I'm not gonna let you die.

—I don't need your permission, son. I'm a general. I'm tired of this place. I'm tired, period. I'm seventy-one years old. I'm allowed.

— . . .

—What? You think I'm sorry to go? You think I have a bucket list I want to get through after all this?

—You don't want to go home?

—I'd like . . . I'd like to live in an old house, alone. By a lake, or a river. Something small. I could sit on the porch and drink coffee, listening to the birds. And no one would come, and I'd never hear another word about war, or aliens, or any of this for the rest of my life. Do you think I can get that?

—Probably not, sir.

—Then no. I'm fine the way things are.

—I'm sorry, sir.

—Sorry for what? Are you apologizing to me because you can't cure cancer? Or because you can't make the world the way I want it to be? Either way, never be sorry about things you have no control over. You'll just give yourself ulcers. Never half-ass anything. Drink plenty of wine. I think that's about as much wisdom as I have to offer. How's your girl?

—She's doing all right. Certainly better than the three of us. She has a day job. She's fifteen, and she has a day job. Home . . . Things are a little rough at home. For one thing, I *really* suck as a schoolteacher. Rose helps me write lessons and stuff. I try my best. It was a lot easier when she was ten. We try to make it about things that she likes as much as we can – apples and pies aren't cool anymore – but it's fairly obvious that we have absolutely no clue what she likes nowadays.

—Apples and pies?

—You know. You have two apples and eleven friends. What does each friend get?

—Nothing. They get squat. I haven't had an apple in five years. I'd shoot the eleven kids if I had to.

—Maybe you should be the one teaching her.

—I was until now.

—What are you talking about?

—Goddammit, Couture! Pay attention to your kid. She doesn't have a day job, she has half a day job. The rest of the time she spends with that young guard trainee, some old man from the soup kitchen, that blue friend of yours.

—Esok? How do you know all that?

—I read tea leaves . . . Because she tells me, you idiot! She might tell *you* if you paid attention. She stops by my place every morning. She usually brings some *yesketats* she gets from the market.

—You like that red juice?

—Oh yeah.

—It's too sweet for me.

—We talk, I show her things.

—What do you talk about?

—Whatever it is she wants to learn. She likes military strategy.

—You're teaching her to fight?

—Do I look like a kung fu master to you? I'm out of breath after I tie my shoes. No! Strategy! Classical stuff: hammer and anvil, oblique order, blitzkrieg, flanking maneuvers – she likes that. We reenact famous battles, with beans and rocks. She's a natural. She doesn't know the names of things, but she has great instinct.

—I didn't know that.

—I know you didn't. You're so busy trying to make all of this 'normal,' making her feel like she's back home, you don't notice what's happening here. I got news for you, son, this ain't home. There's nothing normal about it.

—I just want –

—I know what you want! You're not getting it. Maybe it's time you start wanting something else.

—I don't know what I'm supposed to do.

—You're not 'supposed' to do anything, Couture. You decide. You have no idea what to do, well here's one for you. Get your head out of your ass and get that kid of yours home!

—The Council might rule our way, I –

—The Council? You've been waiting for them for five goddamn years! They're not helping us. How long will it take for you to get that through that thick head of yours? Eva's fifteen now, Couture. Fifteen? Are you gonna wait until she's thirty? Get her away from this place. We don't belong here, son. She doesn't.

—I don't know –

—I don't know what to do . . . Is there an echo in here? Boohoo. You find a way home, and you take it. I told you to make friends. You barely get out of your house. You can't even see what's right in front of your nose. I just told you your daughter spends all her days with an Imperial Guard trainee. What do you think these people do? They pilot big-ass metal robots, that's what they do.

—He can't do it on his own. I already asked. They control all the robots from one place. We'd need someone to let us go. We could try and take that command center by force, but I . . .

—You what? You're afraid it might be dangerous? You don't want to put her in harm's way? She's already in harm's way, Couture. There are riots every day. Someone

184

bombed – well, vaporized – a government building in Osk this morning.

—I didn't know.

—This place is on the verge of revolution, and we're smack-dab in the middle of it. One side blames us, the other one uses us.

—They know we have nothing to do with what's going on.

—Oh, we're involved. We're involved whether we like it or not. Your daughter is. Don't fool yourself into thinking she's safe because they haven't hurt her yet. You get your kid off this rock, you hear me? You need to promise me you'll get her home.

—I'll –

—Goddammit, Couture! You don't try. You do it!

—Yes, sir.

—That's my boy. Now hand me that loaf of bread, will you?

—What? This?

—Are you making fun of my bread?

—You made this . . . thing?

—*You* try making bread with what they have here.

—It looks more like a pancake. Did you use any yeast?

—And how would I do that? Go to the market and ask for fungus? Would you eat that?

—Probably not.

—That's right. Could be someone's athlete's foot. I hate this place. There's nothing good to eat. Not a goddamn thing. You know the first thing I'm gonna do when I'm gone?

—What?

—I'm gonna have the biggest goddamn steak anyone's ever seen. What? I'm dying! You think that's funny?

—You think there's steak in Heaven?

—Oh, I don't know if I believe in Heaven.

—You don't know if you believe in Heaven, but you're sure about the steak.

—Yes. Do you have anything to say about that?

—I . . .

—Be very careful with the next words to come out of your mouth, Couture. You're addressing a brigadier general in the Earth Defense Corps.

—I hope it's bloody as hell, sir.

File No. EE151

Personal File From Esat Ekt

Personal Journal Entry – Dr Rose Franklin

Location: Assigned residence, Etyakt region

They won't do a thing. Eugene is dying, and the Ekt won't lift a finger to help him. It's against the rules. That's not true. It *might be* against the rules. If the Council lets the Etyakt vote stand, then Eugene is a citizen, and they *have* to save his life. But they haven't. They haven't said anything, or done anything, in five years. I wrote to them. I wrote this long letter to the Council of Akyast, telling them we'd gladly accept our fate and stay here if it means saving our friend. Eugene told me not to send it. He said it was a waste of time. I didn't care, of course. I gave the letter to Enatast this morning. I could tell he was uncomfortable. I found out Eugene had given him an even longer letter asking, begging the council to let him die. I can't believe how stubborn that man is.

We're not as close as we used to be, but he's still my friend. I won't let him have the last word on this one, not if it means losing him. The Ekt won't save him, but they also won't stop me from doing it. I just need to cure cancer.

It sounds insane, but I think I know how to do it, sort

of, on paper. Targeted therapy. We were making progress with the idea when we left Earth, developing drugs that target specific DNA mutations. That's just what cancer is. Cells accumulate certain mutations over time and become more and more disconnected from all the mechanisms that are supposed to regulate them, including those that tell the cell to kill itself. At some point they stop caring completely and begin to divide uncontrollably. If I can identify the mutations responsible for Eugene's cancer, and target the right cells . . . I know it's easier said than done – humans have been trying to do just that for decades – but I'm certain it can be done here. They've done it. I've seen it.

The weapon they used against us on Earth did just that. It targeted certain DNA strands and made the cells do something that triggered an immune response against them. It's like an airport sniffer dog. It can be trained to find different things – fruit, drugs, explosives. I need to train mine to find cancer and do the same thing it did on Earth. If I can get the same immune response, but only with cancer cells, Eugene's body will cure itself, theoretically.

I'll need all sorts of samples from Eugene, a way to sequence DNA from healthy and mutated cells. I'll need equipment though it's possible I already have access to everything I need. I don't know what half the things do in the lab where they let me work. My biggest problem is that, even with all the lab equipment in the world, I don't know enough about genetics. I have no idea what I'm doing, or how naïve this idea of mine really is. I never thought I'd say it, but I need Alyssa right now. Short of that, I need to learn, fast, and figure out if this is even remotely possible. I'll have to convince the Ekt I know more than I do, again. I hate being dishonest with them, but I'm not going to let my friend die.

I need to believe I can do this.

File No. 2130

Personal Journal Entry – Eva Reyes

Location: Kaarina Work Camp, near Turku, Finland

So close. We were almost there. We were stopped by local cops, who turned us over to the Russians.

Of course, they knew who I was. They plastered my picture everywhere. Déjà vu all over again. I think I might be the most wanted person here too. This is nuts.

'Bob' managed to convince them he was taking me to this camp. They bought it because we were so close, and no one would lie to get *into* a work camp. They even escorted us to the gate. He said he'd get me out, but I don't see how he can manage that. They'll talk to their bosses at some point, soon, and figure out who he is. Then they'll come for me. I probably have a day at most, maybe two.

There's got to be a way to escape. There are cameras everywhere, but there aren't that many guards. There is no reason for them. These people aren't criminals, they haven't done anything. There are kids everywhere. Pretty much all the Muslims were sent in with their families. Some people even volunteered to come here. Their husbands and wives had a bit too much alien DNA, and they refused to let them go, so they came. This place is no prison. It feels more like a small village than anything else. It's ironic, in a really sad way. There's more closeness here, more love and acceptance, than anywhere else. White, black, brown, Christian, Muslim, all brought together by the greatest injustice of all. But they are together. If you're in here, you're welcome. I must be going out of my mind, but if I had to live anywhere, this is the first place I've seen since we came back where I feel I could have a life. That is until they start slaughtering those people.

They have me in a bunk next to this guy, Bilal. He's just a year older than me. He – this is nuts – he studied plant biology in Helsinki. He worked in a bar to pay for school. There's nothing special about him. Not his DNA. He's not even Muslim. He's a Hindu, but he was born in Pakistan, so . . . It's pathetic. These people can't even do racist right.

I hate this world. People are small. They're ignorant, and they're happy to stay that way. They make an effort to. They'll spend time and energy finding ways not to learn things just to feel comfortable with their beliefs. The cops that turned us in, they weren't scared of the Russians. They genuinely thought they were helping by turning us in. They were served this story that's SO. OBVIOUSLY. BULLSHIT. But they swallowed it. They ate it all, and they asked for seconds. They're happy to buy into this nonsense because they're on the right side of things, and they have someone to blame for everything that's wrong with the world. How cozy that must be, never having to question anything? I thought it would be different. I thought the world would have come together like never before after they were attacked. They'd been hurt. Everyone had. More than anything, they'd been hurt equally, randomly. None of the people who died did anything to deserve it. They were from all walks of life, rich and poor, from every religion. For the first time in history, there was a 'them' everyone could point the finger at. That should have come with an even bigger 'us.' If two kids get beat up by the same school bully, they have a reason to be friends. If I see millions of Chinese people go through the same horror I went through, I should feel some *yokits* sympathy for the Chinese, or I'm a whole new breed of asshole. It happened here. This insanity, it brought everyone here together. There's a 'them': the numbnuts that dragged us here. And there's an 'us': camp people. That's how it's supposed to work. That's how it should be.

Esat Ekt wasn't much better in some ways. But, I don't know, somehow their brand of racism didn't hurt as much. For one thing, it was actually based on race. And they didn't think there was anything intrinsically wrong with the people they oppressed. As much as I hate those Ekt principles, they weren't built on lies. People here are just too stupid to realize they hate people who are exactly like them. Maybe that's what bugs me. Stupidity. I hate it more than I hate evil.

I better learn to live with it, I guess, because I don't think they'll kill me. I wish they would. I don't know what they'll do to me, but it won't be that. It'll be something else. Something without an end. Purgatory. The strangest thing is that this is all just dawning on me. I had hoped . . . somehow I deluded myself into thinking this could all be fixed, that I could go back. I wanted to see the market, Esok, my friends. I wanted to see Ekim, but I won't. I won't see any of it, any of them ever again. It's . . . linear. It moves in one direction, and all of this is behind. What's ahead . . . I don't know what's ahead, but it's never gonna be like before.

I don't know what to do. I could try to recruit people, try to take over this place. If we all went for it, we could easily overwhelm the guards. But these are families. There are kids here, newborns. I can't ask someone with a baby to risk everything for me. I probably can't ask their friends either. They'll denounce me to protect the ones they love. I wouldn't follow me if I were in their shoes. They don't have much of a life in here, but they *are* alive. I don't think they will be for long, but I'm not sure I can convince them of that, not if they don't want to hear it. This isn't . . . sustainable. There are too many of them, and they keep bringing new people in. They won't turn half the world into a refugee camp. At some point, they'll want to make room. At some point, people will have gotten used to these camps. They'll grow tired of all the bad news coming out of them. 'We spend a fortune helping these people, and this is how they repay us?' 'Why should we waste all these resources on the people who tried to kill us when we barely have enough for ourselves?' They'll start with men, the ones with the most alien DNA, then they'll work their way down. When the people in these camps have been dehumanized enough, everyone will be fair game. Women, children. It won't matter. My problem is no one wants to hear that, especially not the mother of a three-year-old playing hide-and-seek behind the barracks. It makes sense. That's why these things work, I guess. I wouldn't risk my child's life unless I was absolutely sure, and it would already be too late if I were. It's the will to live that will kill these people.

Maybe I don't need to find a way out. Maybe there is one already. Wishful thinking, I know, but there must be some sort of black market running in here. If there's one thing you can count on when things go bad, it's free enterprise. Folks in here had money. I'm sure *someone* found a way to take it from them. I just hope it's not the guards. If contraband is coming in, maybe I can go out the same way. Probably not. It doesn't matter. I can't just sit here waiting for the Russian Army to show up.

File No. 2134

Interview between Dr Helen Maher, Director, US Alien Research Center, and Dr Rose Franklin

Location: Johns Hopkins University, Baltimore, Maryland

—Good morning, Dr Franklin. Very pleased to meet you. Welcome back to the United States.

—Thank you. Glad to be back.

—They tell me you've been debriefed.

—For about eight hours, yes. I have to go back tomorrow.

—Nine years is a long time. There's a lot to tell, I'm sure. People wanna know.

—We haven't talked much about our time there. We mostly talked about Vincent.

—The traitor?

—I . . . That's one way to put it.

—What other way is there?

—Well . . . maybe. Like I told them, we weren't close.

—I was under the impression that you were friends.

—We were when we left. We ... We saw things ... very differently over there.

—On – what's it called again? Esat Ekt?

—There. In Russia. We were on opposite sides of everything. I wanted to stay on Esat Ekt, study those people. I thought I should learn about them, get them to know us, so we could find peace. He saw them as the enemy from the start. I would still be there if it weren't for him.

—As a scientist, I envy you.

—Thank you. That makes me wish you had been there instead of him. We didn't talk to each other anymore, until he convinced them it was best to send us back. I couldn't stay anymore because of him. Then we land in Russia and ... we're prisoners. I thought that, no matter how much we fought in the past, we could at least agree on that, find a way to escape. He didn't see it that way. He betrayed me. His daughter too. I think he blames our country for what happened.

—Sadly, he's not the only one. Most of the world does.

—I was told Alyssa Papantoniou works for the US now. Is she here?

—No. We only do basic research here. She works directly for the military.

—OK ...

—Dr Franklin?

—Yes.

—Is there something specific I can do for you today?

—I . . . I was told to meet you here. They drove me. I assumed you're the one who wanted to see me.

—I never asked them to . . . It doesn't matter . . . SO. What would you like to see?

—Have I done something wrong?

—Why do you ask?

—You seemed . . . hostile, just now. Is it something I did in the past? I'm sorry if –

—No, we've never met. Would you like a tour?

—I . . . Yes. I would like a tour if it's not too much trouble. I don't want to take a lot of your time, you must be busy.

—I am.

—Is there anything I can do to help? Now that I'm here. They said they would pick me up at four. That's . . . six hours from now. I can walk around the city, but if I can be of use –

—Ha!

—Have I said something funny?

—Yes, you did. I should be the one asking you.

—I don't understand.

—Obviously. How do I put this? I *like* my job, Dr Franklin. I really do. I can make a difference here. I have a good team of people working for me. I chose *every single one* of them. They're loyal, competent. We've made *so much* progress the last few years.

—That's . . . That's great. I don't understand what you're trying to say. I really don't. Maybe it seems obvious to you, but it's not to me. When I asked you if I could help, I meant just that. I've been gone for a while, but I still think I can contribute. I know Themis better than anyone. I know these robots. Maybe not as much as you do, but enough to be useful, I'm sure of that.

—Dr Franklin, you're . . . They're going to ask you to take my place.

—Me? I . . . I don't even know what you've been doing. You said it yourself, you've made a lot of progress. You got that robot working again. Why would they replace you?

—You really don't know anything, do you?

—That's what I've been trying to say for the last five minutes.

—No one will care if you're up to speed or not. You know enough. They'll trust you more than they trust me.

—Why? I've been gone nine years. I was in Russia with — you just called him a traitor.

—It won't matter. You're a pureblood. You're white.

—I'm white? Surely that can't —

—I'm an A1. That's about as good as it gets, because pure-bloods are so rare. None of them are scientists. Well, you are, but there are only a handful. I'm an A1, but my grand-father was from Tunisia.

—What difference does that make? I'm sorry, I just —

—Muslims don't get government jobs. They get put in *camps*. I'm an atheist, but hey, you can never be really sure, can you?

—That's insane. I understand that a lot of people died just before we left. I understand that people are scared. But this A1, A2 system, it's crazy. Recombination is completely ran-dom, you *know* that. My parents could have had more alien DNA than you have. Your children could be just like me.

—It doesn't matter. People don't know what science was made by 'real' humans and what wasn't. They don't trust anything anymore.

—This feels like a bad dream.

—It's the world, Dr Franklin. You'd better get used to it.

—And Muslims? What could that possibly have to do with anything?

—The first A4s we found were from the Middle East. Most of them are.

—That's not . . . If the story we've been told is true, the first aliens to come here lived in what is now Turkey. It would make sense for more of their descendants to be from —

—Now you're getting it.

—No! I'm not! They came *for* them! A lot of us died, but the ones that did it came here *specifically* to kill those people.

—We don't know if that's true! We don't know if they'll come back for them. We don't know anything. We know they're closer to the aliens than the rest of us.

—Who is? The descendants of the aliens are more alien, yes. People in the Middle East aren't. They're also not all Muslims. Even if they were, it doesn't make any sense . . . Muslims?! Most Muslims are Asians, for crying out loud!

—Asian Muslims don't count.

—I don't even know what that means. You're talking about a religion. There's nothing biological about that. What about Muslims here?

—There might be a connection.

—How? Muslims were victims too. The aliens destroyed Riyadh. Kuala Lumpur.

—Those were large cities with lots of foreigners. Both al-Qaeda and Daesh said Saudi Arabia was an infidel country. Look, I don't have all the answers, but why take the chance?

—You mean you agree with that craziness?

—I mean I can't rule it out.

—Then you're not a very good scientist.

— . . .

—I'm sorry. I shouldn't have said that. I don't know you. I don't know what you've been through.

—It's OK. They said you would have a hard time adjusting. Just give it time.

—I just don't understand. That's all. Borders are closed. People are suspicious of everyone. I understand why people are scared, but wouldn't we be safer, stronger, if we all worked together?

—The world doesn't like us very much anymore. And I don't have the answer to your question. I don't know if this is better. All I know is that we tried it your way before, and a lot of people died.

—There would have been more.

—Are you sure about that?

—Yes!

—Elsewhere, maybe. But here? Our armed forces were spread out all over the world . . . My parents were in New York. My friends. Maybe, just maybe, some of them would still be alive if we'd only taken care of our people.

  That's nonsense. A minute ago you were ready to put your family in a camp, just in case. And don't talk to me about New York. I was there, remember. I lost people too. A lot of us did.

—I know. And you left. Themis was there, and she left. You left everyone behind.

—Themis couldn't fight. And I didn't *leave*. I was locked inside a glass room waiting to die. I watched a friend die right in front of me. So don't talk to me about loss as if I didn't suffer. I survived. Those are two very different things.

— . . .

—And tell me, what would you have done if we'd had all our armed forces? All our tanks, all our planes. Say they were all there, all in New York by some crazy miracle. What would you have done? Bomb the city? Your parents were in it. The Russians tried that in Moscow. We nuked Madrid for no reason, and it didn't help.

—We didn't bomb Madrid. The aliens destroyed it.

—I must remember it wrong, then. Maybe we should have nuked New York. Would that have helped?

—How about I give you that tour, now?

—I think I'll walk the city. It'd be a shame to spend such a nice day inside. But I do have one question.

—By all means.

—The robot, Lapetus, you call it. It's the one I disabled in Central Park, isn't it?

—Yes, it is.

—Then I'm curious. When we assembled Themis, we couldn't get her working without all the pieces. How did you manage to make this one work without one of its legs? We understood so very little about how those pieces work when I left, I –

—We still don't. Well, at least I don't. We do high-level research here, anything connected to Lapetus is handled directly by the military. We don't even have access to it, not to the parts that work. We have the nonfunctioning leg in storage. Would you like to see it?

– No thank you. I know where I need to go.

File No. 2137

Interview between Major
Katherine Lebedev, Russian Main
Intelligence Agency (GRU), and
Vincent Couture

Location: GRU building, Saint Petersburg, Russia

—Vincent, I'd like you to meet Sergeant Vasiliev.

[*It is a pleasure to meet you, Mr Couture.*]

—Hi! So you're my copilot.

[*I think* you *are my copilot.*]

I like him.

—I knew you would.

—Where did you find him?

—Prison.

—Really?

[*I did nothing wrong.*]

—He's right about that. My original idea was to test everyone in work camps –

—How? I didn't think you had a blood test for pilots.

—We still don't. I thought we could bring everyone here and have them try the helmets.

—That's crazy. It would take –

—I assumed we'd find someone after a few thousand tries. The camps are filled with the right kind of people, so part of the job is already done, but you didn't let me finish. I was about to start when I remembered we put everyone with military training in prison instead of camps. We didn't want trained soldiers stirring up trouble.

—So that's where they found you? I bet you were happy to get out of there.

[*I won't miss the food.*]

Your English is pretty good. Why is it that every Russian I meet speaks English?

[*I lived in Canada before. Like you, right?* Bonjour. Je m'appelle Alexander.]

Nice. What'd you do? Were you a spy?

[*I play hockey.*]

Oh! Cool!

[*When do we start? Major said you'd teach me how to fight.*]

I have to teach you how to walk first. Have you ever done any modeling?

[*Is he serious, Major?*]

—I'm afraid he is. Just do what he says, Sergeant.

[*Do I take orders from him?*]

Good question! Vincent is the only one who knows how this thing works, so you kinda have to do what he says. But he's not military. Would you like to be, Vincent? I can make you a captain!

—No, Katherine, I don't want to be a captain in the Russian Army . . . Look, Alex – can I call you Alex? – this thing, it works on trust more than anything else. I can't . . . tell you what to do because by then it'll be too late. You need to . . . I'm a center. You play wing. We need to anticipate each other.

[*She said I have to shoot you if you do anything wrong.*]

Really? What part of trust –

—Only during training, Vincent. After that, we'll have something less . . .

—Crazy?

—I was thinking ominous.

—No, Katherine. Having someone behind you with a gun pointed at your head all day isn't *ominous*. It's insanely stupid, ridiculously dangerous. I think you need more words.

[*I'm sorry. You said trust. I thought you should know.*]

Right . . . Thank you, Alex, for your honesty. And Katherine, I hate to ruin that *ominous* plan of yours but he won't be able to hold a gun, not with the gloves on. They're like hockey gloves.

[*Oh!*]

Exactly.

—All right! We'll think of something else. Why does everything have to be so difficult?

[*So what do we do now?*]

Well, Sergeant, it looks like you won't start training today after all. No, Vincent, I'm not letting you into Themis without some sort of safety measure in place. You can start tomorrow.

—We can start today. We don't need to be inside Themis for now. We can just hold hands for a while.

—What did you just say?

—Hands. Ever tried walking while holding someone's hand? It doesn't work if your pacing is different. You need to adjust speed, distance, so your arms can move in sync. We'll start with that to get our feet moving together. It'll be a mirror image, but it's easy to switch later. Then we'll work on the arms. You can just follow me around. I'm going to exaggerate my arm movements a bit. You have to move like I do. You'll need to walk like that even when I'm not around.

[*This is the stupidest thing I have ever heard in my life.*]

—It sounds *perfect*. I'll let you boys do your thing, then. I don't wanna be a third wheel.

—Don't go, Katherine. I need to talk to you first.

[*This . . . training thing sounded much better when she explained it to me.*]

Oh, don't worry, we'll get to the part where we fall ten times a day soon enough. That reminds me, Katherine, we'll need a place where you don't mind things getting crushed.

—And they say I'm high-maintenance. You can leave us, Sergeant. I'll send for you when we're done here.

[*Yes, ma'am.*]

So?

—Any news about Eva?

—No. We haven't found her yet. She's really good! Or whoever is helping her is really good. Whatever. We'll find her. Don't worry about it.

—You gave me your word she wouldn't be harmed.

—I promised I wouldn't give the order to shoot first. They still need to bring her in. I'm not responsible for what happens if she doesn't want to. You know how she is.

—That's not good enough. I need to know you won't hurt her.

—Hurt her? Why would I do that? But you know we can't let the Americans get their hands on her. If it comes to that, they'll put her down. They'll shoot to kill. No one is going to *hurt* her.

—I won't help you if anything happens to Eva. You can kill me if you want to, but then you'll have nothing.

—Oh, Vincent, Vincent . . . I thought we'd been through this. Do you really think anything's changed because Dr Franklin and your daughter are gone? Look at your hands. How many fingers do you see? Are you *sure*? Oh don't worry, they wouldn't start with you. They'd bring in a little girl and let you watch while they do it to her. They can do things that you and I can't even imagine, Vincent. They can do things to you until there is no *you* left. They can screw with your mind so much you'll be begging for them to hurt you more. They can turn you into a pet.

—You're a sick fuck, Katherine. I hope you know that.

—Me? I'm not the one who wants to do any of this. I'm the one, the only one, stopping them. My boss, he doesn't like this plan. He doesn't like you. He doesn't like you *at all*, Vincent. It's the accent, I think. If this doesn't work out . . .

—If this doesn't work out, what?

—Let's just say you're not the only one who'll spend some quality time with a blowtorch and some bolt cutters.

—You guys watch *way* too much TV. Am I really supposed to fall for this?

—Trust me, Vincent, the GRU can be . . .

—Oh, I know you can do some very nasty shit to people. I have absolutely no doubt about that. I was talking about that Stockholm syndrome thing you're going for. Next

209

thing you know, you'll be asking me out on a date. Just a casual dinner in a dimly lit restaurant. Do you think I'll develop feelings for you? That I'll use Themis to destroy armies . . . out of love? Is that it? I'll admit, if the circumstances were different, and maybe you weren't a psychopath, and the world hadn't gone to shit . . .

—Wow. I don't know what to say, Vincent. I'm . . . hurt. Hey, that dinner thing is a great idea, though. What do you say we get out of here and go for a big steak? I know the perfect place.

—I'm serious, Katherine. I want Eva to be safe. You hear me?

—I'll do my best, Vincent. I promise you I'll do my best. Come now. Steak!

File No. 2138

Personal Journal Entry – Eva Reyes

Location: Kaarina Work Camp, near Turku, Finland

There's a way out. Everyone knows about it. There's a *tataarit* kid – they call him Baba. I have no idea what his real name is. He goes out *every single night* for supplies. Cigarettes, mostly. One hundred percent markup, but Baba can get you anything. He'll even bring you a receipt, so you know you're only getting ripped off a hundred percent. The kid – he can't be more than twelve – makes over two thousand dollars a week, or so he says. I get the feeling it's Baba's dad who pockets the money, but Baba likes to brag. He lives well, that's for sure. New clothes. New phone. He's cocky as hell. I like him a lot.

I asked if he could take me with him. He said no, of course. I've given up on things not being complicated. I tried threatening him, told him I'd tell the guards. He laughed. The guards get 20 percent, so does the chef. It turns out my way out of here is through the kitchen, and the chef is the man with the key. I offered to pay, but he asked to see the money. I really like that kid. I like him enough that I told him who I was. That made him smile. Then he asked for the shirt off my back. Literally. He thinks it will fetch a fortune online. 'Genuine shirt from Eva Reyes, worn on alien planet.' We even took a picture he can use as a certificate of authenticity. I don't know what it is, but there's something about my clothes. Anyway, I hated that shirt. The Russians gave it to me. I might have forgotten to mention that part to Baba. Unfortunately, that priceless fashion item was my *one* shirt, and if I manage to leave this place, I'll do it wearing a tee shirt from a metal band called Nightwish, courtesy of Baba himself. At least it's black. He also gave me enough money for a bus to Turku and the ferry to Mariehamn though I'm supposed to pay him back. I'm not sure how. I didn't ask.

I didn't know if I was being played. It seemed so stupid. How could there be a way out of here, and no one uses it, except for one person who keeps coming back? But it's true. I've seen it. I asked for 'proof of life' before taking off my shirt. It's not a secret hole in the floor, not a breach high up in the fence. There's a door! A *yokits* door! They use it to bring food in, leads right outside. If they wanted to, every single person in here could be out by morning, provided they have money, or the right shirt. Anyone who can beat up a cook can get out! But they're not. They're all staying here. Basically, they don't need the fence or the guards. They can just tell people to stay, and they stay. Stay! There, good boy!

I remember having that conversation with my dad. Not Vincent, my adoptive dad in Puerto Rico. I asked him why people complained about politics all the time but did absolutely nothing about it. I couldn't understand why people keep voting for the very people they loathe. They'll protest a war, but the everyday stuff, small injustices, they just let them slide. Friends making a fortune off government contracts, paying a hundred dollars for a pencil, that type of thing, people complain about it, everyone does, but they won't do a thing. I remember how floored I was when he told me that was a good thing, how we need a certain level of cynicism for society to function properly. If people thought they had real power to change things, if they truly believed in democracy, everyone would take to the streets, advocate, militate for everything. It happens from time to time. Thirty thousand people will block traffic to march for a cause, but they do it believing that the other side couldn't *possibly* feel justified in doing the same thing. What if they did? What if thirty thousand people who believe in one thing marched at the very same time as those who believe in the exact opposite? What if it happened every single day? People who care about other things would also want to be heard. They'd need to scream louder. They'd need their disruption to be more . . . disruptive. People are compliant because they don't expect the system to be fair. If they did, if they thought that was even possible, we'd live in chaos, anarchy. We need apathy, he said, or we'll end up killing each other on the streets.

Did I mention my dad worked for the government?

I didn't believe him then. I'm not sure he believed it either. That whole conversation started because I wanted us to open a shelter for alley cats. I was utterly convinced my parents would agree. Sure, there were some downsides to having tons of cats in our house, but you'd have to be really selfish to let that stop you from saving all those lives. Odds are that civics course was his way of telling me to learn to live with that injustice and not get into an endless argument about cats. He and my mom had raised me to argue. They said they would always welcome a debate based on logic and facts and that they could be convinced of anything if I made my case, but a hundred flea-infested strays probably fell outside their definition of 'anything.' I built it, though. I got a stack of empty boxes from the corner-store trash, and I built a cardboard palace in our yard. I thought of everything. There was a playroom, so they wouldn't get bored. I put all the couch pillows inside to make beds. It was perfect. The rain took the whole thing down after a day or two. The pillows didn't make it. I lost a month's worth of allowance, but I was still proud of myself. If you see something wrong with the world, fix it. Fight. Resist. Don't use cardboard.

That's what I liked about Kara, and Vincent, for that matter. He didn't comply. He would have built that cat shelter, made it three floors high, with a water fountain out front. I don't know if it's all my fault or if it's Kara's death that changed him, but I miss that man.

The town's not far. He said it'll take us twenty minutes to get there. With any luck, I'll be in Mariehamn by the time they notice I'm missing. I'll have to figure out what I want to do if I make it to Sweden. I can't just make a normal life for myself in the middle of this nonsense.

Maybe I can. Maybe I can get a job, watch TV, smile when people make jokes about the people living here. I can stop fighting, stop resisting.

Who am I kidding? I can't get a job. They'll just test my blood over there, and I'll end up living in a Swedish camp instead of a Finnish one. I've never been to Sweden, so a work camp there will be somewhat new. Maybe I can sell my pants and make a fortune, become the Baba of Sweden.

It's all about perspective, really. Just don't call it a prison camp. I could be living the life in a gated community. *Yokits*, I'm nervous. I have to get to Mariehamn first. One step at a time, I guess. One foot in front of the other. I don't know what else I can do. If you see something wrong with the world, fix it. But what if it's the whole world that needs fixing?

File No. EE249

Personal File From Esat Ekt

Personal Log – Dr Rose Franklin

Location: Assigned residence, Etyakt region

I have felt vulnerable, powerless even, since we arrived on this world, but it came with a feeling of excitement, like a child riding a roller coaster for the first time. Now there is nothing but helplessness. My friend is dying, and I can't help him. I can't see the world around me. I can't see anything else.

It was stupid of me to think I could find a cure. I'm not a geneticist. I don't know enough about DNA to even recognize what I'm looking for. I thought I could trick the Ekt into doing some of the work for me, but they saw me coming a mile away. Deception doesn't come naturally to them, and they're not really good at detecting it. Or at least they weren't. They're fast learners. The Ekt won't pass on new knowledge to us, but we, humans, know a hell of a lot more about genetics than I do. I told them I could get information if I were on Earth. I could read papers, talk to people. I don't have access to all the research we've done. I don't have access to anything. I've explained that to them in every way that I could, but they don't believe me, or they don't care. I just need more data. It's not . . . fair. All I want is to save my friend. I have to save him.

I can't find the right mutations. Even if I had found

them, I wouldn't know what to do next. I need to study how their weapon worked, how it found the right cells and what it did to them. They won't let me. I understand why they won't let me play with that weapon, it was designed specifically to kill them, people with Ekt DNA. I understand that *now*. I didn't when I asked them for a sample. They were . . . confused at first. They became agitated and threw me out of the lab. I suppose that 'I promise to be careful' doesn't quite cut it when it comes to weapons of mass destruction. I'll need to find a new place to work in. I get the feeling I'm not welcome there anymore.

I'm not giving up. I don't care what they tell me. I'll do what I have to do. I discovered ancient alien artifacts buried in every corner of the world. I put together a giant robot that can lay waste to entire cities. I stopped an alien invasion, for God's sake. I can save *one man*.

Everything I've done now seems insignificant next to Eugene's life. I've lost people before. I've lost the people closest to me, and I can live with that. I can because there was nothing anyone could have done. But they can save Eugene. They can cure him in a matter of minutes, without effort. I respect, and I even understand, their principles. Where Eva and Vincent see arrogance, I see profound humility. There is a deep respect for life and the universe in their refusal to mess with it. But we're not talking about life as a whole, we're talking about *a* life, my friend's. It might be me who is arrogant, but I don't want to see that life gone so needlessly.

I'll convince them. I'll convince them it's in their best interest to help him. I'll find a way to make them bend their rules. I'll steal the medication if I have to.

File No. 2142

Interview between Dr Rose Franklin
and Dr Alyssa Papantoniou

*Location: United States Central Command (CENTCOM),
MacDill Air Force Base, Tampa, Florida*

—Dr F . . . Franklin. I didn't think we'd meet again.

—I didn't think I'd meet anyone on Earth again, but you're right, you're the last person I expected to call.

—I have sssso many questions. I dd . . . don't even know where to start.

—Why don't you start by answering mine?

—Are we . . . Do you still hate me? I sincerely hope you d . . . don't.

—Do I hate you? That's an . . . interesting way to start the conversation. I . . . I'm not your friend, if that's what you're asking. I'll never forgive you for what you did. But I don't . . . You don't seem as insane as you did before. I guess the rest of the world has caught up with you.

—I'll t . . . take that as a compliment.

—When did you stop working for the Russians?

—They didn't need me after you d . . . disappeared. There was no need to find pilots with Themis gone. Then I learned the Americans were putting Lapetus back together, so I came.

—Just like that. New job. You start on Monday.

—They took some con . . . convincing, but they knew I could help. I did.

—It didn't bother you? Switching sides, again?

—Have I ever misled you into thinking I was a p . . . patriot? Even if I were, I'm a Bosnian. I do what I do for everyone. I don't care where I do it.

—You're a regular Mother Teresa.

—Whatever you think of me, Dr Franklin, I am not responsible for what is happening in the world. If anyone is g . . . guilty of that, it's you.

—I didn't come here to fight with you, Alyssa. I just want to find a way to stop this.

—Stop what?

—All of it. Lapetus. The camps. Everyone hating everyone. How did it come to this?

—Dr Franklin, the free world was destroyed when the aliens came. All these ideas, democracy, the will of the people, everyone being equal, it's based on the belief that, in the end, good will always t . . . tr . . . triumph over evil.

—It did. Didn't it?

—Tell that to the tens of millions that died. They all died in the world's biggest cities, where the power is. P . . . people were scared, and scared people defer to authority. The world also lost Themis. You may have d . . . disabled one of their robots, but it's Themis that gave people hope. Then she was gone. But there it was, lying in the middle of Central Park. Lapetus was inevitable, Dr Franklin. No one could have stopped it.

—You didn't try.

—Me? No. Why would I? Why would I want Earth to be defen . . . defenseless? Why would anyone want that? Do you know why no one, why none of these countries fight back against the Americans?

—Because they can't, Alyssa. They don't fight back because they have nothing to fight with.

—No! They don't fight back because they need Lapetus. They sleep better at night knowing it's there even if it is their enemy that controls it, even if they have to give up some freedom for it. And the camps? The camps are nothing new.

—What are you talking about? Rounding up innocent people, citizens, born and raised in this country, because they happen to have had their father's genes expressed instead of their mother's, or because they call their god by a different name? What are they doing to them, Alyssa? Are they killing them?

—Not many of them. Not for now. But it might happen. People have a very short memory, or a very selective one,

220

I d . . . don't know. You had over one hundred thousand people in camps during the Second World War, so did Canada. They were citizens too. That wasn't in the Middle Ages. Our parents were there.

—I'm not defending what happened during the war, but we were fighting Japan. We're not at war with those people. They haven't done *anything*!

—Does it matter? We have to blame sssomeone. A hundred mmmillion people don't die because . . . these things happen! The human mind doesn't work that way.

—Sure! How about we blame the people that did it?

—Not good enough. That won't make anyone feel better. There's n . . . nothing you can do about them. They're too powerful, and they're not here. It has to be someone weaker, here. Then you can remove those people and feel safer. People need to feel safer.

—You're crazy, Alyssa. Do you know that?

—I'm not saying this is a good thing. I'm saying it's always been this way. We need scapegoats when bad things happen. The Jews poisoned the well.

—What?

—The Black D . . . Death. It killed almost half the world in the fourteenth century. Maybe the Jews were less affected, maybe it was a myth, but people in Europe blamed them for the disease, accused them of poisoning the water. So they threw them out of the cities, or they killed them. They murdered them inside their homes. They burned them alive. In Strasbourg, they brought hundreds of them inside a wooden house and set it on fire. They did this in France, in Germany, in Spain, in Switzerland. This was Europe, the p . . . p . . . pinnacle of civilization. It happened before, and it will happen again. You think the world ch . . . changed while you were gone? It hasn't. This is who we are.

—I'm sorry, Alyssa, but I refuse to believe that.

—Good for you. I choose to be a realist.

—And so you helped with all of it.

—About as much as you did, yes.

—Don't do that, Alyssa. I'm not like you.

—You complained about Lapetus and about the camps. You *gave* them Lapetus. There's no d . . . denying that. It makes no difference whether you intended to or not. I made a genetic test so they could find pilots. They found pilots. Only they didn't stop there, and they started screening everyone. There were aliens among us. People wanted them found.

—We're all aliens, Alyssa. All of us are.

—I know. That was the problem. How do you find them if they're everywhere? Imagine if tall people were to blame. Are you tall? Am I? They made the c . . . camps until they could decide who we're supposed to be scared of. And yes, they used my test to do it. So blame me if you want, I don't care.

—I think there's enough of that going around. I came here to talk about Lapetus.

—Beautiful, isn't he?

—How did you make that test of yours? We couldn't find anyone else who could activate the helmets in Themis.

—Your sample size was too small. I had already made a series of t . . . tests based on the samples I had from your pilots, but it was too precise, too specific. I couldn't find anyone with that much in common with them, but I now had a much larger sample of the po . . . population to look at.

—Who?

—The dead, of course! All one hundred million of them. The aliens made that test for us. They designed that gas to target their own kind. Some people died within seconds of being ex . . . posed to the alien gas. Some spent entire minutes breathing it before they died. If I could figure out who went first, I could narrow it down to a handful of genetic traits. I d . . . did.

—But there can't be that many people with the right profile. We tested hundreds.

—You needed thousands. Sixty-eight thousand. That's how many p . . . people you need to test on average to find one person the robot will respond to. I tested Me . . . Mexicans at first to make sure it worked. We used ICE – Immigration and Cu . . . Customs Enforcement – to get blood samples of everyone they deported. Within a year, we found a few who could pilot.

—Did you use them?

—No. They wanted Americans.

—White Americans, of course.

—Anyone not a Muslim. Apparently, we can only hate so many people.

—That doesn't make any sense. They put people with too much alien DNA in camps because they don't trust them. Yet they want people with even more alien genetics to pilot the robot.

—Ironic, isn't it? Too much alien DNA means you are either locked in a camp, or one of the mmmm . . . most powerful people in the world.

—And they're OK with that?

—If you mean the US government, no. They're not. The pilots are imp . . . implanted with a small explosive device, inside their skull. They can remote-detonate it if needed. It's sss . . . supposed to be painless.

—And how did you get the robot to work? The aliens left because this one was destroyed.

—Disabled, not destroyed.

—How do they control it? Did they make more people like Vincent?

—No, they got the b . . . best engineers they could find and locked them in a room until they figured out a way. They built some contraption – it's a robot, really – that sits on top of the existing controls. The pilot stands about a foot to the side, their legs inside flexible . . . tubes. There are sensors inside that ca . . . capture the human leg movements. The machine translates them into something that matches the alien physiology, then transfers motion to the robot's controls. It's fascinating to watch. I have it on video. Would you like to see?

—Some other time. I want to know how they made it work again. I *disabled* that robot, like you said. It didn't work. It fell apart. The metal in its leg was –

—Dr Franklin, I'm a gen . . . eticist. I know nothing about the metal, or what you d . . . did to it.

—You know it lost a leg. You can't just attach a new one. It doesn't work like that.

—They found a way to convince the rest of the body that the monstrosity they put in its place was the real thing. I don't know how they did that.

—Surely you must know something. It happened here, no?

—All I know is it has to do with the decay rate of the metal where the pieces touch.

—I thought of that when we assembled Themis. I got nowhere with it.

You know, Dr Franklin, it is not entirely impossible that they found someone better than you.

—It's easy to find someone better than me. I just don't think we have the technology to do what you're suggesting. We didn't when I left, anyway.

—If it makes you feel better, they did have some help.

—From whom?

—Come, let me show you. Oh, and Dr Franklin?

—Yes.

—I want you to know I had nnn . . . nothing to do with this.

File No. 2143

Interview between Dr Rose Franklin and Detainee 46275

Location: United States Central Command (CENTCOM), MacDill Air Force Base, Tampa, Florida

—Dr Franklin! What a pleasure!

—Mr Burns! Your face! Who did this to you?

—I believe his name is Keith.

—This is crazy. Someone has to pay for this. Let me –

—No, Dr Franklin, don't. That someone will end up being me. They won't listen to you, and they'll punish me for not being able to convince you that I enjoy being punched in the face repeatedly.

—How did they find you? Who told them about you?

—You did, I'm afraid.

—Me?

—Oh, don't blame yourself. It wasn't your fault. Unfortunately, you don't enjoy the same level of anonymity our late friend did. Apparently, the NSA was curious to see why you flew to Washington during the alien attack and decided to have you followed. They arrested me not long after you vanished, in my favorite restaurant, no less.

—I'm so, so sorry.

—Don't be. There's nothing you could have done. And, you know, this room really isn't so bad when I have it all to myself. My apartment wasn't much bigger. I do miss television, and going out, and pens. They won't give me a pen. I think they're afraid I'll try to kill myself. If these little physical therapy sessions told us anything, it's that I don't like the sight of blood, but they *still* won't give me a pen. But enough about me! I'm not the one who's been on another planet for almost a *decade*. How was it? What does it look like?

—You don't know, do you?

—Why would I? I'm from Michigan.

—It was . . . interesting.

—OK, then. That's all I wanted to know.

—I'm just not sure this is the best place to talk.

—Oh, that! Yes, the only time they turn off the cameras is when Keith pays me a visit. Some other time, then.

—What do they want with you? Why are they keeping you here?

—How did we get here? Good question. They took a blood sample when they first interrogated me, and they have been very interested in me ever since.

—But why here? They keep people with unusual DNA in camps.

—Well, my test results were more interesting than most. Not all, but most. Your blood is much more interesting if you ask me.

—And what do they want with you?

—They want information, mostly. I'm a . . . consultant. They consult me on things. They are very, very enthusiastic about it.

—They beat you up while interrogating you.

—Not exactly. They beat me up, period. Then they come and ask questions. Then they beat me up again to make sure I answer their questions the next time they come.

—What kind of questions?

—Hmmm. Technical questions, mostly. They wanted to know how to get a certain robot to function again. I'm a *technical* consultant.

—What made them think you would know anything about that?

—I'm not sure. I might have said something. I might have said a lot of things while I was being consulted.

—What have you told them?

—I told them . . . I told them everything I knew, I suppose. They can be very convincing, you know. It turns out people like me are very sensitive to certain drugs they have, and I'll admit I have a very low tolerance for pain. Whatever I told them, it seems it wasn't enough because they keep coming back for more. They seem genuinely surprised every time I don't know the answer to a question. I keep explaining to them that the people who really knew died three thousand years ago. I must not be very good at explaining it.

—You're the one who told them how to fix the missing leg.

—I remember them asking about that, yes. Oh yes. They asked about that *many* times. Did it work? They never told me if my solution worked.

—It did. Now they're using that robot to bend other nations to their will.

—That's not very nice.

—No. It's not. I never even thought about what we'd do with that robot after it fell down. I was so happy, so relieved when they all left Earth, I –

—You didn't have time! They took you away. There's nothing you could have done –

—I could have sprayed bacteria all over that robot, disabled every part of it.

—Did you have enough?

—Not at the time, no.

—That's what I thought. How's Eva?

—I don't know. She escaped.

—Escaped? From where?

—I'm sorry. We were being held in Russia. She found a way out of her cell, but I don't know where she is. I'm worried about her.

—She'll be OK. Did she have help? It would be better if she had some help, a friend to look after her.

—I don't know. What are you saying?

—Nothing. Only that if I were in her shoes, I'd like to have a friend to watch over me. Wouldn't you?

—Yes. I'd like that very much. I'd be very grateful.

—You're a nice person, Dr Franklin.

—You used to call me Rose.

—We haven't met in nine years. I don't know how you feel about me anymore.

—Why would I feel any different?

—I can give you a hundred million reasons.

—You feel responsible for what happened? You've been helping us, helping me, all along! You saved . . . so many of us.

—You did all that. I just told you a story or two. Besides, someone has to be held accountable, and since my ancestors are not here . . . They *did* come for people like me, you know.

—I don't think you really believe that.

— . . .

—You know what I'd like? I'd like to hear a story.

—Oh, I think you've heard them all. I'm an old man. Old men don't have any new stories to tell.

—Please? I could really use one now.

—Well, there *is* the one about the blind archer. Have you heard that one before?

—I don't think I have, no.

—Skaði was a great Viking archer and hunter. That wasn't her real name – Skaði is a giantess, a goddess in Norse mythology – but she was so good with a bow . . . So good, she could feed the entire village by herself, and for years she did just that. People said she hunted with her eyes closed, that she could hear the heartbeat of her prey.

She couldn't. That became abundantly clear when Skaði went blind.

—What happened? Was it an accident?

—Oh no. Diabetic retinopathy. Skaði, she developed type 2 diabetes in her early forties, which, at the time, no one had even heard of. Needless to say, it went untreated. It took a few years, but she lost her eyesight completely.

The village survived. There were other hunters, of course. But one year, during a particularly harsh winter, the village ran out of food. Prey was scarce, and the archers weren't nearly as skilled as Skaði. People were starving.

Many of the men were now too weak to hunt. One of the elders suggested they send Skaði on a hunt. Many, including Skaði herself, were quick to point out that she was blind, but the elder quoted from a few myths about Skaði – the goddess, not the diabetic woman. Once you throw religion into the mix, it's easy to lose sight of reality – no pun intended – and somehow everyone agreed to put their fate into the hands of a blind archer, believing the gods would take care of them. The elder offered to accompany Skaði into the forest, in large part because he knew that seeing her trip on a branch five steps in would probably be bad for morale.

They ventured deep into the forest. The wind was blowing, and there were no animal tracks to be found. The elder and Skaði were both ready to give up when a magnificent deer appeared out of nowhere. Skaði, well, she couldn't see a thing. The elder walked in front of her to guide her. A little to the left. A little more. Skaði drew her bow as far as she could. She knew the elder's verbal cues were not enough, and she would surely miss. She remembered what the villagers said about her and quietly summoned her namesake to help her, to let her hear the heartbeat of her prey. And for the briefest of moments, she did. She aimed at the sound and let go of the arrow. It is possible that Skaði did hear a heartbeat at such a distance, unlikely, but possible. Only if she did, it was the elder's heartbeat and not the deer's because her arrow went right through his heart, and he slid to the ground without a sound. Skaði called for him for hours, never found his body. She died the next day when she fell off a cliff trying to get back home.

The moral of the —

—I know what the moral of the story is. You can't do anything if you don't know what's going on.

—I thought it was about not putting too much faith in one person's ability to change things.

—Come closer.

[*Ma'am! DO NOT approach the prisoner! Do not whisper to him!*]

I'll get you out.

[*Ma'am! I'm going to have to ask you to leave!*]

—Thank you for your visit, Dr Franklin. You should go now. My friend Keith and I are about to have a little chat.

PART THREE
Road To Damascus

File No. 2155

Mission log – Capt. Bodie Hough and Lt Barbara Ball, US Marine Corps, Mecha Division

Location: Aboard Lapetus, Muskö Naval Base. Near Stockholm, Sweden

—Hey! Why are we beaming there? We could walk to the Merry Ham.

—It's Mariehamn, with an 'n' at the end, you moron. And it's about a hundred miles. We don't have that kind of time, and they'd see us coming, well, a hundred miles away.

—Are you sure? It looked real close! On the map. You saw it!

—There's a thing at the bottom of the map. Tells you the scale.

[*Lapetus, we don't have all day. You have the coordinates. You are go for launch.*]

—Roger that, Central. Punching it in . . . now. We're . . . here.

—To the left, Bodie.

—OK, I see it. Central, we're about a mile from the pier. We can see the ferry.

[*Roger that. You are looking for a girl, nineteen years of age.*]

I don't see her. I can't tell if –

—Central, this is Lieutenant Ball. We're getting closer, but there are quite a few people here. Can you tell us what she's wearing? They're all very tiny from where we're standing.

[*Stand by. We're asking our source.*]

You're talking to him now? Is your source here?

[*Lapetus, she is wearing a black tee shirt. She should be exiting the ferry building now.*]

. . .

[*Lapetus, do you have contact?*]

There!

—Central, we have eyes on. She saw us too. She's running towards us.

[*Roger that. Just keep her company. We're sending a helo to pick her up. ETA three minutes.*]

—Bodie, look. The ferry building.

—Got it. Central, there are five, no, six people in olive uniforms exiting the building. I repeat, six people, possibly hostiles, coming our way.

[*Where's the girl?*]

Still running. Maybe eight hundred feet from us. Wait. Central, I see flashes of light. Are they shooting at us?

—They're not shooting at us, they're shooting at her!

[*Lapetus, protect the girl at all cost. I repeat, you must protect the girl.*]

—Arming weapon now.

—No, Bodie. They're too close. We'll kill the girl too. Just kneel. I'll pick her up.

—What?

—You heard me. Just kneel!

—All right!

—Come on, girl. Just like King Kong. Climb . . .

I've got her! Get up! Get up! Get up!

—And up we go. I hope she's not afraid of heights. Central, we have her in our hand, but I see trucks on the main road. There's a helo coming from the east. I'm guessing that's not ours.

[*Negative, Lapetus. ETA, two minutes.*]

Central, I don't think they'll feel very welcome. I have a feeling this whole place is about to get very unfriendly. Lieutenant, what do you say we walk her out of here?

—Go! Head south towards the small islands.

—South? But Sweden's that way!

—We can't cross here, Bodie. We need to head south.

—All right. If you say so. Heading south. Central, that helicopter is coming at us *real* fast. It's . . . firing at us. Incoming! Brace for impact!

—Turn around! Turn around!

—Damn! We're hit! We're hit. They hit us in the back.

[*Lapetus, this is Central. Is the girl alive?*]

—Affirmative, Central. I've got her against our chest. She's holding on to my thumb for dear life. Keep heading south, Bodie.

—I am!

—No, that's southwest. We don't want to go there yet.

—Well, it's away from that helicopter. Central, how about some help? We're fine in here, but the girl won't make it if we get hit from the front. I'm running as fast as we can, but I can't outrun a chopper, and we can't fire with a kid in our hands. Can we get some air support?

[*Negative, Lapetus. Our bird is rescue only. F7 is the closest Swedish airbase. We'll have griffins in the air in two minutes. We're looking at another five before they get to you.*]

Central, that's not good enough. The girl will be toast long before they get here.

[*Checking with Swedish Navy. The . . .* Härnösand *is the closest ship to your location. She might get there faster.*]

Can she blow that chopper out of the sky?

[*She's a corvette — 57 mm guns on top. Be advised, Swedish forces will fire warning shots, but they will not engage unless fired upon.*]

Fired upon! What the hell do you think we've been doing out here? He's coming at us again. Incoming!

—Captain!

—Dammit!

—Turn us around, Bodie!

—My leg won't move. We're stuck in mud or something. Turn the body away.

—That's as far as I can – AAARGH! That one hurt.

[*Lapetus, is –*]

We got hit in the shoulder. The girl is . . . She's OK! She's OK! I see her moving.

—Must be one hell of a ride.

—She won't take much more of this. We need to move.

—My leg's free. We're moving again. Lieutenant, can you see the helo? I've lost it.

—I don't see it either. Maybe it's gone.

—I doubt that. It seemed very motivated a second ago.

Got him. He's hiding in the sun. Coming straight at us. Oh, you think you're clever, don't you?

—He's coming fast!

—I'm taking us across.

—No! I don't think we've cleared the –

—He's firing again. I'm turning.

—Ugh. Same shoulder.

—Screw this! I'm heading west.

—Captain! No! You need to clear the trench! Oh, shit.

— . . .

—Back us up! Back us up!

—I'm trying! We're too heavy. The ground keeps giving under our feet.

—Back us up, Captain. Now!

—I can't! It's too steep.

—Keep trying, Bodie!

—I can't do it! We're sinking.

—Central, we walked right into the trench at South Kvarken. We're going down.

—How deep is this thing?

—Ten thousand feet at the deepest.

[*Roger that, Lapetus. What about the girl?*]

I can't keep her above water anymore. Central, we'll lose comms soon. I have to let her go. Dammit! She's still holding on. Come on, girl! Let go!

All right, Central, she's all alone in freezing water. You better get someone here fast. It's a rough sea.

File No. 2157

Debriefing – Colonel Smith, US Army, and Captain Lucas Nilsson, Svenska marinen

Location: Muskö Naval Base. Near Stockholm, Sweden

—You are the captain of the HSwMS *Härnösand*, is that correct?

—Yes. Is Rear Admiral Björkman going to join us?

—No. It's just us.

—What is this? Is this an official inquiry?

—Call it what you want. We just want to know what happened.

—With all due respect – Colonel, is it?

—Yes.

—With all due respect, Colonel. You are an officer in the US Army. I am a captain of the Swedish Navy. I understand that our governments are . . . cooperating, but –

—Captain, with all due respect, I am not asking. Let's not waste any more time pretending you have a choice. You won't like how this ends. Believe me, I have all the authority that I need.

—What do you want to know?

—I want to know why we have a nineteen-year-old in a coma.

—I believe her heart stopped, and she had to be revived.

—The *Härnösand* was less than five minutes away when she went in the water. She should be having cocoa right now, not lying unconscious in a hospital bed. What took you so long?

—I strongly believe I should be having this conversation with Rear Admiral Björkman.

—Capt—

—He should at least be in the room.

—He was unavailable. Don't make me ask again, Captain.

—Ask what? You said we were less than five minutes away. That's how long it took us to get there: less than five minutes. We didn't stop for snacks. It took us another five or six minutes to find the girl.

—Why?

—Why? You didn't lose an aircraft carrier, you lost a tiny human in a really big sea.

—We didn't lose anything.

—Well, your people had her, then they didn't. You can draw your own conclusions. The waves were much bigger than she is. We were almost on top of her when we spotted her waving.

—That's what? Ten minutes in the water.

—Freezing water. Water temperature was three degrees Celsius.

—Three degrees Celsius, that's . . .

—More than two. Less than four.

—I would lose the attitude if I were you. You said she was waving at you. I take it she was still conscious.

—She was. We threw her a life buoy.

—You didn't bring her on board?

—The *Härnösand* is a stealth corvette, not a dive boat. You can't just hop on and off. We had to get a lifeboat down. Problem is, a Finnish attack helicopter showed up. They fired machine guns across our bows, right between us and the girl. She was almost hit. We assumed they'd rather kill her than let us have her, so we backed away. They moved closer. The helicopter was in a better position to extract her than we were. We asked for permission to engage. We were denied. We fired our guns fifty meters from the helicopter. They stopped moving towards the girl, but they stayed to make sure we didn't either.

—There were jets under way.

—Two griffins, but they weren't even in the air yet.

—Why weren't they?

—You'll have to ask them. All I know is there was a problem at the base. The first help we got was a rescue helicopter. One of yours if I'm not mistaken though it didn't have any markings. The Finns fired in the water again when they tried to approach the girl. Your helo moved towards the Finnish helicopter, dangerously close to it. They were in between the Finns' guns and the girl for a few seconds. We grabbed her with the lifeboat before they found a new vantage point. By then, she'd been in the water for a good thirty minutes. She was unconscious. Her heart had stopped. *That's* why she's in a coma.

— . . .

—Will that be all, sir?

File No. EE254

Personal File From Esat Ekt

Personal Journal Entry – Dr Rose Franklin

Location: Assigned residence, Etyakt region

Eugene passed away last night.

I wasn't there.

Vincent and Eva stayed with him until the end. I didn't. I just lay in bed here.

There's this tiny spot on my bedroom wall, top right corner, it lets a little bit of light in all the time. It doesn't matter if I make the wall opaque or not, the outside is always showing through that spot. Last night, there was a star in the middle of it. I couldn't stop staring at it. I kept waiting for it to move past the hole and fade into the wall, but it didn't. It stayed right there, perfectly centered. When planets form, the gas they condense out of always has a small amount of angular momentum, and so they spin on themselves. The sky is always moving. I must have been looking at a ship or a satellite. It's gone now. Someone turned it off two hours ago. I kept on staring, waiting for my star to come back, willing it to come back. Now the sun's up and that spot on my wall is too bright to look at.

I spent two days arguing with regional officials about Eugene's case, asking, begging them to save him. I didn't get the reaction I was expecting. They didn't brush me off. They walked with me all the way to the hospital. They introduced me to doctors. They showed me the medicine. I don't know why. It seems obvious it would just make things worse, but they felt like they had to. There was no cruelty involved. They just wanted to prove that they *could* save him, as if somehow that showed their good intentions. It was touching in some way. They weren't going to do anything – they truly believed it would have been wrong to do so – but they *wanted* to show me that vial. They had such warmth in their eyes when they handed it to me. 'Hey, look! We know your pain is real. You can hold it in your hands.'

Yesterday, I went back and asked them if we could bury him somewhere. They don't bury their dead. I could tell they were puzzled, probably a bit disgusted with the idea, but they wanted to make a gesture. They gave us a spot in fallow lands, somewhere. They said the land wouldn't be used for years, but that they would need to get rid of the bones when it was time to plant again. It was hours away, even in a ship. They wouldn't allow a decomposing body anywhere *close* to where people lived. It didn't matter. I felt like I had accomplished something. I had found a way to honor my friend. Things made sense again. Yesterday, I found out Eugene had prepared a will, if you can call it that. Vincent took me outside and showed it to me. 'I don't want to be buried. I don't want my ashes kept. I don't want any piece of me left on this hellhole. If you ever make it back, tell my family I love them and that I thought of them in the end.' I started crying, shaking. I hit Vincent in the face. I went crazy, batshit, body-out-of-control crazy. I threw rocks at people passing by. I screamed and swung at things that didn't exist until my whole body seized up and I could do nothing but curl up in a ball on the street. Vincent asked for help from passersby, and they carried me back home.

Eugene passed away last night.

I wasn't there.

Did I *want* them to let him die? Eva was right. I *worshipped* these people, what they'd accomplished, the world they built for themselves. I was in awe of their principles and their absolute determination to live by them, no matter what. I drank *ipipyot* until the wee hours with Enatast, talking about the nature of right and wrong. They refused to help a planet struck with some disease they had conquered long ago – exactly like what happened to Eugene, only it happened to *everyone* – and I listened to him with delight as he told stories of distant planets whose names I can't pronounce, of animals that went extinct and made room for new ones to evolve. What if saving that planet denied a whole new species its existence? What if that new life is what the universe needed? I argued with Eva and Vincent about it as if it were philosophy – would you kill Hitler if you could go back in time? – and I ran back to Enatast for comfort when they disagreed with me, like a child who can't remember if the Earth circles the Sun or it's the other way around and goes to her father to set her straight. I saw the death of ten billion people I never met as a form of moral victory. The same thing happened with Eugene, I asked for their help in saving him because I loved that man with every fiber in my being, but I know now there's a part of me that hoped they would say no, that didn't want to see their integrity sullied because of one man, because of me.

I'm a scientist. I find beauty in absolutes. I love the clarity of math, its unwavering dependability. Math will never say one thing and do another one. It will never harm you on purpose because its only purpose is truth. On Esat Ekt, I found that same clarity, that perspicuity, that is so lacking in people on Earth. I found it not because it was there but because I was searching for it. I saw faces in the clouds. I found what I was looking for here because I brought it with me. I know that now. I also know I'm a hypocrite. I marveled at their idealism, applauded them for not wanting to share knowledge with us, but I lied to them to get them to teach me. I lied to them to try to save Eugene. I admired their principles so long as they didn't apply to me.

Eugene passed away last night, and when he did, there was nothing gained, nothing achieved. He just died. In the grand scheme of things, it didn't mean anything. The universe will go on without him as it would have with him. The Ekt will see his death as nature following its course. They won't rejoice. They won't pat themselves on the back for letting him die. There is no malice in them. They watched Eugene die with humility and respect, like we watch the leaves turn to red in the fall. They choose to see the world in a way that gives their life meaning. They choose. It is a choice.

What do *I* choose?

There was a church across from my apartment in Chicago. In the summer, I would watch through the window while grooms greeted their guests at the door. I watched newlyweds leave while everyone cheered. Some left me indifferent and lost my interest before they made it down the steps. Some didn't. The way they smiled or looked at each other. That ignorant bliss, or the moment of doubt when they thought no one was watching. I wondered what their life would be like, and I wished with all my heart it would be a good one. It felt . . . intimate somehow, sharing these precious moments with complete strangers. But it wasn't. I watched through the window. It never occurred to me to get out of my apartment and wish them luck in person. It would have been presumptuous. It was *their* wedding. I wasn't invited, and I didn't want to be.

That is the way of the Ekt. I only now truly understand it. They watch other worlds through a window. Eugene's death was unfortunate – the bride falling down the stairs – but it wasn't their place to save him. It would have been presumptuous. I can't bring myself to hate them. There is a certain nobility to the way they look at things. Only this time, I *was* there. I *was* invited. I couldn't watch my friend die because there was no window to watch it through, and I couldn't bear the reality of it. I lost my friend. I hurt, and that hurt is as real as anything I've seen or touched. There is no objectivity. Everything is perspective.

What does a man's life amount to? What does the life of a thousand, a billion? What is an ant's life worth? I see now that the answer is irrelevant. It's the question that matters. Should the ant let itself die, crushed under the weight of its own insignificance? Or should it live, fight giants, and build magnificent cities underground?

What do I choose?

File No. EE255

Personal File From Esat Ekt

Interview between Dr Rose Franklin and Vincent Couture

Location: Assigned residence, Etyakt region

—Rose! I didn't expect to see you. How are you holding up?

—I'll do it.

—Do w—

—Don't talk, Vincent. Just listen. Six years ago, you told me that the only thing that mattered to you was getting Eva back to Earth.

—I remember that.

—You said you didn't care what happened to me, or to anyone else –

—I –

—I said don't talk. I just want to know if you meant what you said back then. Because if you did, I'm in. I'll make that deal with you right now. We get her home, no matter what the cost. I need that part to be very clear.

—Whatever it takes.

—Do we have a deal?

—We do.

— . . . Vincent?

—What is it, Rose?

—I love you and Eva with all my heart. I hope you know that.

—I do, Rose. We both do.

—Good . . .

File No. 2171

Mission log – Vincent Couture and Sergeant Alexander Vasiliev

Location: One hundred miles north of Chatanga, Siberia, Russia

—Where are we?

—In Siberia, Alex. We're in Siberia.

—It's cold in Siberia. Why are we here?

—Because it's your birthday, and there's absolutely no one anywhere within a hundred miles. There's nothing but rocks and snow from here on end. Do you know what that means?

—We can shoot at things?

—Yes, Alex. We can!

—We can shoot at things!

—We can have sword fights with giant boulders. We can slide on our shield – I've never done that myself. We should definitely try that. But first, we need to practice getting up a few times, so I'm just gonna let myself fall –

—Not on our back! No! Not the back again! AAAAGH! I hate you.

—Then let's get up as fast as we can so we can have some fun.

—We cannot get up lying on our back. You told me fifty times we cannot get up from our back. You said you were never able to do it. We need to roll over first.

—I know what I said, Alex. I'm telling you we can do this. I know we can. Put your hands on the ground. Higher. I'm folding my legs. That's as far as I can go. Push up with your elbows and move your butt forward. Now bend forward . . . And PUSH! PUSH! PUSH! And . . .

—Ouch.

—Yeah. That wasn't even close.

—What makes you think it's even possible?

—It ought to be!

—Can you do it? With your knees bent that way, can you get up?

—Yeah, but there's a lot of wiggling involved. It's hard to wiggle when you only control half your body and you're standing up pretending to be down.

—How about a kick up? I can do a kick up.

—*That* doesn't work with the knees reversed. You end up planting your feet straight, and nothing happens. It doesn't work if you can't bend your toes. Also, she weighs seven thousand metric tons. Let's try again.

—No!

—Come on! Move our butt over our legs, and push! ARGH! You need to push harder.

—You *do* realize I am not really pushing the gigantic robot with my arms?

—I know. I know. Maybe we need to shift the weight more.

—Maybe we need to roll over.

—All right, all right. Roll us over.

—Finally.

—Move us backwards. Knees are bent, now push!

—Ugh! There! This is how you get up.

—I know how to get up! I'm the one who showed you. I just know there is a way to do this. She can teleport herself and destroy cities. She should be able to get back on her feet without rolling over.

—She can't scratch her back.

—Fair enough. But I'm not giving up.

—You do that. Just not with me.

—Hey, Alex, can I ask you something?

—Yes.

—Do you really want to do this?

—Shoot at rocks? Yes. It's fun.

—The whole thing. You know we're not just gonna shoot at rocks. At some point, they'll send us out against real people, and things will go bad for everybody. Do you really want that?

—I volunteered.

—Why?

—It's better than prison.

—Is it?

—I have a wife, three kids.

—You do? I've never seen them.

—I have not seen them in four years. But as long as I do what I'm told, they will be taken care of. They will be safe.

—Is their blood like ours?

—No, they are all A2s. My youngest, Lily, is a pureblood.

—I don't understand. Why do they need to be protected?

—They don't if I do what I'm told.

—They threatened you after you volunteered?

—They call it insurance. You look surprised.

—Not at that. From what I've seen, that's just par for the course. I'm surprised you volunteered. You don't strike me as the war type.

—I will do what needs –

—Alex, stop. That was a compliment. It's why I agreed to pilot with you.

—You did not have a choice.

—I didn't, that's right, but I agreed anyway. I know you'll do what you have to do. I just like that you're not eager to do it.

—I love my country.

—You do? Still?

—I hate the people running my country. But I love Russia. Always will. Like my children. They do things I don't like, but they are still my children. Besides, everyone is doing bad things now. You can't hate everyone.

—No, but close.

—What about you? Do you just not care about your country?

—My country doesn't really exist anymore.

—You know what I mean. You are piloting a Russian war machine.

—Themis isn't Russian. And yeah, I do care. Like I said, my country doesn't exist anymore, but the people in it do. I lived in Chicago when this all started, and I also care about Americans, deeply.

—They will call you a traitor.

—Oh yes. They will. They'll be right, sorta. If a traitor is the opposite of a patriot, then that's what I am.

—You don't like patriots?

—I like the concept. It sounds good. To love the place where you're from, nothing wrong with that, right? It's all good. But is it love, really? Or is it pride?

—I don't understand.

—Well, you can love something that's flawed. It's harder to be proud of it. Can you love something you're not proud of? Much easier if you can do both. That's where it gets messy because you need a reason. You have to have something to be proud *of.* Is it quality of life, education? How would you know? It has to be something much simpler. You, and people just like you. You start believing you're better than everyone else. Other people, well, their culture is messed up, they have the wrong values, they're not as good, not as smart, or they're just plain evil. You can hate them or pretend you're a good person and just be condescending. Everyone else is just as proud as you are for the exact same reasons, but they're wrong, and you're right.

That'd be just fine – you can buy more tanks and go to war with the guy next door – but then you look around and you see those same people *inside* your country. More than that, they want the same rights, the same opportunities, as everyone else. Shit, they could be in charge! So you start taking things away from them, making sure they'll stay where they belong, and let the *real* citizens make the decisions. You step on your own people, you keep them down, because you're proud of your country, because you're a patriot.

—You are a cynical man, Vincent Couture.

—Maybe. Look around, Alex. Do you see anything to rejoice over?

—Yes. There is no one here. We can shoot at things.

—All right, let's do it. Let's practice your aim first. I'll give you the sword. Huh, you'll want to raise your arm. It'll go through the ground with your arm down.

—Whoa.

—Yeah. I know. Just rai— What are you doing?

—Woooo! I'm Luke Skywalker. I'm a Jedi, like my father before me.

—Ha! Let me get us closer to that boulder so you can swing at something real. There, young Padawan.

—That. Is. So. Cool.

—All right, all right. Look to your right. See that boulder wayyyy over there?

—The tall one?

—Yep. The sword is at its longest, that'll give a really narrow beam when we fire. Just aim at the boulder. The sphere we're inside is about the same height as Themis's arm but slightly to the left. That means you need to aim a bit to the right of where you think it'll go. Are you ready?

—Yes! Fire!

—See. Like I told you, a bit more to the right. Lower. No, not that low. That's good. A tiny tiny bit to the right. That's it! Don't move. Firing.

—Whoa. It's just . . . gone.

—That's the idea.

—I thought there would be some kind of explosion. Where did it go?

—The boulder? It didn't go anywhere. Most of it turned into energy. Some of it is in a gaseous state. Technically, nothing was lost . . . I know. Crazy.

—Can we make a wider beam?

—Yeah. I'm setting it to forty-eight. That's 75 percent of the length. The beam will be about twice as wide. Aim at the same spot.

—There is nothing there anymore.

—Well, that nothing will be a hole in a sec. Boom.

—That is a big hole. Do we just leave it there?

—No, we'll fill it up. Oh, wait. Did you forget to bring the giant shovel?

—Very funny. What happens if we make the sword shorter? How large can the beam get?

—At the shortest, too large.

—Let's try it.

—No. Just trust me on this. It's not good.

—Please.

—No . . . There's nothing big enough. Well . . .

—Well what?

—Oh what the hell. Aim over there.

—At what? The mountain?

—I wouldn't call that a mountain, but yeah. There. Ready? Aaaand firing.

— . . .

—Alex, say something.

—I didn't think . . .

—You thought this would be like driving a really big tank, like having the baddest muscle car on the block.

—We could –

—Yes. We could. Do you understand now? Themis was meant to protect us all, not for us to use against one another. She's not a weapon. She's a god.

—Can I ask you a question, Vincent? Why do you do this? You know what she can do. Why are you in here with me?

—Because if I'm not in here, someone else is. Someone who thinks Themis is just a really cool car. Because if I'm not, maybe my daughter is, and I can't have that.

—Have you heard from her?

—Not a thing. They haven't told me anything.

—What is it they say? No news is good news?

—Well, they do say that, but it's bullshit. No news is just the absence of news. And in this case, I don't think they'd tell me if something had happened to her.

—Are you sure?

—Oh yeah. They'd be too afraid of what it would do to my 'motivation.'

File No. 2174

Interview between Dr Rose Franklin and Eva Reyes

Location: Johns Hopkins Hospital, Baltimore, Maryland

—Hi, Eva! No, please, don't get up!

—Hey, Rose. What are you doing here?

—What do you think I'm doing here? I came as soon as I heard. You scared us for a while.

—Us?

—OK, you scared me.

—I swallowed some water.

—Your heart stopped. Your heart stopped for thirty minutes!

—OK, so I died a little. You were dead for years!

—Technically, you didn't die.

—You just said my heart stopped for a half hour!

—I'm just saying you weren't pronounced dead. You were too cold. Doctors can't declare a patient dead while they're in hypothermia. They need to be rewarmed first. I think the saying is: 'They're not dead until they're warm and dead.'

—Still, thirty minutes. Is that a record?

—Sorry. You almost died. You came *this* close. You scared the hell out of me. But you won't make the *Guinness Book of Records*.

—*Yokits.*

—Good news is they say you'll recover completely. How are you feeling?

—I'm high as a kite, so not bad. I don't know what they gave me. I still hurt. My entire body hurts, like I've been dipped in boiling water. I just don't care. Good pills.

—You'll get better.

—How are you, Rose? What have you been doing?

—I'm . . . OK. They offered me a job. I said no.

—What was it?

—Research, like before.

—Why did you turn it down?

—That's what everyone keeps asking. With everything that's happening, it just seemed . . . wrong.

—We could still learn a lot with you in charge.

—Maybe. We've learned a lot before. Look what we did with it. Has anything good come out of anything I've done?

—Besides millions of people being alive instead of dead?

—I'm not sure I had anything to do with that. The Ekt might have left on their own. Now they're using what we did to rob people of their most basic rights, to wage war, to hurt people. I'm not sure I wanna be a part of that anymore.

—What will you do?

—I'm moving back to Chicago. We're kind of famous. I think I can use that to get a teaching job at the university.

—That's good. They offered me a job too.

—Already? I figured they would, but I thought they'd wait at least until you could walk. What did you say?

—What do you mean what did I say?

—You said yes?

—Rose! When I said offered . . . They weren't exactly asking, you know that. I'm an A4, A5. Whatever the biggest A is. What else am I supposed to do? Turn them down, spend the rest of my life in a glass room? No thanks. Maybe, if I'm really lucky, they'll let me live in a camp. I've been there, Rose. It's not everything it's cracked up to be.

—I'm not judging you, Eva.

—It kinda sounds like you are.

—I'm not. Honestly, Eva, I'm not. I don't have all the answers. Vincent thinks –

—I know what my dad thinks. He thinks if the Russians have a robot of their own, if they have Themis, it'll even things out. Maybe he can create a stalemate, stop things from getting worse than they already are.

—He does. That's why he chose to stay. He's risking his life trying to make things better. Even you can see that.

—I know he is. Believe me, I know. People have been reminding me ever since I got here. Poor girl, her dad's a traitor. We're so glad you're not a traitor like your dad.

—Just ignore them.

—Well, he *is* helping Russia.

—You know why!

—I do. But I don't think it's the right move.

—Are you sure you're not letting your personal feelings get in the way? You're not the most objective person when it comes to your dad.

—I'm not the most objective person? Do you hear yourself? Rose. I didn't say I'd like to get my nose pierced. I said I didn't think helping our enemy – the people that took us prisoners, the people who killed Ekim – was the right move. Why are we even having this conversation? Do you think he's right? Honestly, do you think what he's doing will . . . You know what? It doesn't even matter. Say he's right. Are you really OK with things not getting any worse? Is that enough?

—And you think you can make things better by working for the US?

—I think a stalemate only means we get to keep this mess around for ever. Someone has to win before it gets better.

—What good would that do? There are work camps in the US, Eva. We have them *here, now*. Do you really think it would be better? Better than, say, if Russia ruled the world?

—Maybe. Maybe not. The US didn't put me in an aquarium, so I'm partial to them right now.

—Eva, I think you need to –

—I can't just sit and watch, Rose! Tell me what else I can do! Tell me what to do, and I'll do it. But I have to do *something*.

File No. 2176

Interview between Dr Rose Franklin
and Dr Alyssa Papantoniou

*Location: United States Central Command (CENTCOM),
MacDill Air Force Base, Tampa, Florida*

—Dr Franklin. They tell me you t . . . turned down the job at Johns Hopkins. The Alien Research Center isn't the EDC, but it's as close as it gets. I thought you'd j . . . jump at the opportunity.

—I didn't. I . . . They're in good hands with Dr Maher.

—She's an idiot. You'd know that if you spent more than fff . . . five minutes with her. What's the *real* reason?

—I wouldn't know why I was doing it. I don't see the point.

—Knowledge is the point. Why else do we do anything?

—I thought . . . It doesn't feel like we're pursuing knowledge anymore. It's all about beating the other guy.

—Are you hoping to work here instead, because we –

—For the military? No, I don't want your job either, Alyssa. I think this, all of this, is wrong.

—It is far from perfect, I'll give you that. The army has a very nnn . . . narrow perspective on things. But it's what we have. Some research is better than no research.

—That's not good enough. At least it shouldn't be.

—I would be lying if I said I respect your decision.

—That's OK, Alyssa. I didn't expect you to.

—Then may I ask why you're here if it's not for a job?

—I . . . You and I haven't always seen eye to eye.

—You th . . . think I'm a psychopath.

—Alyssa, I –

—Tell the truth, Dr Franklin.

—All right. This isn't exactly how I imagined this conversation going, but here it is. I think you lack empathy, completely. You're egocentric, unable to question your motives, to feel, or at least show remorse. I think you're cold, calculating, that you conceive of right and wrong in almost mathematical terms. I think you're dangerous.

—Thank you for being honest, Dr Franklin. Now if I may do the same. I think you're naïve beyond belief. I think your empathy – and you have *a lot* of it – is a weakness. It blinds you to the g . . . greater picture. You let emotions get in the way of rational judgment, and that is the worst thing a scientist can do. You might be a better human being than I am by anyone's standard, but it is people like you who will bring our world to its end. I think *you're* dangerous.

—I wasn't finished. I *don't* think you're a psychopath. A sociopath, maybe, but you do have a conscience. However uncaring it may be, I think you are guided by a sense of right and wrong. You are egocentric, but I know you wouldn't hesitate to sacrifice yourself if you thought it served your definition of a greater good. You're not a psychopath. You're . . . a utilitarian, in your own heartless way.

—That almost felt like a c . . . compliment.

—It wasn't. I don't want to be your friend, Alyssa. I want you to help me get Mr Burns out of here.

—What? Why would I do that?

—Because he wants to get out of here. Also, because it's the right thing to do, even for you.

—Is it? You called me cold and calculating, so let's ca . . . calculate. Your friend is an inv . . . invaluable asset. He knows more about alien t . . . technology than any of us. We wouldn't have a functional robot without him.

—That's all true.

—He is only helping us because he has no choice.

—Are you sure about that?

—They – I mean US Intelligence – haven't exactly been ge . . . ge . . . gentle with him. They had to exert some pppressure to make him talk.

—How much pressure? I'm willing to bet it didn't take much.

—Some people can handle more pain than others.

—Alyssa, trust me when I say that if he helped you make that robot functional, it's because he wanted you to have a functional robot. With Themis gone, he probably thought that was a good idea. Has he done anything for you since then?

—No.

—And I assume they've kept 'exerting pressure'?

—Yes.

—Can I ask you a personal question? Do you *like* what's happening in the world? Do you like things here in the United States?

—You want me to say I'm against people being imprisoned for no reason, is that it? I am. Nothing good can come of it. It's stupid, baseless. It is not my fault if people are stupid. The real thr . . . threat is not down here, it's up there.

—You might want to rethink that, Alyssa. Now that the Russians have their own robot, they're going to make some bold moves of their own. You know how this could end.

—Yes. But there is nothing I can do to change that. All I can do is continue my work here.

—There's nothing you can do to prevent anything. I was there, Alyssa. If the Ekt come here wanting to hurt us, they will. You can't help. I can't either. I wouldn't have been able to help the last time without Mr Burns. I can't promise you they'll never be a threat, but the Ekt are not coming here anytime soon. They're not the problem. Thermonuclear war, on the other hand . . . We need to fix things down here, Alyssa. This world, the way things are now. Is it even worth protecting?

—Do you have any reason to believe this Mr Burns can do that? Can he stop a war?

—I have no idea, Alyssa. None. I know *I* can't. I don't think you can either. He knows a lot of people. He has friends. Somehow, he's been able to communicate with them, but I'm sure he can do more out there than he can do in here. I just don't see any upside to keeping him. I don't think you do either.

—And if he can't do anything?

—Then we're no worse off than we are now. There's nothing to lose. Just trust him. Trust me. Can you do that, Alyssa? Trust someone?

— . . .

—Will you help me?

—Hello, get me Security –

—What are you doing?

—This is Dr Alyssa Papantoniou. I need Dr Franklin escorted out. I want her access to this ff . . . facility revoked, immediately.

—Alyssa!

—Goodbye, Dr Franklin.

File No. EE380

Personal File From Esat Ekt

Interview between Dr Rose Franklin and Vincent Couture

Location: Assigned residence, Etyakt region

—Vincent, what are you doing here?

—I'm looking for Eva. She didn't come home last night.

—I haven't seen her. I'm sorry.

—It's not your fault if you haven't seen her, Rose. Sorry I woke you up. Go back to bed.

—I'm sure she's fine.

—She was pretty upset when she left. I'm just . . .

—What happened?

—Same thing that always happens. She . . . There's a big protest scheduled for today. She wanted to go. I said no.

—I heard about it. It's supposed to be peaceful. Esok is going.

—It's always peaceful until it's not. There are riots every day now. And I know about Esok, she's one of the organizers. She asked me to come.

—And you said you were busy, I'm sure, but Eva's not like that. Her friends will be there. She just wants to fit in.

—That's just it. I don't want us to fit in. I don't. I know it sounds stupid after seven years, but I still hope the Council lets us leave. I'm not holding my breath, but we have to face the fact that it might be the only way we'll ever see Earth again. Every time we get closer to someone, every time we get involved, in anything, we make it that much easier for the Council to say we belong here. I don't want anyone to think we fit right in. And I sure as hell don't want Eva to feel like she belongs any more than she already does. She's already spent too much of her life here. She doesn't remember half the things she did back on Earth, what a flock of birds looks like, what it smells like just before it rains. This is normal for her now, blue people, tapioca. She actually likes that shit. We made a deal to get her home, Rose, and I'll do whatever it takes, but she won't want to come. You know that, right? We'll have to drag her out of here.

—I know, and I understand where you're coming from, but you can't ask Eva to live like that. She can't keep everyone at a distance, not have any friends. That's not a life. It's our job to get her home. Hers is to be a young woman right now, and this is the only place she has to do it.

—I have a feeling something bad is going to happen, Rose. I thought the bombs, the riots, I thought it would scare ordinary folks away, but these protests are only getting bigger.

—In a way, it's beautiful to watch. People taking their future into their own hands, demanding change.

—Listen to you! Not that long ago, you were all about the great Ekt society.

—I still think what they've built here is amazing in a lot of ways, but you and Eva were right. These people live here, they should have the same rights as everyone else.

—Yeah . . . It's not gonna end well. What they're asking for, it goes against the very principles this world is built on. You take that away, and it could all fall apart . . . I'm not sure they're going to let that happen.

—What do you think they'll do? The Ekt aren't perfect, but they won't exterminate half the population. It won't get that far, you know that.

—It won't. But at some point, they'll consider it. Things will get bad enough they'll actually consider genocide as an option. They'll reject the idea right away because they're not insane, but it'll change everything. Every other bad option will look a whole lot better after that. I don't like it, Rose. People blame us for what's happening, or they blame the Council for what they did to us. Either way, we're right in the middle of it. We need a way out before things get worse.

—We have to talk to the empress.

—We tried that. We can't just walk up to her palace and knock on the door.

—We need to try again. Maybe someone else on her staff. She must have a secretary, something.

—Even if someone agreed to meet us, the empress can't do anything without the Council's say so. She won't break the law just to help the three of us go home.

—Maybe she won't.

—Then what's the point?

—Well, the point is we can't go home without her. We need a ship or a robot to get home. A robot seems easier. We can get Ekim to pilot if we know the coordinates.

—You think he'll do it?

—Whatever it takes, Vincent, remember? But the robots, and I assume the ships, won't go anywhere. They're locked. We need to get Themis moving again, and the empress is the only one that can do that. I don't think we can get it by force, so we need her help.

—Why would she help us?

—Well, for starters, I think a lot of people would be really happy to see us gone. That might be enough.

—And if it's not?

—I'm not sure. I think this ... uprising, whatever you want to call it, it's an opportunity for her. She has to be aware of it.

—I'm not following you, Rose. An opportunity for what? What can the empress do?

—That's exactly my point. She has no power to do anything. There's no global government here anymore.

—There's the Council.

—No. The Council doesn't have the authority to plant a tree. They can only do something if it affects other worlds, and they exist precisely to make sure that doesn't happen. The Council is designed not to do anything. They tried doing something on Earth, see where that got them. It's different with the empress.

—Different how? You just said she has no power.

—That's right. She's an empress, and she has no power. She has no purpose.

—I don't mean to rain on your parade, Rose, but the Ekt don't strike me as the power-hungry type. They gave up an entire empire just to feel a bit safer.

—They did. *Her* empire. Think about it, Vincent. Her ancestors ruled this world. They ruled over thousands of planets. Thousands! A good chunk of the known universe is hers by birthright.

—That was generations ago. I'm not sure that's really on her mind.

—She lives in the past, Vincent. She lives in the palace. That entire building is a symbol of the mighty Ekt empire. Every single thing in there must have a story attached to it. Every tapestry – if they have such a thing – every piece of furniture. She can't go to the bathroom without being reminded that her ancestors had all the power and she has none of it. The Ekt are more advanced in many ways, but, fundamentally, they're not that different from us. Believe me, it's on her mind.

—OK. Say it is. What do you want to do, Rose? Stage a *coup d'état*?

—You mean you and I? Well, no. We can barely make breakfast, we can't stage a *coup*. The empress won't either, it wouldn't work. But I don't think she has to, not if things keep going the way they are. The regions aren't equipped to deal with this, mass protests, terrorist acts on a daily basis. Back home, we'd have called in the army, the National Guard, a long time ago. If this keeps escalating, they'll want to give the empress more power. They'll want the Imperial Guard on the streets. They'll beg her for it.

—I don't see how that helps us. Even if everything you're saying is true, she doesn't need us.

—Maybe she doesn't. Maybe she does. I won't pretend to understand everything there is to know about these people, but the empress does. We have no status here, no power whatsoever. Our one card is that we somehow inspire these people to rebel. That might be useful somehow. I don't know.

— . . .

—Vincent, it doesn't matter if any of this is true. We *need* the empress. She controls our fate. We'll die here if she doesn't help us.

—I'll talk to Enatast again. Maybe he can set it up. But first, I have to find Eva.

—You won't find her now, not if she doesn't want to be found.

—So, what? I just wait for her to come home?

—Well, you know where she'll be this afternoon.

—Right, the protest. Damn, she's stubborn.

—The apple doesn't fall far from the tree.

—I'll tell Esok I changed my mind. Eva and I are going to have a long talk when I get my hands on her. Is it considered bad parenting to ground your child for life?

—Good luck with that.

File No. EE426

Personal File From Esat Ekt

Interview between Vincent Couture and Ipet Estoteks, representative of the empress

Location: Imperial Palace, Osk region

Translated by Vincent Couture

Note: I make her sound very formal in her translation even though she didn't speak any differently than Enatast does. But, man, did she sound entitled! The tone. The posture. The demeanor. It felt as if she'd been waiting her whole life to look down on someone. I took a shower when I came back home.

—Greetings. I'm Vincent.

—Greetings, Vincent.

—How should I address you?

—You may not address me. I represent the empress Iksid-its, daughter of Yotekot, sovereign of the Ekt. My words are hers.

—Thank you – thank the empress? – for granting this meeting.

—Speak now, Vincent Couture.

—OK. I . . . I am here to request assistance in ge—

—You wish to go back to Terra.

—Yes. I do.

—The empress cannot assist you. Only the Council can.

—So I've been told.

—Then why are you here?

—What? I just told you why I'm here. I'm here to –

—Why are you asking the empress for help if you have been told that she cannot help? It seems . . . insane.

—I . . . I'm asking the empress for help because the Council is not helping.

—You should know that the Council will never help you. There are many on Esat Ekt who feel the Council created this problem by visiting your world and needlessly killing so many of your people. There are many on Esat Ekt who feel the Council should be abolished. I can tell you that its members will not compound their mistake by admitting they have committed genocide on an alien species.

—*This* is insane! This. Your people, the Council, they send giants to our world and kill millions of us, then they punish us when it has consequences here. We didn't do anything. You did this.

—Neither I nor the empress approved of the decision, but you are correct.

—What can the empress do to help us?

—The empress, as always, only wishes to help her people. But the law prevents her from doing what she so strongly desires.

—What does that mean?

—The empress does not wish for you to suffer for something you had no part in only to serve the interests of the Council.

—Then send us home.

—Again, our laws, as they stand, prevent the empress from following her heart.

—But . . .

—But what?

—Well, I'm hoping you didn't ask me to come all this way just to tell me that we're going to die here and that there's nothing you can do about it.

—That is precisely why the empress asked you to come here.

— . . . No.

—I do not understand.

—No. You don't meet someone only to tell them that things are utterly hopeless.

—Why not?

—I don't know, you just don't! It's . . . rude.

—It was not our intent to offend you. Perhaps you are still unaccustomed to our ways.

—Sure. I may be a little off when it comes to Ekt customs, but there has to be more. There's something you're not telling me because . . .

—There is nothing more I can say as a representative of the empress.

—Ha! There we go. How about *not* as a representative of the empress?

—Speaking for myself, I would say that your only hope to leave Esat Ekt is to take command of a vehicle yourself.

—We're well aware of that part.

—A giant like the one that brought you here would be your best choice, perhaps the very one that brought you here. But, as you know, the giants are controlled by the empress. Even if you managed to find a pilot capable of taking you home and found your way aboard, the giant would not respond to your commands. One would have to allow you to leave before you could do so.

—Again, not helpful. How would we go about making sure someone does allow it?

—The empress and her army are bound by law to obey the Council. To go against their will is a crime. As I said, the empress is deeply saddened by this situation, and she wishes nothing more than to help you, you and everyone on Esat Ekt. If she were allowed to do so, if she were in charge, she would gladly give each and every one of her subjects, including those with mixed ancestry, the same rights people enjoyed before the Council came to exist. You could come and go as you please. She would resume relations with other worlds, restore the empire to its former glory. But the Council is in charge, not her. Our institutions are strong. They cannot be destroyed with a few bombs. They will survive this period of civic unrest. That said, if the empress were the one to bring this conflict to an end, if she were able to bring down the *Hand of Yetskots* to —

—I'm sorry, the hand of what?

—The *Hand of Yetskots*. That is what they call themselves. They have claimed responsibility for acts of violence in all the districts. If the empress were able to stop them, it would go a long way to help her effect the changes she believes her planet needs. As I said, the empress would do anything to help her people.

—What's any of that got to do with us?

—Several regions have asked the empress for help. They feel that this insurgency must be stopped now before it grows out of control.

—What was your answer? I mean the empress. What did she say?

—The empress will not set herself a task she cannot accomplish. She does not wish to fight people she cannot see, to be bogged down with this situation long enough to lose the confidence of her people. If and when the empress gets involved, her actions must be swift and decisive.

—I'm not sure what I can do to help. I don't know anyone in this *Hand of Yetskots*.

—Your daughter does. A man by the name of Etat Ityets. She is also well acquainted with some of his associates. I would like you to tell me what their names are and where we can find them.

—My daughter? She knows people from the shelter she works at. These people, they're not . . . They organize protests, they don't blow up things. They have nothing to do with that *Hand* of yours.

—I would like you to get me the name and location of everyone involved in organizing protests in Etyakt. Do that, and you will have the gratitude of the empress.

—Her gratitude?

—That in and of itself should be enough.

—Well, it would certainly mean a lot.

—It is also entirely possible that someone will inadvertently unlock a certain giant and allow it to leave this planet unscathed.

—How can I be sure of that?

—I do not wish to appear insensitive, but I do not believe certainty is a luxury you can afford at the moment.

—Fair enough. Quick question, though. What will you do with these people after I give you their names?

—When the time comes, they will be arrested and executed.

—You want to kill them?! But they haven't done anything!

—Everyone has done something. What matters is that the empress will be able to restore peace and tranquility on her world.

— . . .

—You may leave now, Vincent Couture.

File No. 2193

Interview between Major Katherine Lebedev, Russian Main Intelligence Agency (GRU), and Vincent Couture

Location: GRU building, Saint Petersburg, Russia

—Time to go, Vincent!

—Go where?

—We're sending you out.

—I'm not conquering the world for you, Katherine. I told you that already. I'll defend you, but I won't bring another government to its knees.

—No need. The Chinese are doing that part for you. They're walking a million men – for real, a million! – into Korea, and they asked for our help. You'll be an escort.

—North Korea?

—Oh. They just said Korea. Does it matter? I can check if you want.

—The US won't let you –

—You mean they won't let China.

—They won't let you take South Korea. You know that.

—Me? I don't know anything. I suppose we'll find out sooner or later. Probably later. It'll take a while. Like, for ever. When they said they were walking a million men, I thought it was just military talk. But nope. They're on foot. One million of them. Walking. You can see them on satellite, it's impressive, like –

—I'm not doing this.

—Oh, come on! You just said you'll defend us. They're friends, that's kind of like us, don't you think? Let me put it this way. Would you rather a million Chinese get killed?

—I'd rather no one gets killed, but I'm not the one invading another country. The Koreans have the right to defend themselves.

—You're no fun, you know that? Yeah, they do have the right to defend themselves. *Technically.* And they probably will! But they'll lose. Right now, North Korea thinks they just want to walk across their land – actually, they're tickled pink at the idea of marching into Seoul with the Chinese – but they'll know something's up when Beijing launches an airstrike against them.

—I thought those two were friends.

—Oh, they haven't been friends for a while. China tolerated them just to piss off the US, but there's just no reason to anymore. They'll try to blow up every missile site, but they'll miss a few they didn't know about. North Korea will launch whatever they have left. The Chinese will

289

retaliate. We're talking . . . a quarter million dead, at least. That's *before* they walk in. Then it gets ugly, but the Chinese win in the end. There's a million of them. If that's not enough, they can send a million more. Did you know they have more purebloods than anyone else? I didn't. I learn something every day. Anyway, this is how it goes. Lots and lots of people die needlessly. *Or*, you walk in with them, and the Koreans stand down all on their own. You've been there before. They know they can't hurt Themis. You'd be saving . . . countless lives, without firing a single shot. You'd be a hero! Well, you'd be *my* hero anyway.

—What happens then? They won't stay in North Korea. Things will go bad. Will I still be your hero if I start World War III, and this whole place turns into a radioactive wasteland?

—I won't hold it against you, Vincent. I promise.

File No. EE427

Personal File From Esat Ekt

Interview between Dr Rose Franklin and Vincent Couture

Location: Assigned residence, Etyakt region

—She said what?

—She wants us to give her names.

—Whose names?

—Everyone. The people organizing all of this, the marches, the protests.

—You mean Eva's friends?

—I mean everyone. Yes, Eva's friends.

—Vincent, we know these people. Ityets, and Itit and –

—And Esok.

—And she's going to have them killed?

—She's not going to have anyone killed because we're not giving her any names.

—Of course we're not, but this makes no sense at all. What does Esok have to do with any of this? She's not blowing up buildings in Osk.

—That's the thing. She mentioned this superorganized group who, apparently, is responsible for all the terrorist acts. Esok and Ityets are many things, but organized isn't one of them.

—They're also not violent. Ityets would be a Buddhist if we were back on Earth.

—I'm telling you, Rose. She mentioned him by name. I don't understand what the empress has to gain by arresting local organizers.

—My guess . . .

—Yes?

—Say she gets what she wants, and the regions give her more power. It would likely be temporary, right?

—Probably.

—Well, my guess is she doesn't want it to be temporary. She'll want to hit them hard. Arrest as many people as she can. Make sure no one dares to even put up a sign after that.

—Wouldn't that just encourage the people blowing up things to blow up more things?

—Well, she'd have to get them too. All of them.

—On the planet? You can't defeat terrorism on a whole planet, it's not an army you can crush. That's why it's called terrorism. There'd always be one person left somewhere to blow up more things.

—I know what you're saying, Vincent, but imagine for a moment that she can. If she can do *that*, stop all the violence, all the protests, the Ekt everywhere will love her for it. They'd never go back to the way things were.

—Yeah, but she'd anger the people of alien descent even more, wouldn't she?

—I don't know, Vincent. Not if she gives them something they want. No limits on how many children they can have, something like that. Don't forget, everyone they arrest will be labeled a terrorist, and most people here don't condone what they've seen on the big screens. I think she'd be a hero. She might even have enough clout to get rid of that noninterference policy and start dealing with other worlds again. She could get her empire back if this works. The irony is that would probably be a good thing for everyone. For the people here, for those on other worlds. Esok's planet could be saved.

—Great. And all we have to do is get everyone we know murdered for no reason.

File No. 2194

Interview between Dr Rose Franklin and Mr Burns

Location: Medici on 57th, Chicago, Illinois

—Ah! Dr Franklin! Come! Sit!

—Mr Burns! I got your note, but I wasn't sure it was you.

—Do many people leave you notes pretending to be me?

—No, it's just . . . What are you doing here? How did you get out?

—Your friend Alyssa got me out.

—My – Alyssa's not my friend. Are you sure she's the one?

—Yes! I'm sure. I was there! I had to be there. That's an important part of being let out. She walked me out the front door of the building, in the middle of the day! She should have been more surreptitious. They arrested her five minutes after I left. Anyway, it would seem she's more of a friend than you thought.

—I'm having a hard time believing she would do anything out of kindness.

—Well, here I am. But you're right, she is *not* a bundle of joy. Lots of negativity. She didn't laugh at my jokes *once*, and there were some good ones!

—She had me thrown out of the building when I asked for her help.

—With getting me out?

—Yes.

—That makes sense. She's smart. No fun, but smart.

—How is that smart?

—Everyone would know you were involved if you were anywhere near me when it happened. Do I need to remind you how I ended up in there in the first place?

—They'll still suspect me.

—Probably. That's why we're meeting here.

—Your note said: 'Don't change anything. See you soon. Mr Burns.' How did you know I'd be here, and this early?

—It's Saturday! Coffee and cinnamon rolls at Medici, on your way to the Compton lectures.

—But I haven't been to those in, what, almost twenty years!

—You weren't in Chicago. I had a feeling you'd go back to old habits right away.

—Am I that predictable?

—Well, yes. Everyone is. I'd do the same thing. Old shoes, old shirt, a familiar meal. For a moment, the world makes sense again. Oh, and that lecture on Majorana particles sounds *fascinating*. Do you mind if I go with you?

—Aren't you afraid someone will see you?

—The intelligence community at a physics lecture? I don't think so. Though they might come if they read the title. They'd see Majorana and think everyone's there to get high. The CIA is tapping your phones, but no one is following you.

—Good to know.

—Here. Let me pay for those.

—No, no. I got it.

—Dr Franklin, aliens descended upon Earth to find people like me, and they killed one hundred million men, women, and children. Least I can do is buy coffee and cinnamon rolls.

—That was dark. You didn't do anything other than being born, and you helped me when I needed it the most. If anyone is to blame, it's me. I chose to build Themis, I'm buying coffee.

—Do you really blame yourself for all of this? You weren't even here!

—I don't. I thought we were making self-deprecating comments to decide who's paying for breakfast. I used to. Blame myself, that is. I thought everything that happened, every death, every city destroyed . . . I thought that was all because of me. I'd fallen into a hole and caused all that somehow. But I didn't. I didn't gas a hundred million people, the Ekt did. I didn't bomb Madrid or torture people. I didn't break families apart because one of them lost the genetic lottery. I didn't judge or hurt people because of their religion or where they were born. I didn't lock them up. The world did all that. So, no, I don't feel responsible for *all this*. That doesn't make me feel any better. That doesn't help me fix it either. I can't fix . . . *us*. It's people that are broken.

—You're being too hard on people, just like you can be too hard on yourself. People got scared. Rightly so! What happened here nine years ago wasn't anyone's fault. It just happened. People have the right to be emotional, and irrational, from time to time.

—Irrational? We've lost our collective mind! Scientists are ignoring their own findings. People are denying even the most basic scientific facts because it makes them feel better about hurting each other. Do you realize how horrifying that is? We're talking about human beings making a conscious effort, going out of their way, to be ignorant. *Willfully* stupid. They're proud of it. They take pride in idiocy. There's not even an attempt to rationalize things anymore. Muslims are bad because they are, that's all. Why would you need a reason? It's one thing to let your child go blind because you read on Facebook that the measles vaccine would make him autistic, it's another to ship him off to a work camp because he inherited his grandmother's genes instead of Grandpa's. Our entire race is trying to lobotomize itself. It's as moronic and repulsive as someone cutting off their own legs.

—You're not in a happy place right now, are you?

—I'm sorry. It's just . . . Responsible or not, I want things to get better, and I don't know how.

—Let me tell you a story.

—Oh please!

—There was this axolotl.

—Really?

—Yes. An axolotl. It's an amphibian –

—I know what it is. It's a salamander from Mexico.

—Then what's your problem?

—I don't have a problem. There just aren't that many axolotl stories being told.

—I have lots of axolotl stories, thank you very much. May I continue?

—Yes. Yes. I'm sorry.

—There was this axolotl named Jeff. Jeff was sort of a local hero. He had once fought an African tilapia, all on his own, and lived to tell the tale. Axolotls are known for their ability to regrow limbs, but Jeff had lost all four of his legs along with his tail during that David and Goliath moment of his, and none of them grew back to their original size. Suffice it to say that Jeff looked kind of funny.

But regardless of Jeff's physical appearance, he was a good storyteller and little axolotl jaws dropped every time he told the tale of how he lost his tail. Not long after the ordeal, Jeff had decided that he would use what happened to him to do some good, make the salamander world a better place. He began giving motivational speeches to everyone who would listen – and everyone would listen. Even tiger salamanders would stop by to listen to Jeff. He became known across the lake for his pep talks, a little Tony Robbins with gills.

Jeff had a daughter, Lisa, a beautiful lizard-like baby girl with light pink skin and bright, purple gill stalks – they call those rami. Every little girl in town was jealous of Lisa's rami. Lisa was happy – she smiled all the time – but Lisa was also shy, very shy. She faded away in axolotl company and, like any good father, Jeff wanted her to blossom. 'It's OK, Dad,' she said, 'not everyone is a hero like you.'

But Jeff believed *everyone* had it in them to be a hero. After all, there was nothing really special about him. He wasn't the biggest axolotl on the block, nor the baddest, and he had fought a giant tilapia. No one knows how big that tilapia really was; it grew a little every time Jeff told the story. I'm sure even Jeff didn't know anymore. But he had fought a fish, that's for sure. If he, clumsy, nerdy-looking axolotl that he was, could do something like that, surely greatness was within everyone's reach. Lisa too was a hero. She'd just never had the opportunity to show it. All she really needed, Jeff thought, was a push, to be put in a situation where she'd have no choice but to be the best amphibian she could be.

So Jeff took Lisa with him for a long walk. When his abnormally short legs got tired, he found a good spot on top of a rock where they both could rest. He waited, and waited. Lisa wanted to go home, but Jeff told her to be patient. Finally, he spotted an Asian carp coming their way. The carp wasn't as big as the elephantine tilapia he had once wrestled, but Lisa was young, and Jeff figured that vanquishing a midsize carp would be enough for someone her age. Jeff hugged his baby girl, gave her a big kiss, and threw her off the rock, right in the path of the bottom feeder.

The moral of the story is –

—Wait! Wait! What happened? What happened to Lisa?

—The carp ate her, of course. She was just a baby! You didn't really think she was gonna make it, did you?

—I . . . Yes, I did . . .

—You want to know the moral of the story.

—I do!

—The moral of the story is . . . Jeff is a moron. A baby axolotl can't fight a fish! You can't expect babies to do the things adults do. You can't expect anyone to do things they can't do. If you ask me to lift five hundred pounds, I can't. It doesn't matter how much I want to, how much conviction I put into it. It's just not something I can do. Maybe if I'd been training all my life, but not now, not tomorrow. The people on this planet knew nothing of real aliens before Themis was found, they had never seen one until the Ekt came to Earth. Now that I think of it, they still haven't seen one. They've only seen those giant robots but never those inside them. They make first contact, and millions die. Then they learn they're all a bit alien, some more than others. They weren't prepared for this, for any of it. They can't even comprehend what it means about who they are, their place in the universe. All they know is a bunch of people are dead, and their neighbor is more like those who killed them than they are. Fear is a pretty normal reaction if you ask me! The people on this planet are babies! Don't ask them to act like grown-ups. Don't push them in front of a carp.

—You're right.

—I know I'm right! I wouldn't say things if I thought they were wrong!

—We're a bunch of babies, a few billion of them, all scared to death. We're going to kill ourselves if we're left to our own devices. What we need is . . .

—What *do* we need, Dr Franklin?

—We need . . . Jeff.

—What? No! Jeff is a moron! I thought we covered that.

—OK, maybe not Jeff, but you just said it, we're all babies. There aren't any adults around. We need grown-ups. We need adult supervision. There's a reason we weren't prepared. We didn't ask for this. We haven't done anything! Don't take this the wrong way, but this isn't our mess, it's yours, the Ekt's. The Ekt killed millions of us. *They* did. They scared us to death and left us running around chasing our tail because they didn't want to *interfere* any more than they had to. But here's the thing, they *had* to. It's their fault! It's all their fault. They came here three thousand years ago and fundamentally changed who we are. They screwed with the very fabric of life on this planet. *They* are responsible. It doesn't matter that they want nothing to do with it, it's *their* responsibility.

—You break it, you buy it?

—I was thinking more along the lines of 'you make the mess, you clean it up,' but that will do too.

—That is an interesting idea. I like you, Dr Franklin. You're interesting. I'm curious. How do you think the Ekt can clean this up?

—I'm not sure. Perhaps they don't need to do anything. Maybe just being here would be enough. I think part of the problem is that we're still trying to convince ourselves there's something we could do to stop them. We're doing everything we can to maintain the illusion of control. Why do we lock people up? No one *really* thinks they're a threat. We do it because we can. We're doing something. If the Ekt showed us what they're capable of, we'd realize how futile this is.

We've also lost our identity. We were humans. Now we don't know *what* we are. Those alien genes, it's messy. If I have them, am I still me, or am I something else? We're holding on to the idea that we're different, unique. We can't be anything like the Ekt, *we* were made in God's image. Our DNA tells us that's not true, but if we get rid of the people who remind us of that, if we hide the evidence, then we can still pretend. And so we find people who look exactly like us, who come from the same place, believe in the same God, and we make each other feel good by pretending everyone else can't be trusted. I think we'll always be insecure, petty little things, but at least if the Ekt were here, we'd feel *some* connection with the rest of our world. Our late friend once told me: 'redefine alterity and you can erase boundaries.' I believe that's true, only somewhere along the way we've made our own people the 'other' and started hating ourselves.

—Let me get this straight. Your solution to all of Earth's problems is that you don't have a solution, and you want someone else to fix it for you.

—I know how it sounds. I wish I could think of another way. I desperately want to believe there is another way, that the human spirit will conquer, that science will save the day. But the problem *is* us. I don't think we have what it takes to do this on our own. If there were –

—No, no. Stop. I agree with you. It takes a lot of courage to admit your own limits. I admire that.

—You admire the fact that I find myself useless, or that I think our entire species is incapable of taking care of itself?

—A little bit of both. And you are not useless, you just came up with a solution. I personally think it's a good one.

—It's not. They won't come. For starters, we don't even have a way to contact them.

—Of course you do! The Ekt left a device for you to find. It was buried in the chamber you fell in when you were a kid before my ancestor replaced it with a big hand. You should know, we used it to bring you back to life! The Ekt left it here so you could talk to them when the time came.

—It doesn't matter. They still won't come. When we left, things weren't much better there than they are here. They have their own problems to deal with. What happened here on Earth is how their problems started in the first place. I'm fairly certain all they want is to put that entire episode behind them and never look back.

—Then you'll have to give them something they want more.

PART FOUR
Cross The Rubicon

File No. 2195

Mission log – Vincent Couture
and Sergeant Alexander Vasiliev

*Location: Aboard Themis. North of Dandong,
Liaoning Province, China*

—All right, Katherine, we're two or three miles from Dandong. We're going to unstrap and have lunch.

[*Lunch? It's almost six where you are in China!*]

Well, it's one o'clock for us. And it's a sandwich. A sandwich isn't dinner.

[*Sure. You can eat. Where are the Chinese?*]

They're everywhere. We're in China.

[*Ha. Ha.*]

They're about a mile behind us, but they're slow as hell. Why didn't we just meet them at the border? We walked four miles with them, and it took us half a day. Do you know how mind-numbing this is? Our legs are forty times longer than theirs. We almost fell a couple times we have to walk so slow.

[*Poor baby. A million men walking in mud, and you have to walk slowly.*]

They're on a highway. It's in pretty good shape. We're the ones walking in mud on the side of the road.

[*They wanted to make a grand entrance.*]

They're going to be disappointed.

[*Why? No! I don't want to have to call them again! I keep calling with bad news. They hate me.*]

It's getting dark. We can barely see where we step. And there's a residential area up ahead. There won't be enough room for us to walk through.

[*You can walk on the road.*]

We can. But *they* won't be able to after we destroy it. I don't think they want us to walk on houses either. It doesn't really matter anyway. There's a city after that neighborhood. A big one.

[*Your point being?*]

Themis doesn't do cities well.

[*What do you propose?*]

If they really want to cross here, we're just gonna have to beam over and wait for them in the river.

[*You'll be there for hours, alone. So much for that great entrance . . .*]

We can wait *here* for hours and beam over when they're ready to cross into North Korea. I don't care.

[*Fine. I guess I'll have to talk to them after all. Have lunch, I'll get back to you.*]

Good. Just give me a sec, Alex. I'll help you get out of your straightjacket, and we can eat.

—Thank you. I'm starving.

—All right, I'm coming. I suppose now would be a good time to tell you. If the North Koreans start firing before the Chinese march in, I'm bailing us out.

—What?

—Let me take your gloves off. They have to funnel a million men through a bridge. They'll be slaughtered.

—I'm pretty sure that's why we're here.

—Even if we help, Alex. They're fish in a barrel. They'll push through. Maybe half of them will make it. I'm not going to be responsible for half a million dead. If we bail, they won't dare cross that bridge.

—The major will kill us.

—Yeah, Katherine'll be pissed.

—I mean she'll literally kill us. I'm not supposed to tell you, but these little canisters they installed on the ceiling, they're VX gas.

—I knew they weren't something good.

—She can release it remotely.

—She won't. I mean she'll do it if she has to — I don't think she'll even hesitate — but she won't do it for this. Not for the Chinese, not if North Korea fights back. The prize here is South Korea. If it all goes to hell before we even cross the border, it's just not worth it to kill us.

—I'm not sure I want to take that bet.

—Hey, if Katherine's right, the North Koreans will roll out the red carpet for us, and this whole conversation is moot.

[*Vincent, are you there?*]

Yes, Katherine. We just got out of the controls. We were about to eat.

[*Oops. You need to get back in. Lunch will have to wait.*]

What? Why?

[*There is a regiment of Ch'ŏnma-hos tanks lining up across the bridge in Sinuiju. The Chinese want you to get to the river now, make sure they're happy to see you.*]

What if they're not?

[*I think they will be. Now go. Chop. Chop.*]

—I'm hungry. I don't want to die when I'm hungry.

—We're not going to die, Alex. We're going to single-handedly start a global thermonuclear war, and we'll be the only two idiots to survive. We'll have plenty of time to eat our sandwich then. Get your arms in, I'll do the rest. Front is closed. Did you put on weight?

—More muscle.

—Of course. Put your gloves on, Arnold. My turn now. Of all the places we could cross into Korea from, I can't believe they chose this one. I love the sense of irony.

—I don't understand.

—Do you know what the bridge between Dandong and Sinuiju is called?

—Something Chinese?

—It's the Sino-Korean Friendship Bridge.

—Hey, what are friends for?

—I'm all strapped in. Are you ready to get shot at?

—Sure.

—Katherine, our computer tells us we're 6,420 meters from the river at 116 degrees. Can you confirm? I don't want to overshoot the river if we're not welcome.

[*Vincent, the nerds here are nodding.*]

All right. That should do it, give or take a step. Ready, Alex?

—If you say so.

—Friendship Bridge, here we come . . .

—Oh my God!

[*What? Oh my God what?*]

—Relax, Katherine, it's the bridge. It's full of lights. It lights up the water underneath. It's really pretty.

[*Damn, you guys. You almost gave me a heart attack. What about the tanks?*]

We can't see anything with the city lights. It's dark on the Korean side. They can see us, though.

[*Are they firing?*]

Do you think we'd mention the bridge being pretty but forget about the North Korean Army firing at us? I think we're good. Either that, or they're –

—Oh my God!

[*What? Something pretty again?*]

—You could call it that. There's a giant robot full of bright green light on the Korean side of the river.

[*Iapetus is there? In North Korea?*]

I'm afraid so. Should we leave?

[*Stand by.*]

Shit, it's walking towards us.

—What do they want?

—I don't know. I think it just waved at us.

<*Hi, Dad!*>

Fuck.

—Is that – ?

—Yeah. It is.

File No. 2196

Mission log – Warrant Officer Eva Reyes and Lt Barbara Ball, US Marine Corps, Mecha Division

Location: Aboard Lapetus. Seoul, South Korea

—Can I call you Eva?

—As opposed to what?

—You're a warrant officer in the Marine Corps. I can call you ma'am. I can call you chief if you like.

—Eva's fine.

—Good. I'm Barbara.

—Do they often switch pilots on you at the last minute?

—Nope. Never happened before.

—First time for everything, I guess.

—Second time, actually. Both today. I usually ride with Captain Hough. To be honest, he's much better than I am with the legs. I get the arms. Then they tell me I'll ride with Benson, and now you. I don't know what's wrong with them today.

—I know why Captain Hough isn't here. He has a broken arm.

—How do you know?

—I broke it.

—What?

—He touched me.

—Bodie grabbed you?

—He put his arm around my shoulder. I asked him to remove it. He didn't.

—Haha! I'm sorry, that's not funny at all. I can't believe you broke Bodie's arm! He must be so pissed. He's been dying for a combat mission.

—He's a dick.

—Eva, I think you and I are gonna get along fine. Do you know why they removed Benson?

—I think they want me to *prove* myself?

—Why? How? We're just here to scare the Chinese away. They won't cross into Korea with us standing there.

—They might. Themis is with them.

—Shit.

—Shit is right. My father's inside.

— . . .

—You can say it. The traitor, right?

—No. I'm sure he has his reasons . . . Do they expect us to fight?

—Either that, or they think my dad'll back away.

—That's fucked up.

—You can say that again.

—Are you . . . OK with this?

—It doesn't seem like I have much of a choice.

—I'm sorry. I mean that. I'm truly sorry. This is just sick.

[*Lapetus, this is Central, change of plan.*]

Roger, Central. Are you gonna tell us what the new plan is?

[*Themis is at the Yalu River, alone.*]

Where are the Chinese?

[*About eight hours away. Your job is to get Themis to leave before they get there.*]

And just how do you suggest we do that? Ask nicely?

[*We're giving you some operational discretion on this one.*]

How much discretion? Are we clear to engage?

[*Affirmative.*]

. . . Roger that . . . Central, do we have the right crew for this?

[*Lapetus, you have your orders. Turn to 320 degrees, 7 minutes.*]

Are you up for this, Eva?

—Do you think they'll let me leave if I'm not?

—Probably not.

—Then let's just get this over with.

—Central, heading three, two, zero point seven. And change. Awaiting distance. Are we doing this in one jump?

[*Any part of North Korea you'd like to visit along the way?*]

Negative, Central. One jump it is. It just seems a little long if we're to land in a river.

[*Your concerns are duly noted, Lapetus. Unit size sixty-four. Distance three-five-three. In base-8, that's a round one hundred for units, five-four-one for distance.*]

Roger, Central. One-zero-zero. Five-four-one. Ready for jump.

[*Lapetus, you are go for jump.*]

Punching it in now.

. . .

—Uh, Barbara? I don't think we're in the right spot.

—I see that, Eva. Central, this is Lapetus. We're about a quarter mile short of the river on the Korean side. We're standing on some tanks. I repeat. We're standing *on* tanks. More tanks all around. Looks like a whole regiment. I see foot soldiers to the east. It's dark outside but it looks like a lot, five, ten thousand maybe.

[*Can you see Themis?*]

Affirmative. She's in the river right in front of us. We're walking towards them.

—Hi, Dad!

—Did you just wave at them?

—Yep.

[*Iapetus. You should beam into the river, get away from those tanks.*]

Copy that, Central. Punchin— Hot damn! They're firing at us!

[*Beam out of there, Iapetus. Get to the river.*]

Can't do that with our shield working. They're lighting us up like a Christmas tree!

—Barbara, give me a weapon!

—You got it, Eva.

—How does that thing work? Last time I was inside one of these things, we had a sword, not a . . . ball of light.

—Point and I'll shoot.

—They're everywhere! Just shoot!

—Incoming missile, port side! Brace for impact!

—I'd be happier with a shield in my hand. *Yokits!* That hurt!

—Shit. Two more SAM launchers to starboard. Are those tanks ever gonna stop?

—Forget the tanks, let's get rid of those missiles first. Fire!

[*Lapetus, we're showing half a dozen MiGs heading your way. Repeat, six MiGs. ETA 1 minute.*]

—Copy, Central. You can stop with the good news. We're as happ— AAARGH! FUCK! Where did that one come from?

—Behind us, two more trucks with big rockets on top!

—Screw this! Switching to a wide beam. We'll just swing around and wipe them all out.

—There are ten thousand men over there, Barbara. Do we have to kill them all?

—Sorry, Eva, but that's what you get for standing next to the asshole firing missiles at us. What the − ? Central, Themis just appeared in front of us. She's attacking!

—No! She's not! She's firing at the tanks!

—Why is your dad helping us?

—He's not helping us. Vincent's trying to stop us from overloading and wiping out everyone. He's trying to save the Koreans.

— . . .

—Trust me, Barbara! He's not gonna hurt us.

—All right, I'll play. Narrow beam. Point at the SAM launchers.

—Fire! Fire!

—Now to starboard.

—Got it! Fire!

—Behin—

—I know! There! How's that feel?

—I think we got them all?

—Down there. There's one tank left next to our right foot.

—Not anymore. Central, there are no more hostiles. Guys on foot are running away.

[*Is Themis still there?*]

Affirmative. It's just the two of us –

—Barbara!

—AND A BUNCH OF MiGS! Fuck, they're firing. That one's gonna hurt! Brace! Brace! Brace!

—*Yokits!*

File No. 2195 (continued)

Mission log – Vincent Couture
and Sergeant Alexander Vasiliev

Location: Aboard Themis. Sinuiju, North Korea

—Look! The Koreans are firing on Lapetus!

—Yes, Alex. I can see that.

—That's a good thing, isn't it?

—No, Alex, it's not. My daughter is in there.

—At least you know she's alive. Lapetus might get scared and leave.

—I don't think they'll leave. They're in no real danger. They'll just kill a bunch of Koreans for no reason.

—How many tanks do you think there are?

—Katherine talked about a regiment. Do you know how ma— Whoa! That wasn't a tank. They're firing missiles at them!

—Maybe they'll leave now.

— . . .

—Vincent?

—No. They won't. I'm not even sure they can while they're being shot at. What *will* happen is they'll overload and wipe out everything in sight. We're going in.

—What?

—I'm beaming us in. We might be able to stop it.

—Vincent, five minutes ago, you said you would bail if the Koreans attacked us. Now you want to attack the Koreans.

[*Vincent, this is Katherine. We're seeing all sorts of activity on the Korean side. What's going on?*]

—The Koreans are firing.

[*They're firing at you?*]

No, at Lapetus.

[*Good! It might just leave.*]

No! It – Ah screw this! Katherine, I'm taking us there.

[*What? No!*]

The Chinese can't cross that bridge with Lapetus around. There won't even be a bridge if he overloads. Alex, get ready for the sword. And . . . Now!

[*Are we attacking Lapetus?*]

Alex, the sword is at its longest. Get rid of the tanks at our feet, then aim at the ones farthest from Lapetus. I don't want Eva and whoever else is in there to think we're firing at them.

[*You're not firing at them?*]

We have to stop them from overloading, Katherine. The bridge, remember?

[*Vincent, the Koreans just sent out MiGs. They'll be there soon. Very soon. Did I mention I don't like this at all?*]

Alex? How are we doing?

—One. Last. Tank. It's like swatting flies. I'm aiming now, you can fire. Fire! Again! Again! Just keep firing, I'll tell you when to – Oh, we just made a big hole. I'll tell you when to stop . . . Fire!

—This ain't *Star Wars*, Alex. My finger's on the button. It fires when it fires.

—OK, stop. STOP!

—There. I think we got them all. What about those MiGs?

[*Vincent, they're right on top of you!*]

I see them.

—Give me the shield, Vincent.

—I –

—Vincent, the shield!

—It won't turn on. I think we might have drained her. They're firing. Turn our back to them.

—They're firing from both sides!

—I don't know, Alex. Just pick a si— AAARGH! AAAAAARGH!

. . .

Alex, are you all right?

[*What's going on, Vincent?*]

Alex? ALEX!

[*Vincent?*]

I think Alex is unconscious.

[*Fuck. Can you fight Lapetus without him?*]

Fight La— You mean kick them? I can kick them. Oh, wait. I can't even do that. Themis is out of power.

[*Can you get out of there?*]

What part of 'out of power' was unclear? Out, power, or of?

[*You know I can kill you at the press of a button, don't you?*]

Yeah, and leave Themis to the North Koreans. Then again, maybe the Chinese can get her for you. Do you think they'd give her back?

[*I hate you right now, Vincent. I just want you to know that.*]

Don't worry, Katherine. Themis should have absorbed some energy from those missile hits. She'll be back to her old self any minute.

[*Is Lapetus out of power? I'm asking because 'any minute' seems like a really long time if it decides to kill you.*]

I guess we'll find out. By the way, I don't think I thanked you for telling me my daughter was alive and well.

[*Did I forget? We've been so busy down here. You know how it is.*]

I'm switching frequency now.

[*No, don—*]

Hi, Eva! Are you guys OK in there?

<*We're good, Dad. How about you?*>

Oh, that last missile hurt a bit, but we're fine. Peachy.

<*You didn't come all the way here just for me, did you?*>

Well, seeing I had no idea you were still alive a minute ago, I'd say no. Sorry. I would have, though. If you'd called.

<*Don't go there, Vincent. You know why I left.*>

I'm sorry, Eva. I'm sorry for what happened to Ekim. If there was *anything* I could have done to –

<*There* was *something you could have done! You could have left him alone, not put a gun to his head. You could have left the both of us alone.*>

No, Eva, I couldn't have. I'm sorry Ekim died, but if I had to do it all over, I'd make the same choice. I'd do it again.

<*Fuck you, Vincent!*>

I had to get you out of there!

<*WHY? Why? I was happy. Do you think I'm happy* here?>

They were gonna kill you, Eva!

<*You don't know that!*>

Oh, God, Eva. I *do* know that. There's . . . *so much* you don't know. They were going to arrest you for what happened in Eskyaks. They were going to kill you.

File No. EE463

Personal File From Esat Ekt

Personal Log – Dr Rose Franklin
and Vincent Couture

Location: Assigned residence, Etyakt region

—Where's Eva, Vincent?

—I was going to ask you the same thing. I thought she might have gone to your place.

—Did she come home last night?

—She did. She went to bed early. We didn't fight or anything.

—Something's wrong, Vincent. Her picture is on every wall at the market.

—What? What picture? What did you see?

—I went to get some *yat* for breakfast. I was about half-way there, when I noticed everyone was staring at me, more than they normally do. When I got to the market, one woman spit in my face, another tapped me on the shoulder. People wanted to hold my hand. The old man who sells the *yat* gave me a handful of them and wouldn't let me pay. He's never done that. That's when I saw her.

On the large wall, where they show the *esketots* games. She's in all the alleys that run behind the market. That picture, I don't know where it's from. She's staring at the ground, the wind blowing her hair across her face. It's . . . pretty.

—What is she doing?

—It's just her face. That wall must be a hundred feet tall. All we see is her face, and the word *Esant* written underneath.

—*Esant*?

—Yes. I don't know what it means.

—It's a knife. A dagger. The . . . I forget her name. The . . . fortune teller in the blue tent. She has one. It's an ancient thing. I think they used it in ceremonies a long time ago.

—Why would they call her that?

—I have no idea. People here call her a bunch of different things. Eva's hard to pronounce, people don't want to say Evat, that's a man's name. Her friends call her *Yev*. Maybe . . .

—Maybe what?

—Maybe nothing. The vowels are the same, that's all. Did you ask? Did anyone say anything?

—No. I didn't talk to anyone. I didn't know what was going on, so I just ran back here.

—Could it be Ekim making some sort of grand gesture? You know, like a proposal on the giant screen at a baseball game?

—I don't know, Vincent. He didn't strike me as the grand gesture type.

—He might be. He's not as shy when Eva's not around. I think he just knows she'll kill him if he puts her on the spot.

—That would qualify, don't you think?

—Yeah, she'd be mad. I think he would have asked first, anyway. He asked for my permission before he bought her that necklace. Could Ekim even access these walls? Those are run by the government, right?

—They are.

—Maybe he knows someone? Someone who can hack the system, someone at the regional government?

—Vincent, I don't think it's Ekim at all. I think . . .

—What, Rose? You think what?

—I think someone is forcing our hand.

—The empress?

—Who else could do this? Think about it. It's perfect. Either we go for it and give her names. She swoops in and arrests everyone. Or we don't, she does it anyway, but now she has an excuse to get rid of us no matter what. Eva's the poster child for what these people are marching for.

Make her a terrorist, and suddenly everyone asking for more *food* starts to look suspicious.

— . . .

—Vincent?

— . . .

—Vincent, say something!

—We have to turn them in. We have to give the empress what she wants.

— . . .

—We have to find Eva, and we have to turn everyone in.

—They'll kill them, Vincent.

—They'll kill Eva.

—Are you sure about this?

—No matter what, Rose. That's what you said.

—I know what I said. I just . . .

—We'll have to move fast. Her friends will know she's in danger. They'll be hiding her. We have to get to her before the security forces do.

—We don't know if the security forces are even after her, Vincent.

—Yeah, we do. They're here.

File No. EE464

Personal File From Esat Ekt

Interview between Vincent Couture and Opt Enatast

Location: Assigned residence, Etyakt region

—Enatast! Why are you here? Why is security with you?

—Vincent, you and I have espent time together. I do not know how easy your people form reyationships. You are the one Terran I know good —

—Well. Oh, that's right, you still can't do the l's.

—I hope it is not bad for me to say you are my friend.

—Thank you, Enatast. I also think of you as a friend.

—Then you must understand that what I am about to say, I say as a representative of Etyakt and not your friend.

—What is going on, Enatast?

—Where is Eva?

—I don't know. Just tell me why you're here.

—She is wanted for acts of terror.

—The bombings in Osk?

—There have been more bombings in four regions. She was seen near one in Eskyaks.

—This must be a mistake, Enatast. Eva wouldn't – She's never even left this town, let alone the region!

—I have seen the images, Vincent. She was there.

—It doesn't make any sense. Eva can't even make soup. Do you think she knows how to make a bomb? Where would she get it? Why?

—This morning, every region received a message from a group caying itself *Eposk Yetskots, Hand of Yetskots*. They say they put the bomb. They have made demands. More represent . . . ation for part-Ekt.

—What does that have to do with my daughter? Why is her face on every wall in the city?

—We did not send that image, the *Hand of Yetskots* did.

—*Esant*? The dagger?

—Maybe they want to make her a . . . symboy.

—A symbol of what? She's . . . We're all alone here. There're her, me, and Rose.

—What happened to Terra was a bad thing, Vincent. Many many Terrans dead who did nothing to the Ekt. It scared those with non-Ekt ancestors. It united them. They have been divided for many, many times. Some are from pyanets that make war with another. Your Terra has everyone's sympathy. You are victims of a great injustice by the Ekt and, in their mind, want the same thing they want. Eva is young and . . . *epust*, and she is Terran. She is a perfect face for an uprising.

—*Eket eyet akt?*

—We do not know who they are for sure. We have known for many months of a movement in many regions. Your daughter has been meeting with suspect members of the movement.

—She works at the soup kitchen, Enatast! She knows lots of people who are unhappy with the way things work. I know these people! They protest, they march. They don't blow up buildings!

—They are organized, and they are everywhere. There are some in Osk who agree with them. Even in the Guard, they say. They have the means to commit those crimes.

—I'm sure there's an explanation, Enatast. Let's go find her. Let's all go find her, so she can tell us.

—I am sorry, Vincent. I am very sorry. The security forces are searching everywhere. They find her.

—What will happen to her?

—I do not know, Vincent. I am honest when I say I do not.

—I have to f—

—Do not say it to me, Vincent. Do not say anything to me you do not want the security to know.

—I understand. Thanks.

—Good yuck, Vincent.

File No. 2196 (continued)

Mission log – Warrant Officer Eva Reyes
and Lt Barbara Ball,
US Marine Corps, Mecha Division

Location: Aboard Lapetus. Seoul, South Korea

—Eva, this is . . . a bit awkward. Would you rather I turn my comms off?

—No, it's OK. I don't have anything to hide.

What are you saying, Vincent? I might have gotten arrested for something I didn't do, I might have been put on trial, found guilty, maybe, and executed. That's a lot of maybes, don't you think? You don't know that any of it would have happened. Did it ever occur to you to just, I don't know, ask me? You could have talked to me, you know?

[*Lapetus, this is Central. Copy?*]

Hold on, Vincent.

[*Lapetus, this is Central. Copy?*]

Barbara, are you gonna answer that?

—Copy, Central. Lieutenant Ball here.

[*We can still see Themis on satellite.*]

That's right, Central. We're . . . having a little chat.

[*Lapetus, your orders are to get Themis out of there by any means necessary. Are we clear?*]

Crystal, Central. You gave us some discretion on this one. For now we're having a chat. We'll let you know how it goes. Copy?

. . .

Central, do you copy?

[*Copy that, Lapetus. We'll try it your way.*]

All yours, Eva.

—I'm surprised they didn't order us to attack.

—I think they're worried we'd lose. *I* am, anyway.

—Oh, we wouldn't lose now. I don't think Themis can move.

—What?

—I think she's used up all her energy. If I'm right, she's dead as a doorknob.

—I hate to bring this up, your dad being in there and all, but shouldn't we kick their ass while we can?

—We probably should. I wouldn't mind punching him in the face right about now.

—Then why don't we?

—Because I can't move my arms. Lapetus is just as dead as they are.

—How long until we can move again?

—Five, ten minutes if we're lucky.

<*Eva, are you there?*>

Yes, 'Dad.' I'm here. I'm in *yokits* North Korea with an explosive chip in my brain, being shot at by MiG 29s.

<*A chip in your brain? What did they do to you?*>

They can blow our brains out anywhere in the world. Don't tell me they let you pilot Themis without some kind of fail-safe.

<*Gas. Some nasty nerve toxin.*>

How nice. I'm so glad you brought me back here because, hey, I might have been in danger on Esat Ekt.

<*I'm sorry, Eva. You know that's not what I had in mind. I thought . . . I wanted to give you something of a normal life. I thought I was bringing you back to the way things were.*>

Why in the world would I want that, Vincent? Tell me? How could you think for a second that I'd want things to be the way they were? I remember my life here. I was a freak here, a joke. Everyone I loved died. My 'good' memories on Earth are with you inside Themis. Do you get how fucked up that is? People were dying, everywhere.

Millions of them. I was bonding with my dad. That's what you wanted to bring me back to?

<*I didn't have a choice, Eva. There was no time. They were after you. Eskyaks, the Imperial Guard, they were going to find you, and they were going to kill you.*>

That is such bullshit, Vincent! You just thought you knew better than me. You're right, though, you didn't have a choice. That choice was mine. *My* life. *My* choice. You thought you knew better, and you made it for me. I'm not ten anymore, Vincent. I'm *yokits* nineteen years old! You're still making decisions for me like I'm that little girl Kara found in Puerto Rico. Don't pretend you didn't want this. It was you! Eskyaks didn't find me. The empress didn't find me. *You* did. *You* hunted me down.

Barbara . . . get ready.

File No. EE681

Personal File From Esat Ekt

Personal Journal Entry – Vincent Couture

I see her face everywhere. I wish it were my imagination, but they've plastered every alley with my daughter's face. She's on the small leaflets we see lying on the ground. They graffiti her name – the one they've given her – on anything remotely connected to the Council. An entire propaganda machine is built around Eva. Worst of all, it's all fake. As far as I can tell, all of this is a figment of the empress's imagination.

The good news is I found her. Well, not exactly. I found Ekim. He'll take me to her. The empress sent a handful of Imperial Guards to help me. I didn't want them anywhere near me, but they were useful in the end. I don't have anything to bribe anyone with. They have . . . everything, and no reservations about twisting a few arms along the way if it helps. I don't care. I just need to find Eva. Then I give the empress what she wants, and we're gone. That's the deal. She promised to unlock one of the robots – we asked for Themis – and let us leave. All we need is a pilot. I have an idea about that.

I feel like an asshole for using my daughter's boyfriend to find her. He's a sweet kid. But she didn't leave me much choice. She's quick. Eugene must have taught her a lot more than combat maneuvers. She's really good at covering her tracks. It's not easy. The three of us stick out like a sore thumb here. I think people just want to help her. It doesn't mean they all embrace the cause or anything like that. They want to help *her*. They don't talk because they like her, another thing she didn't get from me. Ekim, well, he worships her. He won't let her out of his sight. If he's here, then my daughter can't be too far. He'll take us there. It would break him to know he was betraying her. Poor kid.

That's the thing, though. They're both kids. Ekim is twenty-eight. That's about, I don't know, sixteen for these people. And Eva, well, she's her mother's daughter all right. I'm not sure she knows what she's gotten herself into. This isn't a student protest. The place is on the verge of a full-blown civil war. The bombs they blame her for killed innocent people, some from the security forces. These guys will gun her down if they get to her first. People are scared, especially in Osk. If she's caught, and there's a vote, they'll put her to death. I doubt the Council will go out of its way to save the poster child for the uprising.

I hate the rebellion, the real one, whoever they are. For all their talk about justice and equality, they're just as power-hungry as everyone else. They want their seat at the grown-up table. They don't want to change the system, they want to run it. They've been using all of us since the day we got here, just like the empress is using us now. We're the perfect face to put on what they have to sell. We pose no threat. We look like them. It's a whole lot easier to play the emotion card with us than with reptilians or sentient amoebas.

If these people do exist, they're terrorists. I hate bullies.

You build a revolution on ideas. If the population doesn't buy your ideas, it means they're not ready, or you're wrong. There's this tendency for people to see any fight against the system as a fight for progress. As if the people before them couldn't possibly have gotten anything right. If you're using bombs instead of words, that means you're banking on people giving you what you want out of fear instead of reason. That's never a good sign.

File No. 2195 (continued)

Mission log – Vincent Couture and Sergeant Alexander Vasiliev

Location: Aboard Themis. Sinuiju, North Korea

[*Vincent, are you there?*]

—Not now, Katherine. Oh, thank God, Alex is coming to. Hey there! Nice of you to join us!

—Where are we?

—Same place we were five minutes ago.

—My head hurts. Where are the Koreans?

—They're gone for now. It's just us and Lapetus.

—Are we fighting?

—No, Alex, we're not fighting. We can't move. They can't either.

—How do you know?

—They haven't moved an inch. They haven't shifted their weight. They haven't moved their arms one bit. No one can stay that still for five minutes. I know my daughter can't. It won't last, though. You should get ready.

—Ready for what?

—Eva's pissed. She's getting herself worked up. Watch her fingers.

—What?

—Her fingers. Lapetus's fingers. Whatever. She won't make any big moves. She won't want to lose the element of surprise. She's probably trying to move her pinky, tap her fingers on her leg, something subtle. When it works . . .

—She'll attack us? She's that pissed off at you?

—She doesn't know the half of it.

—That bad, huh?

—I don't know what to tell you, Alex. Have you ever wanted something . . . *so* bad? Nothing but that *one thing* means anything to you. You'd give . . . anything, your life, other people's lives. It doesn't matter. You work at it and you work at it and after a while you can't see anything else. You can't see the people around you. You can't hear them. Then one day, out of the blue, you get it. It finally happens. You're happy. You feel that great sense of accomplishment. Then you start wondering what you've missed along the way while you were chasing that one thing. Would it have meant this much in the end if you'd paid attention to what was around you the whole time?

[*Vincent, if you don't answer me now, I'll fill Themis with VX gas and listen to you twitch and gargle for a minute or two while I eat lunch. I swear, I'll put you on speaker, so I can hold my knish with both hands.*]

Relax, Katherine. We're – Wait. Is that what's bothering you? Having to hold the phone? I'm pretty sure you can put us on speaker without killing us. That has to be its own button. One for twitch and gargle, one that says 'speaker.' If you're not sure, though, don't press anything.

[*Vincent, I have a million Chinese soldiers just itching to shoot at something.*]

I wouldn't come anywhere near us if I were them. This place is about to get ugly.

[*You're going to fight Lapetus?*]

More like Lapetus is going to fight us. As soon as they recharge, I'm pretty sure they'll take a swing at us. You sound worried. I thought that's what you wanted.

[*You're gonna win, right?*]

Well, one of us will.

[*You better win. I want Lapetus.*]

Now you're just being delusional. They're going to beam as far away from here as they can if they feel they're losing. We'll do the exact same thing. No one is going to 'win' if that's what you mean by winning. No one is getting a second robot out of this, Katherine.

[*A girl can dream, Vincent.*]

A girl can dream and eat her knish with both hands.

[*I was serious about the VX gas, you know.*]

No you weren't. You only *think* you were.

[*Dear God. I sense some serious mansplaining coming.*]

Not really. I'd use the same slightly condescending tone if your name was – is there a male version of Katherine? No, really! I can be condescending to everyone. Come on, Katherine. You just threatened to kill me! You, and the Americans for that matter, just didn't think it through. I told you you're not getting a second robot out of this. Why? Because they'll leave before you can get your hands on it. They can only do that if they're alive. That's why this completely insane fail-safe they have in place is useless. They won't kill their pilots because if they do, you'll grab Lapetus. Same reason you won't use that gas. It would mean turning Themis over to them. You're not gonna do that because you're intelligent, incredibly smart, and wise. Did I say smart?

[*You and I are gonna have a talk when you get back here.*]

I have to go now; my daughter is about to punch me in the face.

[*I don't mean to rush you or anything, but Pyongyang isn't going to sit still all day, even if you are.*]

Alex, are you ready for this?

—No.

—Good. Overconfidence is bad.

—Then I'm doing great.

—That makes two of us.

—Didn't you beat that robot before?

—No, that was another one. This one was kicking the living shit out of me and Eva. It came this close. Rose stopped it from killing us.

—That is not particularly reassuring.

—Well, Eva couldn't handle it either.

—How old was she?

—Ten, but that's not the point.

—What is the point?

—I –

—Wait! I think I saw her finger move.

—She'll come at us soon. I wish I knew how. Eugene – General Govender – taught her military tactics.

—Was she any good?

—Apparently. What was that move he said she liked so much? Blitzkrieg? No, that's not it. Flanking maneuvers!

—What is – ?

—Oh, crap!

—Where'd they go?

File No. 2196 (continued)

Mission log – Warrant Officer Eva Reyes
and Lt Barbara Ball,
US Marine Corps, Mecha Division

Location: Aboard Lapetus. Seoul, South Korea

—Ready for what, Eva?

—Can you put us right behind them? Say thirty, forty feet?

—Yeah, I think I can do that. Just tell me when.

—Can you punch it in now and press go when I tell you to?

—Yep. Eva, I gotta tell you, I'm a little nervous about this.

—Does it help if I tell you I'm also scared shitless?

—You fought one of these before. I haven't.

—Yeah. I was inside Themis, fighting . . . this guy, actually. I was just a kid.

—How was it?

—It didn't go well if that's what you mean. I don't remember much. I was trying to hold on to the robot, to Lapetus, but I wasn't strong enough. I felt so small, I *was* so small. I was scared out of my wits, shaking. I was absolutely convinced I was going to die.

—Your father saved you?

—Not really, no. He . . .

—What?

—He was standing where you're standing now. He got out of his station, walked up to mine, and he held me. He held me so I wouldn't let go, but mostly so I'd feel safe. One last big hug. He also thought we were gonna die, but he wanted me to feel safe.

—Did you?

—Yeah. I did. I always felt safe around him.

—Eva, I . . .

—That was a long time ago. A lot's happened since then. He –

—Eva, I'm not judging you. Family's fucked up. I don't really care what kind of issues you and your dad have to work out, but I *really*, really don't think this is the place for that. I don't think you should be here. I think you're endangering the mission, endangering me. Especially me. Not to mention this could start a war.

—What *is* the mission? They told me it was 'to prevent Themis from providing support to the People's Liberation Army.' I'm not fluent in military talk, but I assumed they meant we should kick her ass and make her leave. Am I wrong?

—No, you're not wrong. That's what they want us to do.

—Then, Barbara, and with all due respect to the moron you normally ride with, you have a much better shot with me here than with anyone else. As for starting a war, I didn't come here looking for trouble. To be honest, I didn't want to come here at all. I only signed up hoping I could use Lapetus to get back home.

—Home where?

—Home! Where I grew up. Anyway, it took about two seconds of staring at that console to realize I'd never figure it out. So no, I'm not here to start a war. I'm here now because I'm stuck on Earth, and China is about to invade Korea. *That*'ll start a war. So how about you cut me just a tiny bit of slack, and we find a way to get out of this alive?

—Roger that. Just say when.

—Well, we can't move yet.

— . . . What was it like?

—What was what like?

—Being on another world.

—Well, I was ten when we got there. To be honest, I don't remember much about before. There was just . . . normal. I did – Same thing you do, I guess? I got up every day, ate breakfast. I spent some time with my friends, hanging out, mostly. I worked. I had a job. Have you ever spent any time in another country? Not on vacation, I mean. Like, for real.

—We were a military family. My dad was army. He was stationed in Turkey for about a year. I was young, though. Five years old? I spent most of my time on the base.

—Playing with other kids your age.

—Yeah. There were a bunch of kids.

—That's how it was. The view's different. People don't look the same. Different food. But that's pretty much it. You can change the backdrop, but your life is basically your life anywhere. We're not that original. Anyway, that's how it felt for me. That was my ordinary. This. Now. This is the strange place.

—Why do I find that depre—

—I can move my fingers! Beam us behind them, then turn around as fast as you can.

—And here. We. Go.

—NOW! Turn around! Sideways! Kick them in the back!

—Ugh! That must have hurt. Now what?

—They're shaken up right now. It'll take them a second to realize they're lying flat on their face. Then they'll crouch to try and get up. They won't be able to see us that whole time.

—They will if they roll over.

—They can't get up from their back. They won't roll over. We'll do it for them, though. There! They're moving, get closer so I can grab them. Get ready to push with your right leg, I'll flip Themis on her back.

—All right. We're straddling her.

—Push! Quick! Step on their arms and crouch so I can punch them.

—We have a light cannon, Eva. We can just fire at them.

—Fuck the cannon. They're pinned down. Now bend your legs!

[*Oh shit! . . . Eva, don't do this!*]

Did you stop when I told you not to drag Ekim into this? Now take this you *yokits* ass! UGH! How's that feel?

[*AAAAAGH! Stop it! Fuck! AAAAAARGH! . . . Alex? . . . You broke his arm, Eva, now stop this!*]

Tough luck. He shouldn't have come with you if he didn't want to get hurt. UGH! UGH!

. . .

Oh shit!

—Whoa! They're gone! Where'd they go?

—They beamed away, Barbara. That's where they went!

—From their back?

—GETUSAWAYFROMHERE, NOW!

File No. EE684

Personal File From Esat Ekt

Personal Log – Eva Reyes

Location: Somewhere in the Etyakt region

AAAAHHHH! They shot me! Those red assholes shot me!

[Ayt erktsot!]

Of course I'm hurt. I just said they shot me! My arm's all numb. Some sort of stun gun. I can't feel anything. At least we know they're not trying to kill us. Keep going, Ityets! Here! Down that alley!

Go! Go! I'm right behind you. Damn, these guys are fast. Why can't you run that fast?

[Eyipots oyyetsek Vincent.]

Yeah. I saw him too. Turn here. Hey! Where are you going?

[Ast eyyekt ops ant –]

I don't care where we go! Just shut up and run! They're catching up fast!

They're firing again! Get down! Here! Here! Try that door. Yesss! Close it! Close it! Can you disable it?

[At. At.]

Go! Go!

Wait! Stop!

[Eps eyakak.]

I *have* made up my mind! There's no other door, Ityets. There's no way out! How long do you think that door will hold them?

[Ast . . .]

That's what I thought . . . I think . . . I think this is it, my friend!

Really? You're just going to sit on the floor?

[At.]

All right. I'll finish this log entry and I'll hide the recorder. They'll be so happy to get the both of us, I don't think they'll waste much time searching this place.

My name is Eva Reyes. I'm nineteen years old, and I'm the most wanted person on this planet.

I'm here with Etat Ityets, one of the so-called leaders of the *Hand of Yetskots*. Who comes up with these names anyway? He runs a soup kitchen! He's meditating now. I should try, but I'm too busy being scared we're gonna get caught. I can see the headline already. The Dagger arrested. Yep, that's me: *Esant*, 'The Dagger' . . . Dun-Dun-Duuun. I'm a symbol, apparently. The face of the insurrection. I'm Katniss *yokits* Everdeen. I'm the Mockingjay. Hey, maybe I can change my name. I hate that stupid knife thing.

Hey, Ityets! *Ast eyet ets Mockingjay akt.*

[Akt eyet mockingjay?]

It's a . . . How do I explain bird? Never mind. I guess I'll be The Dagger. Revolution's gotta have a face after all. Only problem is there isn't any. There's no *Hand of Yetskots*. There's no insurgence. None we've heard of, anyway. We have meetings. We hand out leaflets. We have no weapons unless you count kitchen knives, and we sure as hell don't blow up buildings. They vaporized a school in Eskyaks last week. A school! There were no kids inside, but people died. We went there to see if we could help. It's a fairly poor region. Waste of time. There was nothing to help with. Nothing left. Now, they're blaming us for it. Well, not us, me, and this organization that doesn't exist.

The soup kitchen is closed, crawling with security. My guess is they're searching the place for proof. I'm sure they'll find some. If they're willing to destroy a school just so they can frame us for it, I don't see why they wouldn't go the extra mile and plant some evidence.

Now the Imperial Guard is pounding at the door. My father is with them. He has been chasing me, hunting me down, for about a week. We used to be so close. It wasn't that long ago, he'd have faced an entire army just to protect me. That's what fathers do, right? Now . . . Well, now he's brought the army with him.

I wonder why the Imperial Guard is here instead of local security. The empress has no power in the regions. At least, she's not supposed to. It doesn't really matter, I guess. We're still screwed. Ityets has disabled the door. It's basically a solid metal wall now, but they'll break through it soon enough.

Why would anyone want to pin this on me? I'm probably the least important person here. I don't know anyone. I have like five friends. I can't even vote. Why would my father help them? This doesn't make any sense. None of it does.

What do you think they'll do to us? Do you think they'll kill us?

[Ops! *Vincent,* eyet ops ekuktyek atast!]

I don't know anymore, Ityets. I didn't think he'd be the one hunting us either. What are you doing?

[Ast eyoptet.]

You can hear them? What are they saying?

[Eps eyonats itont ikt.]

Step away from the door? *Yokits,* Ityets! Get back! Get back!

File No. 2195 (continued)

Mission log – Vincent Couture
and Sergeant Alexander Vasiliev

Location: Aboard Themis. Sinuiju, North Korea

—What the hell just happened?

—They shot us in the back, or kicked us. I don't know.

—Can you see them?

—No. Push up, Alex, we need to get up!

—I am! What the hell are they doing?

—They're rolling us over! Grab his leg and throw him to the ground! Alex! Grab his leg before he can pin us down!

Oh shit!

—I can't move my arms!

—Eva, don't do this!

[*Did you stop when I told you not to drag Ekim into this? Now take this you* yokits *ass! UGH! How's that feel?*]

—AAAAGH! What do I do?

—I have no fu— AAAAAGH! Stop it, Eva! AAAAAARGH!

—MY ARM!

—Alex?

—I think I dislocated my shoulder.

—You broke his arm, Eva, now stop this!

[*Tough luck. He shouldn't have come with you if he didn't want to get hurt.*]

AAARGH! Screw this! I'm beaming us out of here!

—We're on our back, Vincent! Where can we – AAARGH!

—UP, ALEX! WE'REGOINGUP!

. . .

—Where are we?

—About five hundred feet in the air.

—You're insane!

—Maybe. We're falling. Brace yourself, this is gonna leave a mark!

—FUUUUUUCK MEEEEEE!!!!

File No. 2196 (continued)

Mission log – Warrant Officer Eva Reyes
and Lt Barbara Ball,
US Marine Corps, Mecha Division

Location: Aboard Lapetus. Seoul, South Korea

—MOVE, BARBARA! THEY'RE ABOVE US!

—Abo— AAAAAAARRGH!

— . . .

—Eva, I need help.

—Aagh . . .

—Eva?

—My . . . My left arm's broken.

—Eva, I need help. I –

—I'm here, Barbara.

—I don't know what happened. My legs . . .

—They fell on top of us, Barbara. They beamed into the
yokits sky. Are you OK?

—I can't move my legs.

—Get out of your station, Barbara. I'll come down and beam us away.

—I can't get out. That machine I'm in. I think it broke, crushed my legs inside it. I can't feel them. I can't feel anything from the waist down.

—I'll come help you!

—No, don't. You'll do more harm than good. They'll need to take this thing apart to get me out of it.

—Your face is bleeding.

—Oh . . . I might have broken my nose on the console. Where's Themis?

—She's on her back right next to us.

—What are you doing, Eva?

—I'm dragging us on top of her.

—I won't be able to get up, Eva. It's over.

—Give me the weapon.

—Eva. No.

—Fine. I'll hit with my hands. I'm not giving up, Barbara.

—Jesus Christ, Eva.

[*Eva, are you there?*]

—Fuck you, Dad.

[*Eva, you have to stop! We have to stop!*]

I won't stop! I won't do what you want.

<*Lapetus, this is Central. What's your status?*>

I'm done listening to you.

<*Lapetus, do you copy? Over.*>

My whole life, you tried to tell me what to do. *Yokits*, that hurts! Well, not anymore, Dad. You're done ruining my life. You're –

<*Lapetus, do you co—* >

WHAT, Central? What do you want?

<*What is your current status, Lapetus?*>

Good question, Central. What *is* our status? That contraption of yours crushed the lieutenant's legs. We can't walk. I have one good arm.

<*Lapetus, are you able to retreat?*>

Retreat? I'm losing you, Central. The signal's bad. Real bad.

[*Eva, my copilot's unconscious, maybe dead. I'd leave if I could, but you have to stop.*]

You stole my *yokits* life, Vincent!

File No. 2195 (continued)

Mission log – Vincent Couture
and Sergeant Alexander Vasiliev

Location: Aboard Themis. Sinuiju, North Korea

—Eva, my copilot's unconscious, maybe dead. I'd leave if I could, but you have to stop.

[*You stole my* yokits *life, Vincent!*]

Eva, I'm sorry.

[*You stole my life just so you could get back here! To your life in this . . . cesspool!*]

Oh God, Eva. You don't know what I did, what we had to do to get you back here. You have no idea.

[*Who is we? What did you do?*]

Rose and I, after Eugene died, we swore to each other we would get you back home safe. We thought we could do it, find a way home, but we didn't. We couldn't. We . . . I gave up everything, Eva. I gave up everyone.

[*What does that mean? What did you do, Vincent?! WHAT DID YOU DO!*]

The empress, she offered us a way home. But she . . . She wanted to take over, she needed to make arrests.

[*Oh, no! No! No! No!*]

I did it, Eva. I gave up everyone, all our friends.

[*YOU MOTHERFUCKER!*]

AAAARGH! I did it Eva! I killed them. I gave her Esok's name. She's dead because of me.

[*I'LL KILL YOU!!!*]

DO IT! Do it, Eva! If that's what you want, keep punching! AAARRRGH!!!!

. . .

[*They didn't do anything, you stupid* yokits *asshole! They didn't do it! We didn't do it! There was no* Hand of Yetskots!*]

I know!

[*What?*]

We knew, Eva. We knew from the beginning it was all a sham. We knew the minute the empress told us about the Hand, the minute she said she wanted to swoop in and save the day.

[*And you gave up all our friends anyway! IIIIII HAAAA-AATE YOOOOUUUUU!*]

AAAARGH! Do you think the empress fucking gave a shit whether you did it or not? AAAAGH! COME ON! You can hit harder than this! She was going to get them.

359

She had all of their names! She was going to kill you! I did it, Eva. I gave up everything. I gave up who I was. I turned on everyone I loved. I betrayed an entire fucking planet to save you, Eva.

[*I hate you —*]

I know you do, Eva. If you want to kill me, go ahead! Do you think I care if I live or die after all that? I don't have anything left. I lost you! I was willing to lose you if it meant you could live. I was willing to lose everything. And I have. But you're *alive*. You're alive, Eva. I don't give a shit what happens to me now.

. . .

Do it, Eva! Finish this!

File No. EE463

Personal File From Esat Ekt

Personal Log – Dr Rose Franklin and Vincent Couture

Location: Assigned residence, Etyakt region

—I did it, Rose. It's done.

—Where's Eva?

—Eugene's house. I didn't want to bring her back to our place.

—The Imperial Guard?

—They left with Iyets right after we found him.

—I was hoping they'd escort us to Themis. I suppose we'll have to get there without them. We need to go, now.

—Now?

—Yes, now. Enatast was just here. The insurgents, or so we're told, seized control of . . . *hundreds* of robots. They're marching on Osk right now. There are hundreds more lining up to stop them.

—How can they do that? Take control of the robots?

—I don't think they can.

—It doesn't make any sense, Rose. The empress can put up signs, blow up a few buildings, but I can't imagine the Imperial Guard fighting against itself just to put on a show.

—I don't know, Vincent. All I know is we have to leave before this turns into a full-blown civil war.

—All right, I'll go get Eva. Then we grab Ekim and go. I know where we can find him.

—Do you think he'll do it?

—He doesn't have a choice. I can't fly Themis through space, and I wouldn't know where to go if I did. We're not going anywhere without him.

—This is it, Vincent. It's really happening. Are you OK with all this?

—I don't regret anything if that's what you're asking. Are *you* OK?

—I'm scared. I'll be honest, I'm having second thoughts. I'm not so sure we're doing the right thing. Maybe we could have stopped this.

—You know what, Rose? We didn't start it. We couldn't stop it, but we didn't start it. That'll have to be enough. I'm sure the Ekt will forgive us for not trying to intervene.

—Haha! Must be really nervous. That's not funny at all. What is *that*?

—It's a gun. One of the guards gave it to me.

File No. 2195 (continued)

Mission log – Vincent Couture
and Sergeant Alexander Vasiliev

Location: Aboard Themis. Sinuiju, North Korea

—Finish it, Eva! Just keep hitting if you hate me so much.

. . .

[*I can't hit you anymore, Dad.*]

Eva, I love you. You have no idea how much I –

[*I said* hit, *Dad, not hate.*]

I know, Eva.

[*I mean I literally can't hit you. I can't lift my arm anymore.*]

That's a start, Eva. That's a start. Can you get up?

[*No. My copilot's legs are gone.*]

Mine's unconscious. Does that mean we're done killing each other?

[*Dad, I . . . Yes, we're done killing each other.*]

Good.

[*We're in trouble. I'm in trouble. The —*]

<*Vincent, what the fuck is going on?*>

Hold on a sec, Eva. I gotta talk to Moscow.

We're on our back, Katherine. Lapetus is lying on top of us. I think that about sums it up.

<*We can see that, Vincent.*>

Then why are you asking me?

<*Jeez, Vincent, I don't know. Oh! Yes, I remember now. There are a million Chinese crossing the bridge right now, and the North Korean Army is marching on your location with a few hundred tanks. What else? Oh, the Chinese aren't taking my calls, so . . . If you're not too busy, I'd like to know . . . what the fuck is going on!*>

Well, like I said, we're on our back.

<*Can you, maybe, not be on your back?*>

Maybe, if Alex ever wakes up. He looks pretty banged up.

<*Wake him up!*>

I'm not even sure he's alive, Katherine.

<*Well, you better find a way to get up on your own then, because if the Chinese, or the Koreans for that matter, get to you while you're lying down, they'll take Lapetus, kill your daughter, then they'll come in and shoot you. They'll shoot each other. Yada yada yada, they have two robots and pretty soon all our kids are singing the Chinese national anthem, watching the red flag go up on Mondays.*>

That's sweet of you to worry about me, I —

<Oh, I forgot. Just in case they don't shoot you, I'll have to kill you. You know how much I'd hate to do that. That would be so unpleasant.>

Poor you.

<Yeah, poor me. You'll puke your insides out for a minute or two, then you'll be dead. I'm the one who'll have to live with the guilt — oh, Vincent, the guilt — and all the paperwork. There'll be so. Much. Paperwork, Vincent. You can't even imagine. Also, I'd have lost our one robot on its very first mission, and that won't go too well with my boss. I'm telling you. Bad things will happen to me. Very bad things. Like I said, you need to — >

I can't get up, Katherine. You need a new plan.

<I need! You're the one lying on the ground in North Korea. Can you hold them off?>

Hold them off? You mean kill them?

<No! I meant hold them off. We won't start a war with China for the fun of it, especially if they end up with the robots anyway.>

Not helpful. I can't aim from here without Alex. I can fire a blast all around us, but that's pretty indiscriminate. Let me see if Lapetus can do anything.

<Lapetus? I know your daughter's in there, but they're kind of the enemy, you know.>

Well, I doubt they're looking forward to whatever is in store for them if they get caught, and I don't think the US will be too happy to lose Lapetus either. Right now, I'd say we're allies. You said Beijing wouldn't talk to you. Try

Washington. I'm sure they'd be happy to carpet bomb this place for you if they have planes nearby. For that matter, why don't you? Warn the Chinese beforehand, they'll leave, and we can all have dinner together. I'm starving.

<*Why do you think the Chinese won't take my call? Besides, it wouldn't work. We couldn't bomb the place for ever, and they know we can't send ground troops. They'd just wait and grab the robots afterwards. You need to find a way out of there, Vincent. It's the only way you survive.*>

I'm disappointed in you, Katherine. Now I feel like I picked the wrong country to be blackmailed by.

<*Ooooh. That hurts.*>

Gotta go. I can see the Chinese Army.

Eva?

[*What took you so long?*]

Meh, just Moscow telling me the Chinese are coming, so are the Koreans, and that they'll kill us the minute either of them reaches Themis. How's your day?

[*They just told me the same thing. The US did. They'll blow my head up, Dad. Can you get us out of this?*]

I'm gonna try and send a small blast around us without killing everyone. Maybe they'll keep their distance.

[*You're worried about the Chinese Army?*]

I'm not going to kill a million people just to save the two of us, Eva. Sorry.

[*I get that. But I can learn to live with myself if a dozen of them don't make it and my head doesn't explode.* Yokits! *The North Koreans are closing in too. I don't think we can save everyone, Dad.*]

No, we'll both burst if they start shooting at us. We need to take the Koreans out. Can your robot fire at all? Those big bolts of light would come in pretty handy right about now.

[*My copilot's passed out. I'll get out and see if I can wake her up.*]

All right. I'll send a small blast. Maybe they'll get spooked.

[*Whoa!*]

What?

[*Our leg's gone. You obliterated our leg.*]

I'll buy you a new one. That thing was ugly as hell anyway.

[*She won't wake up, Dad. There's a pool of blood under her legs. She needs help.*]

There's nothing you can do for her, Eva. Not right now. Look at the console. Find the button that looks like an equal sign with a dot above it.

[*There isn't one. They're coming, Dad. The Koreans are coming.*]

I'll send out another burst. There. Did they stop?

[*I don't think so, no.*]

You need to find that button, Eva. Themis hasn't had a lot of time to recharge. She'll run out of energy real quick. You'll have to do it after that.

[*There's no equal sign!*]

Look closer, Eva. It should be on the right.

[*It's not! There isn't one, Dad!*]

There has to be!

[*The console's different! I see the numbers you showed me, but there's no yokits equal sign! Dot, or no dot.*]

<Vincent, we're showing the Chinese and Koreans closing in on your location.>

Yes, Katherine, we can see them too.

<Are they firing at each other?>

No, they're not. I could be wrong, but I'd say you just lost a friend. It looks like the Koreans are going for Lapetus. They're bringing in a bunch of trucks. I see large spools of cable.

<They want to tow Lapetus out of here?>

Best guess is they want to drag him away from Themis.

<Why?>

So they can get to us. Themis is on her back. They can't access the hatch unless they flip us over. They can't do that with Lapetus on top of us.

<Vincent, you know I can't let them take you.>

You mean alive, right? Because they'll 'take me' regardless. I can slow them down, but you need to do something.

<There's nothing we can do, Vincent. You're on your own.>

[*Dad!*]

Oh, shit. I see it. They're tying cable around Lapetus's leg and arm. Eva, I'll send out another burst. That should get rid of those cables, but you need to get back to your station.

[*I'll try.*]

It worked! I got rid of a few trucks, maybe a hundred men.

[*I don't think they got the message, Dad. They're coming back.*]

Are you strapped in?

[*Almost. I can't move my left arm. My shoulder's busted.*]

Well, it looks like they're going after your good arm. See if you can shake it loose. No, wait!

[*For what?*]

Wait until the cable is fixed. You can take out whatever it's attached to. And . . . Now! Now!

[*Yeah! Take that, assholes.*]

Can you see the Chinese?

[*They're coming. Some of them are at your feet. I just flung some sort of crane at them, but they don't seem to care.* Yokits! *We're moving, Dad! They're dragging us away!*]

They have you by the leg.

[*Do something!*]

On it. Cable's gone! I should have gotten the crane too with that burst. Themis must be running low. I don't think she has many more of these left in her. Oh shit!

[*That doesn't sound good.*]

My helmet just turned off. I can't see anything.

[*Can you move?*]

What? No! We're out of juice. It's just you now.

[*What do you want me to do? I don't know what I – NOOOO! They're dragging us again. UGH!*]

What's happening?

[*We just fell off Themis's chest. We're on the ground. The Chinese are moving in.*]

Do they have cables?

[*Yeah, bulldozers too. They're going for your left arm, I think.*]

They're gonna flip us over.

[*Soldiers are climbing on Iapetus. They're on our back!*]

Shake them loose! Don't let them get to the hatch!

[*I'm trying!*]

Just move as hard and as fast as you can!

[*Oh, no, Dad! They're going to kill us if the Koreans get in. Please help me!*]

<*Vincent, this is Katherine. It doesn't look good from where we're sitting. Is there anything you want to tell us?*>

No, Katherine. I don't have anything to tell you. If you have to push that button, I . . . You do what you have to do, but give me a minute first. I want to talk to my daughter. There's time.

[*They keep climbing! I don't wanna die, Dad.*]

I know, Eva. I'm here. I'm here with you. Just like last time, remember?

[*I can't see you. I wish I could see you.*]

Close your eyes. I'm right there. See? You're not alone, Eva.

[*I'm sorry, Dad.*]

You've got nothing to be sorry about. I'm proud of you, Eva. I've always been proud of you. I'm proud of the way you won't let anyone tell you who you need to be, including me. I'm proud of the way you care about people. I'm proud of how you always speak your mind, how you don't pretend to be something you're not. You're my daughter, Eva. I'm proud of that.

[*No! Don't –*]

What?

[*Not you, Dad. Them, they're going to kill us. I don't wanna die. Not like that.*]

Patch me through. Can you do that, Eva, let me talk to them?

[*Yeah . . . I think this is it.*]

Hey! Can you hear me? I'm talking to the American asshole who just told my daughter she was going to die. She says you put something inside her head, some sort of explosive. If that's true, you better hope that thing doesn't go off because if it does, you might as well kill yourself. I know what you're thinking. There's a good chance Moscow will do the same thing and kill me. There's always a possibility the Chinese or Koreans will kill me, but I wouldn't bet on that. You see, I'm not the easiest person to be with. I can be a bit of a dick sometimes, just ask my daughter. My point is if people keep me around, it's not because of my charming personality, it's because I have legs that bend the wrong way, and that's kind of useful if you also happen to have Themis. So on the off chance that I make it through this, I want you to listen to me very carefully. I don't give a shit who this robot belongs to an hour from now. I will fucking kill you. I will mow down whatever place you work at and the house you live in. I will kill everyone you've ever known, your high-school teacher, people you play softball with. I will march down Washington Avenue and turn DC into a fucking sandbox. I will end you and everything you hold dear. There. Will. Be. No United States when I'm done with you, and there is nothing, not a goddamn thing, you can do to stop me. Do you hear me? DO YOU HEAR ME, MOTHER FUCKER? ANSWER ME!

[*They can't answer you, Dad. But they heard you.*]

Now I have a few things to say to *you* in case this doesn't work. Is it just us?

[*Yes, Dad. It's just you and me.*]

I want you to remember your parents in Puerto Rico, how much they loved you. I want you to remember Kara, how she died.

[*What? What's wrong with you? You want to make sure I die depressed, is that it?*]

No! I want you to realize you were loved by a shit ton of people! I know you think I ruined your life, that I stole something from you. I know you blame me for Ekim's death, and you have every right to. It's my fault. Me. None of this is your fault. And maybe you're right, Eva. Maybe I made the wrong call somewhere, and you suffered because of it. If that's the case, then I'm sorry. I'm more sorry than you can ever imagine. But I don't want you to doubt, not for a second, that I did all this because I love you.

[*Dad, there's —*]

Will you shut up and let me speak? You . . . You're the best thing that ever happened to me, Eva. If I fucked that up, it's on me, not you. I want you to know that no one, any-where, was loved more than you were. I guarantee it. I don't care who they are, all those kids that made fun of you, people you idolized when you were young, movie characters. They've got *nothing* on you. I love you, Eva.

. . .

[*Can I talk now?*]

Yeah, Eva, you can talk now. You can talk my ear off.

[*There's another giant robot standing at our feet.*]

PART FIVE
Never Land

File No. 2197

News Report – Miranda Patel, BBC

Location: London, UK

London is in chaos. Approximately twenty minutes ago, an all-too-familiar giant robot appeared in Regent's Park, mere steps away from the memorial honoring the victims of the first alien attack nearly two decades ago. Moments later, two more materialized side by side in Trafalgar Square. While Londoners remained surprisingly calm in our previous encounters with the aliens, they are showing no such composure this time around. Mass panic has set in. There is looting across town. All the major roads are blocked. There have already been dozens of casualties, people trampled trying to evacuate their offices, vehicles plowing through crowds. The city has issued a statement asking people to stay in their homes and avoid the streets, but the memory of those thousands of bodies lying on the pavements is still fresh in the minds of Londoners, and most will do anything to escape the –

I am just told that more of these giant killers, a lot more, have appeared . . . everywhere. Reports continue to come in as we . . . It appears we are witnessing a full-scale alien invasion. New York, Washington. We are getting images from Washington now. There are four, no, five robots surrounding the White House.

Back to the UK, while Londoners are on the run, it is unclear where they can run *to*. We have a preliminary list of cities where metal giants have been spotted. Here we go: Aberdeen, Belfast, Birmingham, Bristol, Derby, Doncaster, Edinburgh, Glasgow, Leeds, Liverpool, Manchester, Newcastle-upon-Tyne, North Lanarkshire, Nottingham, Rotherham, Salford, Sheffield, Stockport, Stoke-on-Trent, Swansea, and York. As I said, this list is preliminary. We are getting continuous reports from . . . This is a picture of the Stockton Cricket Club in Stockton-on-Tees. As you can see, there seems to be nowhere to hide.

So far, no sign of the deadly gas that killed tens of millions. The aliens have not made their intentions known, but the sheer number of robots would indicate they are not on a mission of peace. Whatever their objective is, it would appear they will achieve it without resistance on anyone's part, as no state has dared to challenge the invader. It should come as no surprise since our last attempt at a military response right here in London had nothing but cataclysmic consequences. I believe I speak for anyone who has seen the crater that once was Madrid when I say that we should –

I am in shock. It has been only a few minutes, but already, the United States, and now the UK, have signalled their unconditional surrender to the aliens. Whether their message has been heard and understood remains to be seen, but – More reports of surrender. China – we do not have video at this time, but there are apparently over *two hundred* robots in China alone – China has just joined the growing list of countries to lay down their arms. We should hear from Her Majesty's Government on that subject shortly. I suspect the American capitulation will have a domino effect on other nations as well.

We can see — This is central London from above, and we can see smokestacks everywhere. There are fires erupting throughout the city. I am urging everyone to *stay inside* until the streets are safe again.

I . . . This is a historic moment. The United Nations is broadcasting, as we speak, on all available frequencies, the unconditional surrender of the human race. Our fate, your fate, is now in the hands of extraterrestrials.

We are getting live feeds from Russia now, several other countries as well. We will air those momentarily, but I — Let us all take a moment to let the events that just unfolded sink in. I, for one —

This just in. The alien invaders have apparently responded and issued a statement of their own. It is addressed not to the UN, but to all nations. It should be available to us in a moment. I repeat. The aliens have issued a — Oh! I am told we are broadcasting it right now. This is the first communication we have with an alien race.

[*Citizens of Terra. My name is Opt Enatast. I wish to speak with Rose Frankyin.*]

File No. 2198

Interview between Dr Rose Franklin and Opt Enatast, representative of Esat Ekt

Location: United Nations Headquarters, New York, New York

—Greetings, Rose Frankyin. It is good to see you again. The Otok Akitast sends its regards.

—Thank you. Did you really have to mention my name?

—I did not know how to find you.

—I suppose so. You said the Council sends its regards?

—They do.

—I thought the empress had —

—The empress tried to take power. She created a fictious terrorist group in —

—Fictitious.

—Sorry, Rose Frankyin. A fic . . .

—Fictitious.

—Fic . . . titious terrorist group.

—When we left, there were hundreds of robots marching on Osk.

—Many hundreds. Empire Guards pretending to fight other Empire Guards. They surrendered fast. The empress had hundreds arrested to . . . be punished.

—We gave her some of those names. She asked us to.

—And she promised to send you home. I know.

—How?

—Vincent sent me the names on the day you departed. He asked me to protect a woman named Esok.

—So *you* stopped the empress?

—The Counciy did. I onyi said to them what I knew. The empress was arrested and executed. Her younger sister is now empress of Esat Ekt.

—That . . . is . . .

—You were hoping the empress would succeed.

—No. I – I didn't want all those people killed for something they didn't do, but the people in our region, the illegal ones, life might have been better for them if . . .

—It *might* be better. Not perfect, but better. What is the word? Concessions. They had to be made to cam the popuyation.

—What kind of concessions?

—More food. Two seats on the Otok Akitast, on the Counciy.

—Two? What can they do with two seats? Their vote will barely count at all.

—Yes. But their voice wiy be heard. Every day. The rest of the Counciy members have to yook at them when they vote. It take time but there wi— Change come.

—I hope so. We don't have much time, Enatast. They – Our people will expect you to make a statement.

—I do not know what to say, Rose Frankyin.

—I do. I prepared something. Can you read this?

—If there are not too many hard sounds.

—Try it now. I tried not to use too many words with l's.

—My name is Opt Enatast. I come from a pyanet cayed Esat Ekt, birt . . . birthp . . .

—Birthplace.

—It is a hard word.

—You can say home.

—Home of the robot Themis. I understand that many tongues are spoken on your world and I ask your for-giv . . . egiveness for speaking the one I was taught.

Yet me begin by stating what should be obvious by now. There are X of our robots on your pyanet.

—Don't say X. I didn't know how many there were.

—Two thousand and forty-eight.

—Wow. Say that instead of X. Keep reading.

—They have been instructed not to attack – that is true, Rose Frankyin – but they wiy defend themselves if fired upon – that is also true. I urge your governments to use restraint, for you do not possess the knowyedge, technoyogy of fire . . . epower to defeat us. Do not send more of your peopye to their deaths. It would be futiye. We accept your surrender. We are in controy and the terms of our reyationship will be dictated by us . . . Rose Frankyin?

—Yes.

—I cannot say that. That is not true. We do not want Terra to surrender. Why would you surrender to us? We are onyi here to –

—I know. I know. But that was the deal. There are certain things I am asking you to say that won't make sense to you. You just have to trust me that those things have to be said.

—I was given instructions by the Counciy, I –

—Did they tell you to kill us all?

—NO! We –

—Then that means you accept our surrender. If someone surrenders to you, you either accept it or you keep on fighting until they're all dead.

—I see. Then we accept.

—Keep reading.

—This is the third time we visit Terra. The first time, thousands of years ago, changed who you were. Not knowing that, we visited you again and caused the death of many . . . many Terrans. It is my hope that our third visit wiy have more positive consequences. We are not your enemy. We are not conquerors. We wiy be gone soon, and we have no desire to return. We are . . . indebted to the Terran peope for what you suffered and we have now been asked to repay that debt. We cannot bring back the dead, repair the damage we have caused. I have no doubt that many of you wiy continue to fear and hate us after we are gone. We accept your judgment. However, if that fear persists, it must not cause more suffering. We wiy make sure of that. That is our way to make amends. You may see it as a gift or a curse.

What does a curse mean?

—A bad thing.

—Oh. You said it hep if we come.

—I know, but some people will be scared. Keep going.

—We have no desire to ruye your pyanet, your yives, your evoyution —

—Why don't you just skip that sentence?

—Yes. Yes. You are the masters of your destiny. Whether Terrans eth . . . rive, or perish is up to you. Our one purpose is to make sure you reach that fate together as a race, the Terran race.

Whatever your disputes or disagreements, you have to

384

find a way to end them. *You* do. And you must do it ensuring that everyone is given the same rights, the same protections, no matter their circumstances, origins, or faith. You must act as one. I have been made aware of an organization named the United Nations which serves that purpose.

I have not been made aware of anything. What are the United Nations?

—It's where we are. It's . . . a little bit like the Council of Akitast.

—Good . . . I understand that this organization functions according to a set of ruyes, and you may continue to run it as you see fit. We wiy contact you from time to time and ask about your progress. We may send a representative to witness the way you govern. At any time, if we find that a group of Terrans, however smay, is deprived of its rights, is without food or care, is imprisoned without cause, suffers from a disease you can treat or cure, we wiy come back.

Rose Frankyin. We won't come back. We agreed to come here because of what you promised.

—I know, but you need to say you will.

—I cannot say what is not true.

—Enatast, if you really want to help, you have to pretend.

— . . .

—Can you say with absolute certainty that the Ekt will never come here again?

—Rose Frankyin! Do you think I am stupid?

—I'm sorry. But I really need you to say this. We all do.

—I must think.

—Continue.

—From this moment on, you wiy function according to the doctrines of equayity and cooperation. We hope you can do so of your own voyition, but we won't hesitate to impose those principles upon you if we have to.

We do not want to interfere with other races, and it is with great reservation that we agreed to come. However, our presence here many generations ago may have changed more than just your genetics, and we consider your kind reyated to ours, your fate connected with ours. We are, in part, responsibe for what you are, and we must accept responsibiyity for what you become. We won't abandon you in the chaos that we have created on Terra.

The Counciy cannot agree to this.

—They *are* responsible. You tell them that. Or you don't tell them. They don't have to know. Besides, everything you just read is true, Enatast. Your people did this.

—That is not the Ekt way.

—It could be.

— . . . We understand that our presence here is causing fear and confusion, and we won't stay any more than we have to. We have given specific instructions to one of your peope, Drrr—

—Doctor. Dr means doctor.

—Doctor Rose Frankyin. She wiy be our representative on Terra. Is there more?

—No. This is it. I can take care of the rest.

—I hope I do not make a bad bad mistake.

—You'll do great. I can have our people set up a microphone if you want to send that message from here.

—I mean that I hope using your words is not a mistake. I can read your message from one of the giants. But I would yike to see Vincent before we go.

—He's inside Themis. Can you find her?

—I can. Do I bring her here?

—Yes. There is another robot with her. Bring them both here if you can. Eva is in there.

—Rose Frankyin.

—Yes?

—I wiy use your words even if I do not agree with them.

—Thank you.

—I have one request.

—The whole planet just surrendered to you. I'm pretty sure you can get anything you want.

—Vincent said there are things that yive in the sky on Terra.

—Things in the sky . . . Birds?

—Yes. If you can find one, I would very much want to see a . . . bird before I go.

—Would a pigeon – Never mind. You don't know what that is. Yes, there are birds across the street. I'll take you. You can even feed them if you want.

—Thank you, Rose Frankyin. Do you have what you promised us?

—Yes. I do.

File No. 2200

Interview between Dr Rose Franklin
and Vincent Couture

*Location: United Nations Headquarters,
New York, New York*

—What the hell just happened, Rose? One minute, I'm with Eva in North Korea, then some giant robot appears right next to us. Next thing I know, Themis and Lapetus are in the parking lot in front of the old EDC hangar. Now Enatast is here? I just heard his speech on TV.

—It's a long story, Vincent.

—Then you better start talking. Did he say: 'Resistance is futile'?

—No, he did not.

—Sure sounded like it. His English is getting good, though.

—I helped with his speech a little.

—You did? Did *you* do this? Did you get the Ekt to come here?

—I didn't know what else to do, Vincent.

—What did you do?

—I . . . called them?

—With what?

—The . . . I don't know what it's called. The thing they used on me, to bring me back after I died. It's also used for communication. I sent them a message about two weeks ago. I didn't know if they received it. I guess they did.

—What was the message? Please invade us?

—Not in so many words. I told them we – our people – were hurting, and hurting each other. I told them we had lost sight of our identity and we were . . . terrified, and lost. That discovering we were related to them robbed us of our past and destroyed our future. That we were killing each other trying to cling to an outdated notion of humanity. I told them it was their fault. All of it. Whether they want to admit it or not, they are responsible. They came here thousands of years ago, and they changed us. They made us into something different. They tried to fix it and killed millions of us instead, scared us into insanity. They did that. I told them they couldn't simply wash their hands of it.

—Are you . . . ? Rose! Your alien friend, didn't he tell you – maybe it wasn't you, our nameless friend, whatever – that the Ekt would just . . . wipe us out? Isn't that what he said? They'd send us into oblivion and let us evolve from scratch all over again if they thought . . .

—He was wrong.

—Oh, well, if he was wrong. Sorry I even mentioned it. There I was thinking we risked total annihilation.

—Think about it, Vincent. They killed a few million of us, and that sent their world into a civil war. Their people – half of them anyway – see us as ... I don't know ... cousins. We're related to them. What do you think would happen if they killed all of us? Anyway, they didn't.

—You didn't care.

—I thought it was worth ... Look. We needed help. We ... It was their mistake. We couldn't fix this. We don't have what it takes. We just don't. They could do it. They could make things right.

—By force?

—I try to convince myself it's something else. Supervision? We're children, Vincent. We're all children. We were thrown into a grown-up world before our time. I thought ... I thought we needed some adults to show us right from wrong.

—Yeah, that makes sense, maybe. It sounded a bit like bullshit when you said it, though.

—What do you want me to say, Vincent? That I believe in the human spirit? In our innate ability to face even the most insurmountable odds? I wish that were true, Vincent. I wish.

—We could have done more.

—Who? You and I? Eva? We're not superheroes, Vincent. We got lucky a few times, but we can't control the entire world. You thought you could help with Themis. Eva thought the same thing. Where did that get us? We had two of these insanely powerful weapons on Earth, and you and your daughter were each in control of one of them. What did you do? You pounded each other to the brink of death. We're not . . . We're not heroes. No one is. Every movie we watch, every book we read, we see people who can solve every problem, face every danger all on their own. But in real life, Vincent, we just call the cops. That's what I did.

—I don't know, Rose, I –

—They were *executing* people!

—It's not the first time. Probably not the last.

—It's the first time we did it everywhere. It's the first time there isn't *anyone* to say: Hey! Stop this. This is *wrong*. We've lost our collective mind. If that had happened to me, you'd have appointed a guardian. If I had gone insane, put my own life in danger, you –

—Stop. Stop. I understand why you did it, Rose. I'm not sure I agree, but I understand. What I don't get is how you got the *Ekt* to agree. They . . . This goes against everything they believe in. You just said, their world was sent into chaos the last time they came here, and now they're . . . We just surrendered to them, Rose! The whole planet surrendered to them! Interference doesn't even begin to . . . From what I know of them, the Ekt would want absolutely no part in this. They'd want the opposite of this.

—You're right. They wouldn't have come. They wouldn't have considered it. We had to give them something. How did he put it? We had to offer them something they wanted more.

—And what's that?

—What they came for the last time they were here.

File No. 2202

Interview between Dr Rose Franklin and Mr Burns

Location: United Nations Headquarters, New York, New York

—Are you sure you want to go through with this?

—Dr Franklin, I'm a man of my word. Besides, I'm not sure they'd take no for an answer after coming all this way. There are so many of them! That message of yours must really have made an impression.

—They'll execute you right away, you know that? You and all your people.

—Well, not right away. It will seem like right away, but it'll take a good ten days to get back there. Technically, we have a few days to live.

—I don't want you to die for us. I don't want you to die period.

—I hope so! That's a horrible thing to wish on someone! I don't particularly want to die either, to be perfectly honest.

—Then don't do it.

—Dr Franklin, there are nearly two thousand people in the hangar behind us. I'm sure none of them are eager to meet their maker, but all of them chose to come because they thought it was the right thing to do. A lot of them were locked up in camps waiting to be executed, they didn't take much convincing. For over three thousand years, our entire lives were spent making sure no one knew we existed. When that changed, and millions of people died, most of us had a hard time dealing with the responsibility. For many, this is some kind of relief, knowing that no one will suffer because of us anymore.

—No one suffered because of you. You've never done anything wrong.

—Sins of the father, Dr Franklin.

—Somehow, you don't strike me as the biblical type.

—Oh, I love the Bible! So many stories in there. Do you know the one about Balaam and the talking donkey? There's one about two bears shredding forty-two kids to pieces because one of them called someone 'baldy.'

— . . .

—Does it help if I tell you it doesn't hurt at all? I mean, I've never been there, and, who knows, they might have gone all medieval since then, but I was told that back in the day, they vaporized people with an energy beam. As far as I know, that's painless. You would know! Did it hurt when you died?

—I didn't die. The other Rose Franklin did.

—So complicated!

—What I was trying to say is —

—Dr Franklin, I get it. You feel bad because I and two thousand of my friends and family are going to die. You feel responsible. You've said that, a lot. It's cute the first hundred times, but it really gets old after a while. You couldn't have forced us to do this. The simple fact is that my ancestors couldn't keep it in their pants, and they messed with your gene pool. You're probably better off, but that *is* the reason the Ekt came here and killed tens of millions of people. There's always a chance they'd come again to finish the job. You have this thing hanging over your head, and I don't think your species can move forward while it's there, so we'll just remove it. Life's been around for millions of years. Whether I die tomorrow or fifty years from now really doesn't mean anything in the grand scheme of things. We're all dying. If I can do some good while doing it, why not? Also, we get a free trip!

—Please stop joking about this.

—I'm not joking! I know you think of me as the 'alien guy,' but I was born in Michigan! I've never left this rock. You have! Does that seem fair? You've been to their world and, from what you tell me, it's an interesting place. I wish it were under different circumstances, but I'm happy to go. OK, so there's the dying thing at the end, but nothing's perfect. Do you think the astronauts who died in the Columbia shuttle wasted their lives? They went into friggin' space! That is the coolest thing anyone can do, besides traveling to a whole other world in a different galaxy inside a giant alien robot, but that's not the point. Don't feel bad for us! We're going into space! Now if you really want to help: When I said don't feel bad, I meant don't feel *too* bad. You can feel a little bad. There is one thing you can do.

—Name it. Anything.

—There is this tiny little bakery on Fifty-third Street. It can't be more than a ten-minute walk from here. They sell the best pistachio eclair you've ever tasted. If I miss anything from Earth it will be – no, it won't be that, it'll be the purri and chutney I had in Kerala – but this is close. Do you think I could get one of those eclairs before I go?

—Sure. I'll send someone in a minute.

—I . . . You probably can't get two thousand of them, but do you think you can get the whole store? I'd like my friends and family to enjoy a little treat before we leave. That, and I'd feel like an ass eating an eclair in front of all of them.

—I'll see what I can do.

—Thank you!

—No, thank you, for everything.

—Oh, don't thank me yet. Well, you can thank me for the other things, like saving your life – that's probably worth some thanks – but this plan of yours might not work at all. There are plenty of people left on Earth with a bunch of alien DNA. You could end up right back where you started. Then again, it might work. With any luck, the Ekt will have scared people enough that the UN will mean something again. You'll have the EDC, again. Themis and – what's his name? – the other robot will be there to protect you if need be, but you'll stop killing each other with –

—I'm sending her back. I'm sending them both back.

—What? You went through a lot of trouble to put that robot together, and by you, I mean *you* you. Seems a shame to do all that just to give her away.

—We're not ready.

—Are you sure about that?

—I am. I thought we were. I really wanted to believe we were evolved enough to handle this. But we're not.

—You didn't strike me as a pessimist, Dr Franklin.

—I'm not. I'm not a pessimist.

— . . .

—Do you mind if I tell you a story? I've heard many of yours, now I feel it's my turn. It's a true story.

—Oh, I'd love to hear it.

—There's a homeless man. I met him before we went to Esat Ekt. I'd see him around here from time to time. I think he went to the men's shelter down on Thirtieth. We talked . . . maybe twice. Nothing more. Anyway, I saw him again yesterday on my way here. He was sitting on the stairs in the little park across the street. I wouldn't have recognized him, but he recognized me. He said he was looking for a friend. He was worried the aliens might have hurt her. He told me they met there every Tuesday around lunchtime. She bought him chai tea. You should have heard him describe the tea, as if it were the rarest thing on the planet. She lent him a new book each week, and they'd discuss it at the park over chai. He hadn't seen her in a few weeks. I told him maybe I could help find her. Her name's Sarah, he said. He didn't know much more than that, but he mentioned she wore a scarf on her head. I told him I'd do what I could. I had a hunch she might have worked at the UN. Sure enough. Sarah Smith, born Sara Dhanial in Karachi, Pakistan. She is – she *was* – an interpreter at the UN. Diplomats and their staff weren't rounded up like the rest of the population, but Sara lost her job and they sent her to a camp in Connecticut. I went back to the park and told him what I knew. He was sad, obviously. I offered to buy him some food. He said no, but he asked if I could spare some change. I didn't have any, so I renewed my offer to buy him something with my card. He thought about it for a minute, then told me he'd like a couple bags of chai, but that if it was too expensive, he'd settle for one. Then he asked how much a bus ride to Connecticut would cost him. He dug into his pocket and started counting how much money he had. He wanted to bring her tea. He seemed genuinely surprised when I started crying. The point is: There is decency in this world. We just need to look for it. Given enough time, I have absolutely no doubt it will flourish again. Then, maybe.

I said we're not ready now. Not yet. That's not pessimism. I can't make the forest grow faster because I want it to. I can't will it to grow. It takes time. I hoped it could happen during my lifetime, but I don't think it can. All I can do is plant some seeds, take care of the seedlings, and hope someone else does it after I'm gone.

—You're a good storyteller, Rose Franklin. I will miss you.

—I'll miss you too, so much.

—Are you trying to make me cry, Dr Franklin? I didn't think I would be, but I'm a little emotional. Dying is fine, I prepared myself for the dying part, but the idea of leaving this world for good is . . .

—I'm happy to go with you if you don't want to be alone.

—Alone? I'm going with all my friends and family. Alone is the last thing going through my mind right now. Besides, didn't you spend the last nine years trying to leave that planet? I'd have to be incredibly selfish to ask you to go back just to keep me company. You're needed here, Dr Franklin. You have a world to rebuild.

—Me? No. I'm not rebuilding anything. I'm just here to remind everyone of what will happen if they don't.

—I can think of no one I'd rather have to remind me. I don't think we have much time, Dr Franklin. Let's do something about those eclairs, shall we?

File No. 2205

Interview between Dr Rose Franklin
and Vincent Couture

*Location: United Nations Headquarters,
New York, New York*

—Did they all leave?

—Yes, Vincent. They did.

—You don't seem happy. I can tell you everyone else is relieved that they left as promised.

—Did you have any doubts?

—It crossed my mind. My point is you should be all smiles. You got what you wanted.

—It's not that. I can't stop thinking about Mr Burns. Did you see all those people boarding the Ekt ships? It was like watching cattle being led to the slaughterhouse. These people did nothing but help us. And now they'll die. For nothing.

—It was their choice, Rose. They knew what they were walking into when they boarded those ships. They did it because they thought it was worth it. Don't dishonor them by suggesting it wasn't.

—Maybe you're right. It just feels . . . like one more wrong thing to end a long list of wrongs.

—Since we're talking about doing things for nothing, why the hell would you ask them to take Themis back? Lapetus, I understand, he was ugly and missing a leg. But Themis? We went through a lot of trouble – all of us – to put her together. You friggin' died, Rose. I killed you for that. A lot of people died so we could have that robot. Now that the cat's out of the bag, and the Ekt know we have it, what's the downside to keeping her?

—I'm surprised, Vincent. I thought – Haven't you been paying attention? They were using her to kill people. Our people!

—They can still do that. They'll just use tanks or drop a buttload of bombs on each other. But we'll be defenseless if some bad alien dudes decide to drop by.

—That's what you're worried about, Vincent? Evil little green men?

—Well, yeah.

—How long have we known each other?

—Counting the other Rose or not?

—I know you better than that, Vincent Couture. Why don't you tell me what's really bothering you?

— . . .

—You can tell me.

—What am I gonna do?

—What?

—I don't know what I'm supposed to do. I . . . I tried being something else on Esat Ekt, but here . . . Here I'm the guy with the weird knees.

—Now you get to be something more.

—What about Eva? She'll have a hard time giving that up, I'm sure.

—I thought you wanted her to have a normal life.

—She made it abundantly clear I had to reexamine my definition of normal. We both made compromises. By we, I mean mostly me.

—Eva's nineteen, Vincent. She has her whole life ahead of her. There's plenty of time for her to figure out what she wants to do. And you know they'll offer you a job. The two of you have spent nine years on another world dealing with all kinds of aliens. They'll have something for you to do at the EDC, even if it doesn't involve a two-hundred-foot giant robot. If that's not what you want to do, then do something else. Isn't there anything you always wanted to do but never had the chance?

—Maybe. What will *you* do? They must have offered *you* a job. You're the 'emissary to the alien world.' You're the friggin' chosen one.

—I'm not sure anyone really trusts me after what I've done, but they offered me my old job back.

—Great! I'm happy for you.

—I said no.

—What? Why?

—Do I have to say it? Eva might not want a regular job, a regular life, but I do. Oh, Vincent, I really do. I want to go home and not worry about my day. I want to take a bath, read a book. I want to take a bath three times a day if I want to. I want . . . small things. I've had enough of the big ones.

—You'll miss it.

—Yeah, I will. That doesn't mean I'd be happy doing it. Maybe someday. Maybe I'll come back, but for now, I need to take care of me. Just me.

—What will you do all day?

—Same thing I've been doing these past few weeks. I teach at the University of Chicago, mostly undergrads. It feels . . . good. Every time a student's eyes light up when I talk about atomic weight, I feel . . . like I've accomplished something. Like maybe he or she'll save the world someday.

—Fair enough. I'd say you've earned it. We'll miss you, Rose. And let's face it, if we're ever in real trouble, we'll get you whether you like it or not. I mean, we had this giant machine that could destroy entire cities, but we've never really done anything with it. It was always you, Rose. Just you. This is your movie. The rest of us are just extras in it.

File No. 2367

Interview between Eva Reyes
and Vincent Couture

Location: Themis Toy Store, Montreal, Canada

—No, Dad! I'm not pretending to do things at the cash register just so you can film this.

—Come on! It's our first day!

—Your first day, Dad. I told you a million times, I'm only doing this until I find something else.

—Fine. But you'll love it so much, you'll beg me not to hire someone.

—In your dreams. Some of us have grown up, you know. I don't want to spend the rest of my life playing with dolls.

—Dolls! Do you know what you're holding in your hand right now? That's a vintage Leia in her Hoth outfit from something called The Vintage Collection. It's a vintage remake of a vintage figure. Meta vintage. There are lessons about the universe, life constantly repeating itself, buried inside that thing. It's 3.75 inches of wisdom, and before you roll your eyes at me, you should know I've seen you playing with the *Walking Dead* figures when you thought I wasn't watching. I was watching, and I saw you playing with *dolls*, like you said.

—That's different! It's Daryl! I like Daryl.

—You didn't think the little crossbow could fire, did you?

—No. That *is* pretty cool.

—There's hope for you, Eva. There is hope.

—I wouldn't count on it. I've been thinking –

—Uh-oh . . .

—Maybe I could be a pilot.

—You mean join the army?

—What's wrong with that?

—Nothing. There's absolutely nothing wrong with that. I'd miss you, that's all. They'd be lucky to have you.

—What do you think Kara would say?

—She'd say . . . She'd say that you should do whatever makes you happy. Go for it. Never give up. She'd be proud of you, you know.

—And you?

—Am I proud of you? Hell yeah! I was proud the minute I found out you existed.

—Would you be proud of me if I were in the army?

—Eva, it's you I'm proud of, not your job or the uniform you wear. I'd be proud of you no matter what you do. I'd be *real* proud of you if you worked at the toy store with your dad.

—I don't think it's me, Dad. I don't think I'd be happy being cooped up all day.

—With toys.

—Even with toys. It's . . . weird . . . We've been through so much, I – I'm just not sure I can do normal anymore. I go to the park, and I sit on a bench, and it's beautiful, and calm. So calm. I watch people having a picnic with their kids and it's cool, but all I'm thinking is how much fun we'd have wrecking that park with Themis. There are days I wake up, and I hate myself for wishing something bad would happen. I wish we'd get her back and I could swing that giant sword again. Am I a horrible person for thinking that?

—Eva, I've had that thought so many times. I know the feeling. Believe me. It took me ten years to get over it and stop wishing for the apocalypse. You're the one who got me over it, you know. Having you around, it just . . . I spent all my life trying to figure out who I was and what I wanted. Then you showed up, this brash little thing that wouldn't listen to anyone.

—Hey!

—Then I realized that was it. That was the thing that mattered to me. I didn't care what I did or what happened to me anymore. You're the one thing that matters now.

— . . .

—Eva, there's something I have to tell you.

—What is it?

—When Kara died, she – What? Are you OK?

—I can still see it, Dad. Kara falling backwards into that white cloud. It's . . . weird. There are things I can barely remember. It feels like a lifetime ago, but –

—Some of it feels like it happened this morning . . . I don't know if you remember, but the army went back to the UN for her body a few days after the attack.

—You wanted us to scatter her ashes. We never did.

—In a helicopter, right! We can still do that. They found her ashes in a locker room along with all our stuff. Apparently, they cataloged our personal effects after we disappeared and put everything in boxes. It all arrived this morning. Here.

—My – Kara's gopher!

—Oh, it's yours! I forgot how banged up that thing was.

—Thank you!

—There's something else. She had two envelopes on her when she died. One was a letter for me.

—What'd she say?

—She . . . You know what? I won't tell you. It's between me and her. But it's what convinced me to let you try Themis. The second envelope was for you.

—What's in it?

—I don't know.

—You haven't read it?

—No, I thought it was . . . It's between you and her. She told me to give it to you when the time came.

—What does that mean?

—She said I'd know.

—Did you?

—Come to think of it, I did. It was your fourteenth or fifteenth birthday. You were arguing with Rose. I looked at you, and it hit me. Right there and then. Boom! You weren't my little girl anymore. You were this . . . amazing young woman I barely knew. It was scary, and touching. You were so . . . You looked like you could take on the world. That day, I thought about the letter, only it was inside my locker in New York, millions of miles away, so . . .

— . . .

—What is it, Eva?

—I don't know. I'm afraid to open it.

—Why?

—I don't know! I just am!

—Well, she'd never even met you when she wrote it, so I don't think she'd have had anything bad to say to you.

—You're an idiot, Dad. When Kara died, I'd only known her for two days. I *didn't* know her, really. But I have this image of her, this person I've constructed in my head. I've added . . . details to that person over the years, whenever you talk about her, things like that, but deep down, that's still who she is to me. That image I put together at ten years old over a couple days. That's Kara to me. That's my mother. I'm afraid whatever's in that letter won't match. I'm afraid I'll realize I was wrong the whole time, that I didn't know her at all. I'm afraid I'll lose her all over again.

—Only one way to find out. I don't think you'll lose her, Eva. Your mother was many things, but mysterious isn't one of them. She was the most honest, transparent person I've ever met, except for you. What you saw is what you got. I'd say that image of yours can't be that far off. And you know I'm here, right? If you ever want to talk about Kara. You know her more than you think, trust me on that, but there are plenty of stories about your mom I'd love to share with you. If you want.

—Yeah. It looks like we're going to have plenty of time to talk anyway.

—Why do you say that?

—We've been open for four hours, and we haven't had a single customer.

—We haven't . . . I like that.

—*Yokits* . . .

File No. 1613

Hi, Eva!

*I told Vincent to give you this 'when you were ready,' so I don't
know if you're ten or thirty. I hope I've been gone at least a little
while. I'd like for this to be a good moment, I don't want it to be
sad. Yes, I'm gone if you're reading this letter, but I was very
much alive when I wrote it. I don't think I've ever felt more alive.
I found you.*

  *I'm in Cuba. The sun is about to set. It's been insanely hot
and muggy all day, but a nice breeze just picked up a minute ago.
It feels . . . I don't really know what I'm feeling. I'm scared, for
you and for me. I'm also excited, full of hope. It's an odd mix of
good and bad, the calm before the storm. I'm looking at you right
now. That's a lie. I'm looking at the window where they're
keeping you. But I know you're in there. I saw you today with
them. You were so tiny next to those men. You must have been
terrified, but there was such resilience, such defiance in your eyes. I
know that look.*

  *I miss your father right now. I want to share this with him. I
want him to see what I see. I want him to see you. He's plan B. If*

all goes well, you'll never have to read this, and I'll just bring you home. I'm hoping there's a home to bring you back to, but one thing at a time. Earth is being attacked by alien forces, and there's a strong possibility all of us will be dead soon. Rough week.

I should be aboard Themis right now, fighting back, but I came to find you instead. I'd be lying if I said I thought about it for a long time, and it seemed like the right choice. I didn't choose. I just . . . left. You're not alone, Eva. You just don't know it yet. I'll keep you safe, and if I can't, Vincent will. I seriously hope it's me. I'd rather not die, obviously, but I also have a plan. No one dies in my plan. If I fail, and your father is the one who comes to find you, I don't think he'll care who lives or dies. He'll machete his way through an entire army if that's what it takes.

I have to warn you, Eva. Your dad is one big pain in the ass. He's stubborn, doesn't listen. He thinks he's smarter than everyone — he often is, but that's not really the point — and you're probably more mature now than he'll ever be. Of course, there's a flip side to that. He'll play with you not because he wants to please you. He'll play because he loves to play. His heart is even bigger than his ego if you can imagine. He'll protect you when you don't need to be protected. He'll jump in front of a train for you. He won't think twice. He'll do it because it would kill him if anything happened to you. He'll make stupid calls, that I can promise you. It won't be long before you're the grown-up in the family.

I need to ask a favor of you. I want you to take care of him for me. You're just a kid, but I've seen you go through hell, and I know you can overcome anything. He can't. Not anymore. You have to be there for him. You have to protect him, from danger, from himself. More than anything, you have to live. You've lost a parent. You've lost three of them if you're reading this. Trust me when I say that Vincent won't survive losing a child.

So when you're my age, and he still treats you like you're ten, when he turns the entire world upside down to make sure you're OK, when he does something incredibly stupid because he's worried about you, let him. Don't change who you are. Don't become something you're not, but let him have his moments. Be his little girl from time to time. He'll need that. He'll need you more than you can understand. He's been waiting for you his whole life.

The sun's going down. It looks like you'll spend the night. There's this little bar across the street. I think I'll have a mojito, watch the sun set, and call it a day.

So long, Eva. I'll see you soon.

Kara

Epilogue

File No. 2379

Interview between Dr Rose Franklin
and Vincent Couture

Location: Medici on 57th, Chicago, Illinois

—Vincent! It's so good to see you! How long has it been? A year?

—Can't be.

—It has to be. How old is Eva?

—She'll turn twenty-one in – Wow. I can't believe it's been that long.

—You're all set up? How's the toy business?

—It's good! I'm not making any money, but it's a lot of fun.

—Where's Eva? Is she still living with you? Last we spoke, you told me she was working at the store.

—That lasted a whole three months.

—That's not bad.

—I know! I had to fire her.

—Fire her? What'd she do?

—She stayed, that's what she did. I just wanted to spend some time with her. I thought she'd be gone after a week or two, but she stayed. I just couldn't do that to her any longer. It was like watching a tiger pacing in its cage. She was good, though, sold way more than I did.

—Where is she now?

—Sweet home Alabama.

—What?

—She's in Fort Rucker. Flight school.

—For the army?

—Yep. She blew through basic combat training – go figure – then the warrant-officer-school thing, and now she's training on the Apache. Believe it or not, she has a knack for it.

—That fast?

—Yeah. It's fast. She also had good letters of recommendation.

—How are you two going to see each other?

—I'm not sure. We'll see where she gets posted. I might need to sell the store. I was hoping she'd be a Canadian helicopter pilot, but the choppers are more fun on this side of the border. Bigger guns. She likes *big* toys.

—God help us all.

—She already has an offer from the EDC.

—What does the EDC need with helicopter pilots?

—They're putting together a . . . conventional strike force, developing new tech. State-of-the-art experimental stuff.

—Who's running it? Don't tell me they got Alyssa to run it?

—Ha! No, but she does work there.

—I . . . Who did they put in charge?

—You're going to love this. Remember Katherine from Russia?

—No! Really?

—Yep.

—Wow. They're building weapons.

—Well, yeah. Just in case harsh language fails to stop an alien invasion.

—I don't like this at all, Vincent.

—Then you're really not going to like this. There's someone here who'd like to say hello . . . Come in!

—Mr Burns!

[*You seem surprised, Dr Franklin!*]

I saw you. I saw you board the Ekt ship and leave. You and everyone else.

[*I did. As far as the me on that ship is concerned, I've been gone over a year . . . I suppose I've been dead over a year.*]

But –

[*Oh, come on, Dr Franklin! I said I was willing to die. I didn't say I was stupid. I couldn't watch thousands of people – my family, my closest friends, me! – vanish into nothingness for no good reason.*]

How did you – ?

[*Same way we brought you back, of course! Before we left, we each scanned ourselves with the device we used on you – when was that? – nineteen years ago! Wow! We're not getting any younger. We scanned ourselves and stored the information. That was . . . mindlessly boring. You should have seen the line for the machine! I asked a friend of ours – your daughter met him, Mr Couture! – to make us whole again when it was safe. I guess it was safe!*]

—Was it – What was his name? – Bob?

[*Yes! Bob! He sends Eva his best. He says . . . let's see if I can remember. Oh yes!* ArtÄl'nyj gorshùk g£shhe kipÆt. *Something like that.*]

What does it mean?

[*How should I know? It's in Russian.*]

I'll tell her he said hi.

[*You do that. It's funny, all my life, I wanted to visit the planet of my ancestors, and I finally did! But I don't remember anything about it because I wasn't even there. Ironic, isn't it?*]

—I don't know what to say. I don't –

[*What, Dr Franklin? You don't what? I know you're happy to see me, even if you're making that face right now. Seriously, you look like you just drank a whole glass of sour milk.*]

—I think Rose is worried the Ekt will find out you're alive and come back.

—No, Vincent. They won't. The Council just needed a victory of sorts after all that happened. I don't think they could care less about what goes on here.

[*That's the spirit. And who knows? The universe isn't the most friendly place. You might need some old fool with stories to tell someday.*]

I'm sure we will, Mr Burns. I'm sure we will.

[*Speaking of stories, you never told me about the time you fell into that giant metal hand.*]

Of course I have! You know all about it. You even told me you played a part in all that.

[*No, no, no! I told you we made sure you'd be the one studying that hand when you were older, but we didn't know anything about you until you fell into that hole. I'd love to hear that story.*]

Some other time, maybe?

[*Do you have anything better to do right now? Don't answer that, I already know the answer.*]

—I've never heard that story either, Rose.

[*See! Everyone wants to hear it. Please!*]

—All right . . . It was my eleventh birthday. I'd gotten a new bike from my father . . .

Acknowledgments

It's over. I wrote a *yokits* trilogy. I'm not quite sure what emotion I'll settle on in the end. For now, I'm happy. I'm sad. I'm proud. I want to thank Seth, my agent, Will, Rebecca and everyone at Gernert. I owe all of you drinks for the rest of your lives. Jon Cassir at CAA. My editors – I've had a few. Mark, thank you for giving this series a home. Mike, who is now being chased by zombies all day – killing a hundred million people with you was a lot of fun. Mouahaha! Sarah! You're amazing. I'm still in awe at your work on this. You get it. You truly get it. I hope we get to do this again. Everyone else at Del Rey, Alex, David, Emily, Erika, Keith, Scott, Tricia, I love you all. You're family to me. To the entire PRH audio team, you've made something truly special. Let's not forget my three UK editors – like I said, I've had a few. Alex, Emad, Jillian, thank you for putting that big face in the UK sky. Thanks to my nineteen other editors around the world. Thank you, Dave Kaiser, for helping with Bob's Russian. He says: '*Bolshoe spasibo!*' To everyone who's worked on that series in one way or another, thank you.

To Barbara, former president of Bot Bot publishing, can you believe how far we've come? This is the thing I started writing on my iPhone while you were reading. I wouldn't be here without you. To my son, Theodore. You're the inspiration for all this, so keep asking questions, lots of questions. And don't worry, we'll get you more Themis toys.

To the Themisphiles – yep, that's what I call you, most incredible readers in the universe – one huge thank-you. Mucho, domo merci beaucoup! *Eyesunt yesk!* Some of you have already asked if there'll be more Themis Files. We'll see. I have a few things I'm working on, but I'm not closing the door on that universe. Mr Burns has more stories to tell, I'm sure. I hope he saves me some Kung Pao chicken.

So . . . now what?